G.A. HENTY

By Sheer Pluck

A Tale of the Ashanti War

by

G. A. Henty

ILLUSTRATED BY GORDON BROWNE

PrestonSpeed Publications

PENNSYLVANIA

A note about the name PrestonSpeed Publications:
The name PrestonSpeed Publications was chosen in loving memory of our fathers,
Preston Louis Schmitt and Lester Herbert Maynard (nicknamed "Speed"
for his prowess in baseball).

By Sheer Pluck
A Tale of the Ashanti War
by G. A. Henty
© 2005 by PrestonSpeed Publications
Published by PrestonSpeed Publications,
51 Ridge Road, Mill Hall, Pennsylvania 17751.

Various terminology, words, and phrases used in the original Victorian printing of *By Sheer Pluck* have
been changed or eliminated to meet today's standards and sensibilities. The historical, educational, and
entertainment value of *By Sheer Pluck* reveals little known details about life amongst the tribes, the
peoples of the region, and their interaction with the colonial settlers.

This book is printed on acid-free paper, and its binding materials have been chosen
for strength and durability.

Heirloom Hardcover Edition ISBN 1-887159-77-0 (cloth)
Popular Softcover Edition ISBN 1-887159-78-9 (trade pbk)

PRINTED IN THE UNITED STATES OF AMERICA

PrestonSpeed Publications
51 Ridge Road
Mill Hall, Pennsylvania 17751

INTRODUCTION

G. A. Henty did not compose a "My dear lads" for the story *By Sheer Pluck*. His readers were familiar with the historic events described in this story. For the Henty readers of the time, the Ashanti War was a much talked about current event. Moreover, the Ashanti War was very real and familiar to the author as Henty covered it on the scene as a war correspondent.

CONTENTS

ILLUSTRATIONS

OUT WITH THE SCOUTS.

BY SHEER PLUCK

CHAPTER I

A FISHING EXCURSION

"NOW, Hargate, what a fellow you are! I've been looking for you everywhere. Don't you know it's the House against the Town boys. It's lucky that the Town have got the first innings; they began a quarter of an hour ago."

"How tiresome!" Frank Hargate said. "I was watching a most interesting thing here. Don't you see this little chaffinch nest in the bush, with a newly hatched brood? There was a small black snake threatening the nest, and the mother was defending it with quivering wings and open beak. I never saw a prettier thing. I sat quite still and neither of them seemed to notice me. Of course, I should have interfered if I had seen the snake getting the best of it. When you came running up like a cart-horse, the snake glided away in the grass, and the bird flew off. Oh, dear! I am sorry. I had forgotten all about the match."

"I never saw such a fellow as you are, Hargate. Here's the opening match of the season, and you, who are one of our best bats, poking about after birds and snakes. Come along; Thompson sent me and two or three other fellows off in all directions to find you. We shall be half out before you're back. Wilson took James' wicket the first ball."

Frank Hargate leaped to his feet, and, laying aside for the present all thoughts of his favourite pursuit, started off at a run to the playing field. His arrival there was greeted with a mingled chorus of welcome and indignation. Frank Hargate was, next to Thompson the captain of the Town eleven, the best bat among the home boarders. He played a steady rather than a brilliant game, and was noted as a good sturdy sticker. Had he been there, Thompson would have put him in at first, in order to break the bowling of the House team. As it was, misfortunes had come rapidly. Ruthven

1

and Handcock were bowling splendidly, and none of the Town boys were making any stand against them. Thompson himself had gone in when the fourth wicket fell, and was still in, although two wickets had since fallen, for only four runs, and the seventh wicket fell just as Frank arrived panting, on the ground.

"Confound you, Hargate!" Thompson shouted, "where have you been? And not even in flannels yet."

"I'm very sorry," Frank shouted back cheerfully, "and never mind the flannels, for once. Shall I come in now?"

"No," Thompson said. "You'd better get your wind first. Let Fenner come in next."

Fenner stayed in four overs, adding two singles as his share, while Thompson put on a three and a two. Then Fenner was caught. Thirty-one runs for eight wickets! Then Frank took the bat, and walked to the ground. Thompson came across to him.

"Look here, Hargate, you have made a nice mess of it, and the game looks as bad as can be. Whatever you do, play carefully. Don't let out at anything that comes straight. The great thing is to bother their bowling a bit. They're so cocky now, that pretty near every ball is straight on the wickets. Be content with blocking for a bit, and Handcock will soon go off. He always gets savage if his bowling is collared."

Frank obeyed orders. In the next twenty minutes he only scored six runs, all in singles, while Thompson, who was also playing very carefully, put on thirteen. The game looked more hopeful for the Town boys. Then there was a shout from the House, as Thompson's middle wicket was sent flying. Childers, who was the last of the team, walked out.

"Now, Childers," Thompson said, "don't you hit at a ball. You're safe to be bowled or caught if you do. Just lift your bat, and block them each time. Now, Frank, it's your turn to score. Put them on as fast as you can. It's no use playing carefully any longer."

Frank set to to hit in earnest. He had now got his eye well in, and the stand which he and Thompson had made together, had taken the sting out of the bowling. The ball which had taken Thompson's wicket was the last of the over. Consequently the next came to him. It was a little wide, and Frank, stepping out, drove it for four. A loud shout rose from the Town boys. There had only been one four scored before, during the innings. Off the next ball Frank scored a couple, blocked the next, and drove the last of the over past long leg for four. The next over Childers strictly obeyed orders, blocking each ball. Then it was Frank's turn again, and seven more went up on the board. They remained together for just fifteen minutes, but during that time thirty-one had been added to the score. Frank was caught at cover point, having added twenty-eight since Thompson left him, the other three being credited to Childers. The total was eighty-one—not a bad score in a school match.

"Well, you've redeemed yourself," Thompson said, as Frank walked to the tent. "You played splendidly, old fellow, when you did come. If we do as well next innings we are safe. They're not likely to average eighty. Now get on your wicket-keeping gloves. Green and I will bowl."

The House scored rapidly at first, and fifty runs were put on with the loss of four wickets. Then misfortune fell upon them, and the remaining six fell for nineteen. The next innings Frank went in first, but was caught when the score stood at fifteen. Thompson made fourteen, but the rest scored but badly, and the whole were out for forty-eight.

The House had sixty-one to get to win. Six wickets had fallen for fifty-one runs, when Thompson put Childers on to bowl. The change was a fortunate one. Ruthven's stumps were lowered at the first ball. Handcock was caught off the second. The spirits of the Town boys rose. There were but two wickets more, and still ten runs to get to win. The House played cautiously now, and four overs were sent down without a run. Then off a ball from Childers a four was scored, but his next ball levelled the outside stump. Then by singles the score mounted up until a tremendous shout from the House announced that the game was saved, sixty runs being marked by the scorers. The next ball, the Town boys replied even more lustily, for Childers' ball removed the bails, and the game ended in a tie. Both parties were equally well satisfied, and declared that a better game had never been played at Dr. Parker's. As soon as the game was over Frank, without waiting to join in the general talk over the game, put on his coat and waistcoat and started at a run for home.

Frank Hargate was an only son. His mother lived in a tiny cottage on the outskirts of Deal. She was a widow, her husband, Captain Hargate, having died a year before. She had only her pension as an officer's widow, a pittance that scarce sufficed even for the modest wants of herself, Frank, and her little daughter Lucy, now six years old.

"I hope I have not kept tea waiting, mother," Frank said as he ran in. "It is not my beetles and butterflies this time. We have been playing a cricket-match, and a first-rate one it was. Town boys against the House. It ended in a tie."

"You are only a quarter of an hour late," his mother said smiling, "which is a great deal nearer being punctual than is usually the case when you are out with your net. We were just going to begin, for I know your habits too well to give you more than a quarter of an hour's law."

"I'm afraid I am horridly unpunctual," Frank said, "and yet, mother, I never go out without making up my mind that I will be in sharp to time. But somehow there is always something which draws me away."

"It makes no matter, Frank. If you are happy and amused I am content, and if the tea is cold it is your loss, not ours. Now, my boy, as soon as you have washed your hands we will have tea."

It was a simple meal. Thick slices of bread and butter and tea, for Mrs. Hargate could only afford to put meat upon the table once a day, and even for that several times in the week fish was substituted, when the weather was fine and the fishing-boats returned well laden. Frank fortunately cared very little what he ate, and what was good enough for his mother was good enough for him. In his father's lifetime things had been different, but Captain Hargate had fallen in battle in New Zealand. He had nothing besides his pay, and his wife and children had lived with him in barracks until his regiment was ordered out to New Zealand, when he had placed his wife in the little cottage she now occupied. He had fallen in an attack on a Maori pah, a fortnight after landing in New Zealand. He had always intended Frank to enter the military profession, and had himself directed his education so long as he was at home.

The loss of his father had been a terrible blow for the boy, who had been his constant companion when off duty. Captain Hargate had been devoted to field sports and was an excellent naturalist. The latter taste Frank had inherited from him. His father had brought home from India—where the regiment had been stationed until it returned for its turn of home service four years before he left for New Zealand—a very large quantity of skins of birds which he had shot there. These be had stuffed and mounted, and so dexterous was he at the work, so natural and artistic were the groups of birds, that he was enabled to add considerably to his income by sending these up to the shop of a London naturalist. He had instructed Frank in his methods, and had given him one of the long blow-guns used by some of the hill tribes in India. The boy had attained such dexterity in its use that he was able with his clay pellets to bring down sitting birds, however small, with almost unerring accuracy. These he stuffed and mounted, arranging them with a taste and skill which delighted the few visitors at his mother's cottage.

Frank was ready to join in a game of football or cricket when wanted, and could hold his own in either. But he vastly preferred to go out for long walks with his blow-gun, his net, and his collecting boxes. At home every moment not required for the preparation of his lessons was spent in mounting and arranging his captures. He was quite ready to follow the course his father proposed for him, and to enter the army. Captain Hargate had been a very gallant officer, and the despatches had spoken most highly of the bravery with which he led his company into action in the fight in which he lost his life. Therefore Mrs. Hargate hoped that Frank would have little difficulty in obtaining a commission without purchase when the time for his entering the army arrived. Frank's desire for a military life was based chiefly upon the fact that it would enable him to travel to many parts of the world, and to indulge his taste for natural history to the fullest. He was but ten years old when he left India with the regiment, but he had still a vivid recollection of the lovely butterflies and bright birds of that country.

His father had been at pains to teach him that a student of natural history must be more than a mere collector, and that like other sciences it must be methodically studied. He possessed an excellent library of books upon the subject, and although Frank might be ignorant of the name of any bird or insect shown to him he could at once name the family and species.

In the year which Frank had been at school at Dr. Parker's he had made few intimate friends. His habits of solitary wandering and studious indoor work had hindered his becoming the chum of any of his school-fellows, and this absence of intimacy had been increased by the fact that the straitness of his mother's means prevented his inviting any of his school-fellows to his home. He had, indeed, brought one or two of the boys, whose tastes lay in the direction of his own, to the house to show them his collections of birds and insects. But he declined their invitations to visit them, as he was unable to return their hospitality, and was too proud to eat and drink at other fellows' houses when be could not ask them to do the same at his own. It was understood at Dr. Parker's that Frank Hargate's people were poor, but it was known that his father had been killed in battle. There are writers who depict boys as worshippers of wealth, and many pictures have been drawn of the slights and indignities to which boys, whose means are inferior to those of their school-fellows, are subject. I am happy to believe that this is a libel. There are, it is true, toadies and tuft-hunters among boys as among men. That odious creature, the parasite of the Greek and Latin plays, exists still, but I do not believe that a boy is one whit the less liked, or is ever taunted with his poverty, provided he is a good fellow. Most of the miseries endured by boys whose pocket-money is less abundant than that of their fellows are purely self-inflicted. Boys and men who are always on the look-out for slights will, of course, find what they seek. But the lad who is not ashamed of what is no fault of his own, who frankly and manfully says, "I can't afford it," will not find that he is in any way looked

BLOWN OUT TO SEA

down upon by those of his school-fellows whose good opinion is in the smallest degree worth having.

Certainly this was so in the case of Frank Hargate. He was never in the slightest degree ashamed of saying, "I can't afford it;" and the fact that he was the son of an officer killed in battle gave him a standing among the best in the school in spite of his want of pocket-money. Frank was friends with many of the fishermen, and these would often bring him strange fish and sea creatures brought up in their nets, instead of throwing them back into the sea.

During the holidays he would sometimes go out with them for twenty-four hours in their fishing-boats.

His mother made no objection to this, as she thought that the exercise and sea air were good for his health, and that the change did him good. Frank himself was so fond of the sea that he was half disposed to adopt it instead of the army as a profession. But his mother was strongly opposed to the idea, and won him to her way of thinking by pointing out that although a sailor visits many ports he stays long at none of them, and that in the few hours' leave he might occasionally obtain he would be unable to carry out his favourite pursuits.

"Hargate," Ruthven, who was one of the oldest of the House boys and was about Frank's age, that is about fifteen years old, said a few days after the match, "the Doctor has given Handcock and Jones and myself leave to take a boat and go out this afternoon. We mean to start soon after dinner, and shall take some lines and bait with us. We have got leave till lock-up, so we shall have a long afternoon of it. Will you come with us?"

"Thank you, Ruthven," Frank said; "I should like it very much, but you know I'm short of pocket-money, and I can't pay my share of the boat, so I would rather leave it alone."

"Oh, nonsense, Hargate!" Ruthven answered; "we know money is not your strong point, but we really want you to go with us. You can manage a boat better than any of us, and you will really oblige us if you will go with us."

"Oh, if you put it in that way," Frank said, "I shall be glad to go with you; but I do not think," he went on, looking at the sky, "that the weather looks very settled. However, if you do not mind the chance of a ducking, I don't."

"That's agreed then," Ruthven said; "will you meet us near the pier at three o'clock?"

"All right. I'll be punctual."

At the appointed hour the four lads met on the beach. Ruthven and his companions wanted to choose a light rowing boat, but Frank strongly urged them to take a much larger and heavier one.

"In the first place," he said, "the wind is blowing off shore, and although it's calm here it will be rougher farther out; and, unless I'm mistaken, the wind is getting up fast. Besides this it will be much more comfortable to fish from a good-sized boat."

His comrades grumbled at the extra labour which the large boat would entail in rowing. However, they finally gave in and the boat was launched.

"Look out, Master Hargate," the boatman said as they started; "you'd best not go out too far, for the wind is freshening fast, and we shall have, I think, a nasty night."

The boys thought little of the warning, for the sky was bright and blue, broken only by a few gauzy white clouds which streaked it here and there. They rowed out about a mile, and then laying in their oars, lowered their grapnel and began to fish. The sport was good. The fish bit freely and were rapidly hauled on board. Even Frank was so absorbed in the pursuit that he paid no attention to the changing aspect of the sky, the increasing roughness of the sea, or the rapidly rising wind.

Suddenly a heavy drop or two of rain fell in the boat. All looked up.

"We are in for a squall," Frank exclaimed, "and no mistake. I told you you would get a ducking, Ruthven."

He had scarcely spoken when the squall was upon them. A deluge of rain swept down, driven by a strong squall of wind.

"Sit in the bottom of the boat," Frank said; "this is a snorter."

Not a word was said for ten minutes, long before which all were drenched to the skin. With the rain a sudden darkness had fallen, and the land was entirely invisible. Frank looked anxiously towards the shore. The sea was getting up fast, and the boat tugging and straining at the cord of the grapnel. He shook his head. "It looks very bad," he said to himself. "If this squall does not abate we are going to have a bad time of it."

A quarter of an hour after it commenced the heavy downpour of rain ceased, or rather changed into a driving sleet. It was still extremely dark, a thick lead-coloured cloud overspread the sky. Already the white horses showed how fast the sea was rising, and the wind showed no signs of falling with the cessation of the rain-storm. The boat was labouring at her head rope and dipping her nose heavily into the waves.

"Look here, you fellows," Frank shouted, "we must take to the oars. If the rope were a long one we might ride here, but you know it little more than reached the ground when we threw it out. I believe she's dragging already, and even if she isn't she would pull her head under water with so short a rope when the sea gets up. We'd better get out the oars and row to shore, if we can, before the sea gets worse."

The lads got up and looked round, and their faces grew pale and somewhat anxious as they saw how threatening was the aspect of the sea. They had four oars on board, and these were soon in the water and the grapnel hauled up. A few strokes sufficed to show them that with all four rowing the boat's head could not be kept towards the shore, the wind taking it and turning the boat broadside on.

"This will never do," Frank said. "I will steer and you row, two oars on one side and one on the other. I will take a spell presently. Row steadily, Ruthven," he shouted; "don't spurt. We have a long row before us and must not knock ourselves up at the beginning."

For half an hour not a word was spoken beyond an occasional cheery exhortation from Frank. The shore could be dimly seen at times through the driving mist, and Frank's heart sank as be recognized the fact that it was further off than it had been when they first began to row. The wind was blowing a gale now, and, although but two miles from shore, the sea was already rough for an open boat.

"Here, Ruthven, you take a spell now," he said.

Although the rowers had from time to time glanced over their shoulders, they could not, through the mist, form any idea of their position.

When Ruthven took the helm he exclaimed, "Good gracious, Frank! the shore is hardly visible. We are being blown out to sea."

"I am afraid we are," Frank said; "but there is nothing to do but to keep on rowing. The wind may lull or it may shift and give us a chance of making for Ramsgate. The boat is a good sea-boat, and may keep afloat even if we are driven out to sea. Or if we are missed from shore they may send the life-boat out after us. That is our best chance."

In another quarter of an hour Ruthven was ready to take another spell at the oar.

"I fear," Frank shouted to him as he climbed over the seat, "there is no chance whatever of making shore. All we've got to do is to row steadily and keep her head to wind. Two of us will do for that. You and I will row now, and let Handcock and Jones steer and rest by turns. Then when we are done up they can take our places."

In another hour it was quite dark, save for the gray light from the foaming water around. The wind was blowing stronger than ever, and it required the greatest care on the part of the steersman to keep her dead in the eye of the wind. Handcock was steering now, and Jones lying at the bottom of the boat, where he was sheltered, at least from the wind. All the lads were plucky fellows and kept up a semblance of good spirits, but all in their hearts knew that their position was a desperate one.

CHAPTER II

A MAD DOG

"DON'T you think, Hargate," Ruthven shouted in his ear, "we had better run before it? It's as much as Handcock can do to keep her head straight."

"Yes," Frank shouted back, "if it were not for the Goodwins. They lie right across ahead of us."

Ruthven said no more, and for another hour he and Frank rowed their hardest. Then Handcock and Jones took the oars. Ruthven lay down in the bottom of the boat and Frank steered. After rowing for another hour Frank found that he could no longer keep the boat's head to wind. Indeed, he could not have done so for so long had he not shipped the rudder and steered the boat with an oar, through a notch cut in the stern for the purpose. Already the boat shipped several heavy seas, and Ruthven was kept hard at work bailing with a tin can in which they had brought out bait.

"Ruthven, we must let her run. Put out the other oar, we must watch our time. Row hard when I give the word."

The manœuvre was safely accomplished, and in a minute the boat was flying before the gale.

"Keep on rowing," Frank said, "but take it easily. We must try and make for the tail of the sands. I can see the light-ship."

Frank soon found that the wind was blowing too directly upon the long line of sands to enable him to make the light-ship. Already, far ahead, a gray light seemed to gleam up, marking where the sea was breaking over the dreaded shoal.

"I am afraid it is no use," he said. "Now, boys, we had best, each of us, say our prayers to God, and prepare to die bravely, for I fear that there is no hope for us."

There was silence in the boat for the next five minutes, as the boys sat with their heads bent down. More than one choking sob might have been heard, had the wind lulled, as they thought of the dear ones at home. Suddenly there was a flash of light ahead, and the boom of a gun directly afterwards came upon their ears. Then a rocket soared up into the air.

"There is a vessel on the sands," Frank exclaimed. "Let us make for her. If we can get on board we shall have a better chance than here."

The boys again bent to their oars, and Frank tried to steer exactly for the spot whence the rocket had gone up. Presently another gun flashed out.

"There she is," he said. "I can see her now against the line of breakers. Take the oar again, Ruthven. We must bring up under shelter of her lee."

In another minute or two they were within a hundred yards of the ship. She was a large vessel, and lay just at the edge of the broken water. The waves, as they struck her, flew high above her deck. As the boat neared her a bright light suddenly sprang up. The ship was burning a blue light. Then a faint cheer was heard.

"They see us," Frank said. "They must think we are the life-boat. What a disappointment for them! Now, steady, lads, and prepare to pull her round the instant we are under her stern. I will go as near as I dare."

Frank could see the people on deck watching the boat. They must have seen now that she was not the life-boat; but even in their own danger they must have watched with intense interest the efforts of the tiny boat, adrift in the raging sea, to reach them. Frank steered the boat within a few yards of the stern, then Jones and Ruthven, who were both rowing the same side, exerted themselves to the utmost, while Frank pushed with the steering oar. A minute later, and they lay in comparatively still water, under the lee of the ship. Two or three ropes were thrown them, and they speedily climbed on board.

"We thought you were the life-boat at first," the captain said, as they reached the deck; "but, of course, they cannot be here for a couple of hours yet."

"We were blown off shore, sir," Frank said, "and have been rowing against the wind for hours."

"Well, my lads," the captain said, "you have only prolonged your lives for a few minutes, for she will not hold together long."

The ship, indeed, presented a pitiable appearance. The masts had already gone, the bulwark to windward had been carried away, and the hull lay heeled over at a sharp angle, her deck to leeward being level with the water. The crew were huddled down near the lee bulwarks, sheltered somewhat by the sharp slope of the deck from the force of the wind. As each wave broke over the ship, tons of water rushed down upon them. No more guns were fired, for the lashing had broken and the gun run down to leeward. Already there were signs that the ship would break up ere long, and no hope existed that rescue could arrive in time.

Suddenly there was a great crash, and the vessel parted amidships.

"A few minutes will settle it now," the captain said. "God help us all."

At this moment there was a shout to leeward, which was answered by a scream of joy from those on board the wreck, for there, close alongside, lay the life-boat, whose approach had been entirely unseen. In a few minutes the fifteen men who remained of the twenty-two, who had formed the crew of the wreck, and the four boys, were on board her. A tiny sail was set and the boat's head laid towards Ramsgate.

"I am glad to see you, Master Hargate," the sailor who rowed one of the stroke-oars shouted. He was the man who had lent them the boat. "I was up in the town looking after my wife, who is sick, and clean forgot you till it was dark. Then I ran down and found the boat hadn't returned, so I got the crew together and we came out to look for you, though we had little hope of finding you. It was lucky for you we did, and for the rest of them too, for so it chanced that we were but half a mile away when the ship fired her first gun, just as we had given you up and determined to go back; so on we came straight here. Another ten minutes and we should have been too late. We are making for Ramsgate now. We could never beat back to Deal in this wind. I don't know as I ever saw it blow much harder."

These sentences were not spoken consecutively, but were shouted out in the intervals between gusts of wind. It took them two hours to beat back to Ramsgate, a signal having been made as soon as they left the wreck to inform the life-boat there and at Broadstairs that they need not put out, as the rescue had been already effected. The lads were soon put to bed at the sailors' home, a man being at once despatched on horseback to Deal, to inform those there of the arrival of the life-boat, and of the rescue of the four boys who had been blown to sea.

Early next morning Frank and Handcock returned to Deal, the other two lads being so exhausted by their fatigue and exposure that the doctor said they had better remain in bed for another twenty-four hours.

It is impossible to describe the thankfulness and relief which Mrs. Hargate experienced, when, about two in the morning, Dr. Parker himself brought her news of the safety of her boy. She had long given up all hope, for when the evening came on and Frank had not returned, she had gone down to the shore. She learned from the fishermen there that it was deemed impossible that the boys could reach shore in face of the gale, and that although the life-boat had just put out in search of them, the chances of their being found were, as she herself saw, faint indeed. She had passed the hours which had intervened in prayer, and was still kneeling by her bedside, where little Lucy was unconsciously sleeping, when Dr. Parker's knock was heard at the door. Fervent, indeed, was her gratitude to God for the almost miraculous preservation of her son's life, and then, overcome by the emotions she had experienced, she sought her couch, and was still asleep when, by the earliest train in the morning, Frank returned.

For some time the four boys were the heroes of the school. A subscription was got up to pay for the lost boat, and close as were Mrs. Hargate's means, she enabled Frank to subscribe his share towards the fund. The incident raised Frank to a pinnacle of popularity among his school-fellows, for the three others were unanimous in saying that it was his coolness and skill in the management of the boat, which alone kept up their spirits, and enabled them to keep her afloat during the gale, and to make the wreck in safety.

In the general enthusiasm excited by the event, Frank's pursuits, which had hitherto found few followers, now became quite popular in the school. A field-club was formed, of which he was elected president, and long rambles in the country in search of insects and plants were frequently organized. Frank himself was obliged, in the interests of the school, to moderate the zeal of the naturalists, and to point out that cricket must not be given up, as, if so large a number withdrew themselves from the game, the school would suffer disaster in its various engagements with other schools in the neighbourhood. Consequently the rule was made that members of the club were bound to be in the cricket-field on at least three days in the week, including one half-holiday, while they were free to ramble in the country on other days. This wise regulation prevented the "naturalists" from becoming unpopular in the school, which would assuredly have been the case had they entirely absented themselves from cricket.

One Saturday afternoon Frank started with a smaller boy, was one of his most devoted followers, for a long country walk. Frank carried his blow-gun and a butterfly net, Charlie Goodall a net of about a foot in depth, made of canvas, mounted on a stout brass rim, and strong stick, for the capture of water-beetles. Their pockets bulged with bottles and tin boxes for the carriage of their captured prey.

They had passed through Eastry, a village four miles from Deal, when Frank exclaimed, "There is a green hairstreak. The first I've seen this year. I have never caught but one before."

Cautiously approaching the butterfly, who was sunning himself on the top of a thistle, Frank prepared to strike, when it suddenly mounted and flitted over a hedge. In a moment the boys had scrambled through the gap and were in full pursuit. The butterfly flitted here and there, sometimes allowing the boys to approach within a few feet and then flitting away again for fifty yards without stopping. Heedless where they were going, the boys pursued, till they were startled by a sudden shout close to them.

"You young rascals, how dare you run over my wheat?"

The boys stopped, and Frank saw what, in his excitement, he had not hitherto heeded, that he was now running in a field of wheat, which reached to his knee.

"I am very sorry, sir," he said. "I was so excited that I really did not see where I was going."

"Not see!" shouted the angry farmer. "You young rascal, I'll break every bone in your body," and he flourished a heavy stick as he spoke.

Charlie Goodall began to cry.

"I have no right to trespass on your wheat, sir," Frank said firmly; "but you have no right to strike us. My name is Frank Hargate. I belong to Dr. Parker's school at Deal, and if you will say what damage I have caused, I will pay for it."

"You shall pay for it now," shouted the farmer, as he advanced with uplifted stick.

Frank slipped three or four of his clay bullets into his mouth. "Leave us alone or it will be worse for you," he said as he raised the blow-gun to his mouth. The farmer advanced, and Frank sent a bullet with all his force, and with so true an aim that he struck the farmer on the knuckles. It was a sharp blow, and the farmer, with a cry of pain and surprise, dropped the stick.

"Don't come a step nearer," Frank shouted. "If you do, I will aim at your eye next time," and he pointed the threatening tube at the enraged farmer's face.

"I'll have the law of you, you young villain. I'll make you smart for this."

"You can do as you like about that," Frank said. "I have only struck you in self-defence, and have let you off easily. Come along, Charlie, let's get out of this."

In a few minutes they were again on the road, the farmer making no attempt to follow them, but determined in his mind to drive over the next morning to Deal to take out a summons against them for trespass and assault. The lads proceeded silently along the road. Frank was greatly vexed with himself at his carelessness in running over half-grown wheat, and was meditating how he could pay the fine without having to ask his mother. He determined upon his return to carry some of his cases of stuffed birds down to a shop in the town, and he felt sure that he could get enough for these to pay for any damage which could have been inflicted, with a fine for trespassing, for he had seen stuffed birds exposed in the windows for sale, which were, he was sure, very inferior to his own both in execution and lifelike interest.

After proceeding a few hundred yards along the road they met a pretty little girl of seven or eight years old walking along alone. Frank scarcely glanced at her, for at the moment he heard a shouting in the distance and saw some men running along the road. For a moment he thought that the farmer had despatched some of his men to stop him, but instantly dismissed the idea, as they were coming from the opposite direction and could by no possibility have heard what had happened. They were lost sight of by a dip in the road, and as they disappeared, an object was seen on the road on the near side of the dip.

"It is a dog," Frank said. "What can they be shouting at?"

The dog was within fifty yards of them when the men again appeared from the dip and recommenced shouting. Frank could now hear what they said. "Mad dog! mad dog!"

"Get through the hedge, Charlie, quick," Frank cried. "Here, I will help you over, never mind the thorns."

The hedge was low and closely kept, and Frank, bundling his comrade over it, threw himself across and looked round. The dog was within ten yards of them, and Frank saw that the alarm was well founded. The dog was a large cross-bred animal, between a mastiff and a bull-dog. Its hair was rough and bristling. It came along with its head down and foam churning from its mouth. Frank looked the other way and gave a cry. Not twenty yards off, in the middle of the road, stood the child. She, too, had heard the shouts, and had paused to see what was the matter. She had not taken the alarm, but stood unsuspicious of danger watching, not the dog, but the men in the distance.

Frank placed the blow-gun to his mouth, and in a moment his pellet struck the animal smartly on the side of the head. It gave a short yelp and paused. Another shot struck it, and then Frank, snatching the water-net from Charlie, threw himself over the hedge, and placed himself between the child and the dog just as the latter, with a savage growl, rushed at him.

Frank stood perfectly cool, and as the animal rushed forward, thrust the net over its head; the ring was but just large enough to allow its head to enter. Frank at once sprang forward, and placing himself behind the dog kept a strain upon the stick, so retaining the mouth of the net tightly on his neck. The animal at first rushed forward dragging Frank after him. Then he stopped, backed, and tried to withdraw his head from the encumbrance which blinded him. Frank, however, had no difficulty in retaining the canvas net in its place, until the men, who were armed with pitchforks, ran up and speedily despatched the unfortunate animal.

"That's bravely done, young master," one of them said; "and you have saved Missy's life surely. The savage brute rushed into the yard and bit a young colt and a heifer, and then, as we came running out with forks, he took to the road again. We chased 'um along not knowing who we might meet, and it gave us a rare turn when we saw the master's Bessy standing alone in the road, wi' nout between her and the dog. Where have you been, Miss Bessy?"

"I've been to aunt's," she said, "and she gave me some strawberries and cream, and it's wicked of you to kill the poor dog."

"Her aunt's farm lies next to master's," the man explained; "and little miss often goes over there. The dog was mad, missy, and if it hadn't been for young master here, it would have killed you as safe as eggs. Won't you come back to the farm, sir? Master and mistress would be main glad to thank you for having saved missy's life."

"No, thank you," Frank said; "we are late now and must be going on our way. I am very glad I happened to be here at the time;" so saying Frank and Charlie proceeded on their way to Deal.

On reaching home he at once picked out four of his best cases of stuffed birds. The cases he had constructed himself, for his father had encouraged him to depend upon himself for his amusements. He had asked Charlie to come round to help him to carry the cases, and with these he proceeded to a shop where he had seen such things offered for sale.

"And you really did these yourself?" the man said in surprise. "They are beautifully done. Quite pictures, I call them. It is a pity that they are homely birds. There is no great sale for such things here. I cannot give you more than five shillings each, but if you had them in London they would be worth a great deal more."

Frank gladly accepted the offer, and feeling sure that the pound would cover the damage done and the fine, which might be five shillings apiece for trespassing, went home in good spirits. The next morning the doctor was called out in the middle of school, and presently returned accompanied by the farmer with whom they had had the altercation on the previous day. Frank felt his cheeks flush as he anticipated a severe reprimand before the whole school.

"Mr. Gregson," the doctor said, "tells me that two of my boys were out near his place at Eastry yesterday. One of them gave him his name, which he has forgotten."

"It was I, sir," Frank said rising in his place; "I was there with Goodall. We ran on Mr. Gregson's ground after a butterfly. It was my fault, sir, for, of course, Goodall went where I did. We ran among his wheat, and I really did not notice where we were going till he called to us. I was wrong, of course, and am ready to pay for any damage we may have caused."

"You are welcome," the farmer said, "to trample on my wheat for the rest of your born days. I haven't come over here to talk about the wheat, though, I tell you fairly I'd minded to do so. I've come over here, Dr. Parker, me and my missus who's outside, to thank this young gentleman for having saved the life of my little daughter Bessy. She was walking along the road when a mad dog, a big brute of a mastiff, who came, I hear, from somewhere about Canterbury, and who has bit two boys on the road, to say nothing of other dogs and horses and such like; he came along the road, he were close to my Bess, and she stood there all alone. Some of my men with pitchforks were two hundred yards or so behind; but law, they could have done nothing! when this young gentleman here jumped all of a sudden over a hedge and put himself between the dog and my Bess. The dog, he rushed at him; but what does he do but claps a bag he'd got at the end of a stick over the brute's head, and there he holds him tight till the men comes up and kills him with their forks. Young gentleman," he said, stepping up to Frank and holding out his hand, "I owe my child's life to you. There are not many men who would have thrown themselves in the way of a mad dog, for the sake of a child they knew nothing of. I thank you for it with all my heart. God bless you, sir. Now, boys, you give three cheers with me for your school-mate, for you've got a right to be proud of him."

Three such thundering cheers as those which arose had never been heard within the limits of Dr. Parker's school from the day of its foundation. Seeing that farther work could not be expected from them after this excitement, Dr. Parker gave the boys a holiday for the rest of the day, and they poured out from the school-room, shouting and delighted, while Frank was taken off to the parlour to be thanked by Mrs. Gregson. The farmer closed his visit by inviting Frank, with as many of his school-fellows as he liked—the whole school if they would come, the more the better—to come over to tea on the following Saturday afternoon, and he promised them as much strawberries and cream as they could eat. The invitation was largely accepted, and the boys all agreed that a jollier meal they never sat down to than that which was spread on tables in the farmer's garden. The meal was called tea, but it might have been a dinner, for the tables were laden with huge pies, cold chicken and duck, hams, and piles of cakes and tarts of all sorts. Before they started for home, late in the evening, syllabub and cake were handed round, and the boys tramped back to Deal in the highest of glee at the entertainment they had received from the hospitable farmer and his wife. Great fun had been caused after tea by the farmer giving a humorous relation of the battle with which his acquaintance with Frank had commenced, and especially at the threat of Frank's to send a bullet into his eye if he interfered with him. When they left a most cordial invitation was given to Frank to come over, with any friend he liked to bring with him, and have tea at the Oaks farm whenever he chose to do so.

CHAPTER III

TOUGH YARN

"YOU had a close shave the other night," one of the boatmen remarked to Frank, as a few days after the adventure he strolled down with Ruthven and Handcock to talk to the boatman whose boat had been lost, "a very narrow shave. I had one out there myself when I was just about your age, nigh forty years ago. I went out for a sail with my father in his fishing-boat, and I didn't come back for three years. That was the only long voyage I ever went. I've been sticking to fishing ever since."

"How was it you were away three years?" Handcock asked, "and what was the adventure? Tell us about it."

"Well, it's rather a long yarn," the boatman said.

"Well, your best plan, Jack," Ruthven said, putting his hand in his pocket and bringing out sixpence, "will be for you to go across the road and wet your whistle before you begin."

"Thank ye, young gentleman. I will take three o' grog and an ounce of 'bacca." He went across to the public-house, and soon returned with a long clay in his hand. Then he sat down on the shingle with his back against a boat, and the boys threw themselves down close to him.

"Now," he began, when he had filled his pipe with great deliberation and got it fairly alight, "this here yarn as I'm going to tell you ain't no gammon. Most of the tales which gets told on the beach to visitors as comes down here and wants to hear of sea adventures is just lies from beginning to end. Now, I ain't that sort, leastways, I shouldn't go to impose upon young gents like you as ha' had a real adventure of your own, and showed uncommon good pluck and coolness too. I don't say, mind ye, that every word is just gospel. My mates as ha' known me from a boy tells me that I've 'bellished the yarn since I first told it, and that all sorts of things

23

have crept in which wasn't there first. That may be so. When a man tells a story a great many times, naturally he can't always tell it just the same, and he gets so mixed up atween what he told last and what he told first that he don't rightly know which was which when he wants to tell it just as it really happened. So if sometimes it appears to you that I'm steering rather wild, just you put a stopper on and bring me up all standing with a question."

There was a quiet humour about the boatman's face, and the boys winked at each other as much as to say that after such an exordium they must expect something rather staggering. The boatman took two or three hard whiffs at his pipe and then began.

"It was towards the end of September in 1832, that's just forty years ago now, that I went out with my father and three hands in the smack, the *Flying Dolphin*. I'd been at sea with father off and on ever since I was about nine years old, and a smarter boy wasn't to be found on the beach. The *Dolphin* was a good sea boat, but she wasn't, so to say, fast, and I dunno' as she was much to look at, for the old man wasn't the sort of chap to chuck away his money in paint or in new sails as long as the old ones could be pieced and patched so as to hold the wind. We sailed out pretty nigh over to the French coast, and good sport we had. We'd been out two days when we turned her head homewards. The wind was blowing pretty strong, and the old man remarked, he thought we was in for a gale. There was some talk of our running in to Calais and waiting till it had blown itself out, but the fish might have spoilt before the wind dropped, so we made up our minds to run straight into Dover and send the fish up from there. The night came on wild and squally and as dark as pitch. It might be about eight bells, and I and one of the other hands had turned in, when father gave a sudden shout down the hatch, 'All hands on deck.' I was next to the steps and sprang up'em. Just as I got to the top something grazed my face, I caught at it, not knowing what it was, and the next moment there was a crash, and the *Dolphin* went away from under my feet. I clung for bare life, scarce awake yet nor knowing what had happened. The next moment I was under water. I still held on to the rope and was soon out again. By this time I was pretty well awake to what had happened. A ship running down channel had walked clean over the poor old *Dolphin*, and I had got hold of the bobstay. It took me some time to climb up on to the bowsprit, for every time she pitched I went under water. However, I got up at last and swarmed along the bowsprit and got on board. There was a chap sitting down fast asleep there. I walked aft to the helmsman. Two men were pacing up and down in front of him. 'You're a nice lot, you are,' I said, 'to go running down Channel at ten knots an hour without any watch, a-walking over ships and a-drowning of seamen. I'll have the law of ye, see if I don't.'

" 'Jeerusalem!' said one, 'who have we here?'

" 'My name is Jack Perkins,' says I, 'and I'm the sole survivor, as far as I knows, of the smack, the *Flying Dolphin*, as has been run down by this craft and lost with all hands.'

" 'Darn the *Flying Dolphin*, and you too,' says the man, and he begins to walk up and down the deck a-puffin' of a long cigar as if nothing had happened.

" 'Oh, come,' says I, 'this won't do. Here you've been and run down a smack, drowned father and the other three hands, and you're look-out fast asleep, and you does nothing.'

" 'I suppose,' said the captain, sarcastic, 'you want me to jump over to look for 'em. You want me to heave the ship to in this gale and to invite yer father perlitely to come on board. P'raps you'd like a grapnel put out to see if I couldn't hook the smack and bring her up again. Perhaps you'd like to be chucked overboard yourself. Nobody asked you to come on board, nobody wanted your company. I reckon the wisest thing you can do is to go for'ard and turn in.' There didn't seem much for me to do else, so I went forward to the forecastle. There most of the hands were asleep, but two or three were sitting up yarning. I told 'em my story and what the captain had said.

" 'He's a queer hand is the skipper,' one of 'em said, 'and has not got a soft place about him. Well, my lad I'm sorry for what's happened, but talking won't do it any good. You've got a long voyage before you, and you'd best turn in and make yourself comfortable for it. '

" 'I ain't going a long voyage,' says I, beginning to pipe my eye, 'I wants to be put ashore at the first port.'

" 'Well, my lad, I daresay the skipper will do that, but as we're bound for the coast of Chili from Hamburg, and ain't likely to be there for about five months, you've got, as I said, a long voyage before you. If the weather had been fine the skipper might have spoken some ship in the Channel, and put you on board, but before the gale's blown out we shall be hundreds of miles at sea. Even if it had been fine I don't suppose the skipper would have parted with you, especially if you told him the watch was asleep. He would not care next time he entered an English port to have a claim fixed on his ship for the vally of the smack.'

"I saw what the sailor said was like enough, and blamed myself for having let out about the watch. However, there was no help for it, and I turned into an empty bunk and cried myself to sleep. What a voyage that was, to be sure! The ship was a Yankee and so was the master and mates. The crew were of all sorts, Dutch, and Swedes, and English, a Yank or two, and a sprinklin' of natives. It was one of those ships they call a hell-on-earth, and cussing and kicking and driving went on all day. I hadn't no regular place give me, but helped the black cook, and pulled at ropes, and swabbed the decks, and got kicked and cuffed all round. The skipper did not often speak to me, but when his eye lighted on me he gave an ugly sort of look, as seemed to say, 'You'd better ha' gone down with the others. You think you're going to report the loss of the smack, and to get damages against the *Potomac*, do you? We shall see.' The crew were a rough lot, but the spirit seemed taken out of 'em by the treatment they met with. It was a word and a blow with the mates, and they would think no more of catching up a handspike and stretching a man senseless on the deck than I should of killing a fly. There was two or three among 'em of a better sort than the others. The best of 'em was the carpenter, an old Dutchman. 'Leetle boy,' he used to say to me, 'you keep yourself out of the sight of de skipper. Bad man dat. Me much surprise if you get to de end of dis voyage all right. You best work vera hard and give him no excuse to hit you. If he do, by gosh, he kill you, and put down in de log, Boy killed by accident.'

26

"I felt that this was so myself, and I did my work as well as I could. One day, however, when we were near the line I happened to upset a bucket with some tar. The captain was standing close by.

" 'You young dog,' he said, 'you've done that a purpose,' and before I could speak he caught up the bucket by the handle and brought it down on my head with all his might. The next thing I remember was, I was lying in a bunk in the forecastle. Everything looked strange to me, and I couldn't raise my head. After a time I made shift to turn it round, and saw old Jans sitting on a chest mending a jacket. I called him, but my voice was so low I hardly seemed to hear it myself.

" 'Ah, my leetle boy!' he said, 'I am glad to hear you speak again. Two whole weeks you say nothing except talk nonsense.'

" 'Have I been ill?' I asked.

" 'You haf been vera bad,' he said. 'De captain meant to kill you, I haf no doubt, and he pretty near do it. After he knock you down he said you dead. He sorry for accident, not mean to hit you so hard, but you dead and better be tossed overboard at once. De mates they come up and take your hands and feet. Den I insist dat I feel your wrist. Two or three of us dey stood by me. Captain he vera angry, say we mutinous dogs. I say not mutinous, but wasn't going to see a boy who was only stunned thrown overboard. We say if he did dat we make complaint before consul when we get to port. De skipper he cuss and swear awful. Howebber we haf our way and carry you here. You haf fever and near die. Tree days after we bring you here de captain he swear you shamming and comed to look at you hisself, but he see that it true and tink you going to die. He go away wid smile on his face. Every day he ask if you alive, and give grunt when I say yes. Now you best keep vera quiet. You no talk 'cept when no one else here but me. Other times lie wid your face to the side and your eyes shut. Best keep you here as long as we can, de longer de better. He make you come on deck and work as soon as he think you strong enough to stand. Best get pretty strong before you go out.'

"For another three weeks I lay in my bunk. I only ate a little gruel when others were there, but when the skipper was at dinner

Jans would bring me strong soup and meat from the caboose. The captain came several times and shook me and swore I was shamming, but I only answered in a whisper and seemed as faint as a girl. All this time the *Potomac* was making good way, and was running fast down the coast of South America. The air was getting cool and fresh.

" 'I tink,' Jans said one evening to me, 'dat dis not go on much longer. De crew getting desperate. Dey talk and mutter among demselves. Me thinks we have trouble before long.'

"The next day one of the mates came in with a bucket of water. 'There! you skulking young hound,' he said as he threw it over me; 'You'd best get out, or the skipper will come and rouse you up himself.'

"I staggered on to the floor. I had made up my mind to sham weak, but I did not need to pretend at first, for having been six weeks in bed, I felt strange and giddy when I got up. I slipped on my clothes and went out on deck, staggered to the bulwarks and held on. The fresh air soon set me straight, and I felt that I was pretty strong again. However, I pretended to be able to scarce stand, and, holding on by the bulwark, made my way aft.

" 'You young dog,' the skipper said, 'you've been shamming for the last six weeks. I reckon I'll sharpen you up now,' and he hit me a heavy blow with a rattan he held in his hand. There was a cry of 'Shame!' from some of the men. As quick as thought the skipper pulled a pistol from his pocket.

" 'Who cried 'Shame?' " he asked looking round.

"No one answered. Still holding the pistol in his hand he gave me several more cuts, and then told me to swab the deck. I did it, pretending all the time I was scarce strong enough to keep my feet. Then I made my way forward and sat down against the bulwark, as if nigh done up, till night came. That night as I lay in my bunk I heard the men talking in whispers together. I judged from what they said that they intended to wait for another week, when they expected to enter Magellan Straits, and then to attack and throw the officers overboard. Nothing seemed settled as to what they would do afterwards. Some were in favour of continuing the voyage to port, and there giving out that the captain and officers had been washed overboard in a storm; when, if all stood true to each other, the truth could never be known, although suspicions might arise. The others, however, insisted that you never could be sure of everyone, and that some one would be sure to peach. They argued in favour of sailing west and beaching the ship on one of the Pacific islands, where they could live comfortably and take wives among the native women. If they were ever found they could then say that the ship was blown out of her course and wrecked there, and that the captain and officers had been drowned or killed by the natives. It seemed to me that this party were the strongest. For the next week I was thrashed and kicked every day, and had I been as weak as I pretended to be, I'm sure they would have killed me. However, thanks to the food Jans brought me, for I was put on bread and water, I held on. At last we entered the straits. The men were very quiet that day, and the captain in a worse temper than usual. I did not go to sleep, and turned out at the midnight watch, for I was made to keep watch although I was on duty all day. As the watch came in I heard them say to the others, 'In ten minutes' time.' Presently I saw them come out, and joining the watch on deck they went aft quietly in a body. They had all got handspikes in their hands. Then there was a rush. Two pistol shots were fired, and then there was a splash, and I knew that the officer on watch was done for. Then they burst into the aft cabins. There were pistol shots and shouts, and for three or four minutes the fight went on. Then all was quiet. Then they came up on deck again and I heard three splashes, that accounted for the captain and the two other mates. I thought it safe now to go aft. I found that six of the men had been killed. These were thrown overboard, and then the crew got at the spirit stores and began to drink. I looked about for Jans, and found him presently sitting on the deck by the bulwark.

" 'Ah, my leetle boy!' he said, 'you have just come in time. I have been shot through the body. I was not in de fight, but was standing near when dey rushed at de officer on watch. De first pistol he fire missed de man he aim at and hit me. Well, it was shust as well. I am too old to care for living among de black peoples, and I did not want a black wife at all. So matters haf not turned out so vera bad. Get me some water.'

"I got him some, but in five minutes the poor old Dutchman was dead. There was no one on deck. All were shouting and singing in the captain's cabin, so I went and turned in forward. Morning was just breaking when I suddenly woke. There was a great light, and running on deck I saw the fire pouring out from the cabin aft. I suppose they had all drunk themselves stupid and had upset a light, and the fire had spread and suffocated them all. Anyhow, there were none of them to be seen. I got hold of a water-keg and placed it in a boat which luckily hung out on its davits, as Jans had, the day before, been caulking a seam in her side just above the water's edge. I made a shift to lower it, threw off the falls, and getting out the oars, rowed off. I lay by for some little time, but did not see a soul on deck. Then, as I had nowhere particular to go, I lay down and slept. On getting up I found that I had drifted two or three miles from the ship, which was now a mere smoking shell, the greater part being burnt to the water's edge. Two miles to the north lay the land, and getting out an oar at the stern I sculled her to shore. I suppose I had been seen, or that the flames of the ship had called down the people, for there they were in the bay, and such a lot of creatures I never set eyes on. Men and women alike was pretty nigh naked, and dirt is no name for them. Though I was but a boy I was taller than most. They came round me and jabbered and jabbered till I was nigh deafened. Over and over again they pointed to the ship. I thought they wanted to know whether I belonged to it, but it couldn't have been that, because when I nodded a lot of 'em jumped into some canoes which was lying ashore, and taking me with them paddled off to the ship. I suppose they really wanted to know if they could have what they could find. That wasn't much, but it seemed a treasure to them. There was a lot of burned beams floating about alongside, and all of these which had iron or copper bolts or fastenings they took in tow and rowed ashore. We hadn't been gone many hundred yards from the vessel when she sunk. Well, young gentlemen, for upwards of two years I lived with them critturs. My clothes soon wore out, and I got to be as naked and dirty as the rest of 'em. They were good hands at fishing, and could spear a fish by the light of a torch wonderful. In other respects they didn't seem to have much sense. They lived, when I first went there, in holes scratched in the side of a hill, but I taught 'em to make huts, making a sort of axe out of the iron saved. In summer they used to live in these, but in winter, when it was awful cold, we lived in the holes, which were a sight warmer than the huts. Law, what a time that was! I had no end of adventures with wild beasts. The way the lions used to roar and the elephants—"

"I think, Jack," Ruthven interrupted, "that this must be one of the embellishments which have crept in since you first began telling the tale. I don't think I should keep it in if I were you, because the fact that there are neither lions nor elephants in South America throws a doubt upon the accuracy of this portion of your story."

"It may be, sir," the sailor said, with a twinkle of his eyes, "that the elephants and lions may not have been in the first story. Now I think of it, I can't recall that they were; but, you see, people wants to know all about it. They ain't satisfied when I tell 'em that I lived two years among these chaps. They wants to know how I passed my time, and whether there were any wild beasts, and a lot of such like questions, and, in course, I must answer them. So then, you see, naturally, 'bellishments creeps in; but I did live there for two years, that's gospel truth, and I did go pretty nigh naked, and in winter was pretty near starved to death over and over again. When the ground was too hard to dig up roots, and the sea was too rough for the canoes to put out, it went hard with us, and very often we looked more like living skelingtons than human beings. Every time a ship came in sight they used to hurry me away into the woods. I suppose they found me useful, and didn't want to part with me. At last I got desperate, and made up my mind I'd make a bolt whatever came of it. They didn't watch me when there were no ships near. I suppose they thought there was nowhere for me to run to, so one night I steals down to the shore, gets into a canoe, puts in a lot of roots which I had dug up and hidden away in readiness, and so makes off. I rowed hard all night, for I knew they would be after me when they found I had gone. Them straits is sometimes miles and miles across; at other times not much more than a ship's length, and the tide runs through 'em like a mill-race. I had chosen a time when I had the tide with me, and soon after morning I came to one of them narrow places. I should like to have stopped here, because it would have been handy for any ship as passed; but the tide run so strong, and the rocks were so steep on both sides, that I couldn't make a landing. Howsomdever, directly it widened out, I managed to paddle into the back water and landed there. Well, gents, would you believe me, if there wasn't two big allygaters a-sitting there with their mouths open ready to swallow me, canoe and all when I came to shore."

"No, Jack, I'm afraid we can't believe that. We would if we could, you know, but alligators are not fond of such cold weather as you'd been having, nor do they frequent the sea-shore."

"Ah, but this, you see, was a straits, Master Ruthven, just a narrow straits, and I expect the creatures took it for a river."

"No, no, Jack, we can't swallow the alligators, any more than they could swallow you and your canoe."

"Well," the sailor said with a sigh, "I won't say no more about the allygaters. I can't rightly recall when they came into the story. Howsomdever, I landed, you can believe that, you know."

"Oh yes, we can quite believe, Jack, that, if you were there, in that canoe, in that back water, with the land close ahead, you did land."

The sailor looked searchingly at Ruthven and then continued:

"I hauled the canoe up and hid it in some bushes, and it were well I did, for a short time afterwards a great—" and he paused. "Does the hippypotybus live in them 'ere waters, young gents?"

"He does not, Jack," Ruthven said.

"Then it's clear," the sailor said, "that it wazn't a hippypotybus. It must have been a seal."

"Yes, it might have been a seal," Ruthven said. "What did he do?"

"Well, he just took a look at me, gents, winked with one eye, as much as to say, 'I see you,' and went down again. There warn't nothing else as he could do, was there?"

"It was the best thing he could do anyhow," Ruthven said.

"Well, gents, I lived there for about three weeks, and then a ship comes along, homeward bound, and I goes out and hails her. At first they thought as I was a native as had learned to speak English, and it wasn't till they'd boiled me for three hours in the ship's copper as they got at the colour of my skin, and could believe as I was English. So I came back here and found the old woman still alive, and took to fishing again; but it was weeks and weeks before I could get her or anyone else to believe as I was Jack Perkins. And that's all the story, young gents. Generally I tells it a sight longer to the gents as come down from London in summer; but, you see, I can't make much out of it when ye won't let me have 'bellishments."

"And how much of it is true altogether, Jack?" Frank asked. "Really how much?"

"It's all true as I have told you, young masters," the boatman said. "It were every bit true about the running down of the smack, and me being nearly killed by the skipper, and the mutiny, and the burning of the vessel, and my living for a long time—no, I won't stick to the two years, but it might have been three weeks, with the natives before a ship picked me up. And that's good enough for a yarn, ain't it?"

"Quite good enough, Jack, and we're much obliged to you; but I should advise you to drop the embellishments in future."

"It ain't no use, Master Hargate, they will have 'bellishments, and if they will have 'em, Jack Perkins isn't the man to disappint 'em; and, Lord bless you, sir, the stiffer I pitches it the more liberal they is with their tips. Thank ye kindly all round, gentlemen. Yes, I do feel dry after the yarn."

CHAPTER IV

A RISING TIDE

THE HALF year was drawing to its close, and it was generally agreed at Dr. Parker's that it had been the jolliest ever known. The boating episode and that of the tea at Oak Farm had been events which had given a fillip to existence. The school had been successful in the greater part of its cricket matches, and generally every one was well satisfied with himself. On the Saturday preceding the breaking up Frank, with Ruthven, Charlie Goodall and two of the other naturalists, started along the sea-shore to look for anemones and other marine creatures among the rocks and pools at the foot of the South Foreland. Between Ruthven and Frank a strong feeling of affection had grown up since the date of their boating adventure. They were constantly together now; and as Ruthven was also intended for the army, and would probably obtain his commission about the same time as Frank, they often talked over their future, and indulged in hopes that they might often meet, and that in their campaigns they might go through adventures together.

Tide was low when they started. They had nearly three miles to walk. The pools in front of Deal and Walmer had often been searched, but they hoped that once round the Foreland they might light upon specimens differing from any which they had hitherto found. For some hours they searched the pools, retiring as the tide advanced. Then they went up to the foot of the cliffs, and sat down to open their cans and compare the treasures they had collected. The spot which they had unwittingly selected was a little bay. For a long time they sat comparing their specimens. Then Frank said, "Come along, it is time to be moving." As he rose to his feet he uttered an exclamation of dismay. Although the tide was still at some little distance from the spot where they were sitting, it had already reached the cliffs extending out at either end of the bay. A brisk wind was blowing on shore, and the waves were already splashing against the foot of the rocks.

The whole party leaped to their feet, and seizing their cans, ran off at the top of their speed to the end of the bay. "I will see how deep the water is," Frank exclaimed; "we may yet be able to wade round." The water soon reached Frank's waist. He waded on until it was up to his shoulders, and he had to leap as each wave approached him. Then he returned to his friends.

"I could see round," he said, "and I think I could have got round without getting into deeper water. The worst of it is the bottom is all rocky, and I stumbled several times, and should have gone under water if I could not have swam. You can't swim, Ruthven, I know; can you other fellows?"

Goodall could swim, as could one of the others. "Now, Ruthven," Frank said, "if you will put your hand on my shoulder and keep quiet, I think I could carry you round. Goodall and Jackson can take Childers."

But neither of the other boys had much confidence in their swimming. They could get thirty or forty yards, but felt sure that they would be able to render but little assistance to Childers, and in fact scarcely liked to round the point alone. For some time they debated the question, the sea every minute rising and pushing them farther and farther from the point. "Look here, Frank," Ruthven said at last; "you are not sure you can carry me. The others are quite certain that they cannot take Childers. We must give up that idea. The best thing, old boy, is for you three who can swim to start together. Then if either of the others fail you can help them a bit. Childers and I must take our chance here. When you get round you must send a boat as soon as possible."

"I certainly shall not desert you, Ruthven," Frank said. "You know as well as I do that I'm not likely to find a boat on the shore till I get pretty near Walmer Castle, and long before we could get back it would be settled here. No, no, old fellow, we will see the matter out together. Jackson and Goodall can swim round if they like."

These lads, however, would not venture to take the risk alone, but said that they would go if Frank would go with them. "Chuck off your boots and coats and waistcoats," Frank said suddenly, proceeding to strip rapidly to the skin. "I will take them round, Ruthven, and come back to you. Run round the bay you and Childers, and see if you can find any sort of ledge or projection that we can take refuge upon. Now, then, come on you two as quick as you can." The sea had already reached within a few feet of the foot of the cliff all round the bay. "Now, mind," Frank said sharply, "no struggling and nonsense, you fellows. I will keep quite close to you and stick to you, so you needn't be afraid. If you get tired just put one hand on my back and swim with the other and your legs; and above all things keep your heads as low as possible in the water so as just to be able to breathe."

The three lads soon waded out as far as they could go and then struck out. Jackson and Goodall were both poor swimmers and would have fared very badly alone. The confidence, however, which they entertained in Frank gave them courage, and they were well abreast of the point when first Jackson and then Goodall put their hands on his shoulders. Thanks to the instructions he had given them, and to their confidence in him, they placed no great weight upon him. But every ounce tells heavily on a swimmer, and Frank gave a gasp of relief as at last his feet touched the ground. Bidding his companions at once set off at a run, he sat down for two or three minutes to recover his breath. "It is lucky," he said to himself, "that I did not try with Ruthven. It's a very different thing carrying fellows who can swim and fellows who can't. What fools we've been to let ourselves be caught here! I had no idea the tide came so high, or that it was so dangerous, and none of us have ever been round here before. Now I must go back to Ruthven." Frank found it even harder work to get back than it had been to come out from the bay, for the tide was against him now. At last he stood beside Ruthven and Childers.

"We can only find one place, Frank, where there is any projection a fellow could stand upon, and that is only large enough for one. See!" he said, pointing to a projecting block of chalk, whose upper surface, some eight inches wide, was tolerably flat.

"There is a cave here, too, which may go beyond the tide. It is no depth, but it slopes up a bit."

"That will never do," Frank said; "as the waves come in they will rush up and fill it to the top. Don't you see it is all rounded by the water? Now, Childers, we will put you on that stone. You will be perfectly safe there, for you see it is two feet above this greenish line, which shows where the water generally comes to. The tides are not at spring at present, so though you may get a splashing, there is no fear of your being washed off."

The water was already knee-deep at the foot of the rocks, and the waves took them nearly up to the shoulders. Ruthven did not attempt to dispute Frank's allotment of the one place of safety to Childers. Frank and he placed themselves below the block of chalk, which was somewhat over six feet from the ground. Then Childers scrambled up on to their shoulders, and from these stepped on to the ledge. "I am all right," he said; "I wish to Heaven that you were too."

"We shall do," Frank said. "Mind you hold tight, Childers! You had better turn round with your face to the cliff, so as to be able to grip hold and steady yourself in case the waves come up high. The tide will turn in three quarters of an hour at the outside. Now, then, Ruthven, let's make a fight for it, old man."

"What are you going to do, Frank?"

"We will wade along here as far as we can towards the corner, and then we must swim for it."

"Don't you think it's possible to stay here," Ruthven said, "if the tide will turn so soon?"

"Quite impossible!" Frank said. "I have been nearly taken off my feet twice already, and the water will rise a yard yet, at least. We should be smashed against the rocks, even if we weren't drowned. It must be tried, Ruthven. There is no other way for it. The distance is a good deal farther than it would have been if we had started at first; but it isn't the distance that makes much matter. We've only got to go out a little way, and the tide will soon take us round the point. Everything depends on you. I can take you round the point, and land you safely enough, if you will lie quiet. If you don't, you will drown both of us. So it's entirely in your hands. Look out!" At this moment a larger wave than usual took both boys off their legs, and dashed them with considerable force against the cliff. Frank seized Ruthven, and assisted him to regain his feet. "Now, old fellow, let me put you on your back. I will lie on mine and tow you along. Don't struggle; don't move; above all, don't try and lift your head, and don't mind if a little water gets in your mouth. Now!"

For a moment Ruthven felt himself under water, and had to make a great effort to restrain himself from struggling to come to the surface. Then he felt himself lying on his back in the water, supported by Frank. The motion was not unpleasant as he rose and fell on the waves, although now and then a splash of water came over his face, and made him cough and splutter for breath. He could see nothing but the blue sky overhead, could feel nothing except that occasionally he received a blow from one or other of Frank's knees, as the latter swam beneath him, with Ruthven's head on his chest. It was a dreamy sensation, and looking back upon it afterwards Ruthven could never recall anything that he had thought of. It seemed simply a drowsy pleasant time, except when occasionally a wave covered his face. His first sensation was that of surprise when he felt the motion change, and Frank lifted his head from the water and said, "Stand up, old fellow. Thank God, here we are, safe!"

Frank had indeed found the journey easier than that which he had before undertaken with the others. He had scarcely tried to progress, but had, after getting sufficiently far out to allow the tide to take him round the point, drifted quietly.

"I owe my life to you, Frank. I shall never forget it, old fellow."

"It's been a close thing," Frank answered; "but you owe your life as much to your own coolness as to me, and above all Ruthven, don't let us forget that we both owe our lives to God."

"I sha'n't forget it," Ruthven said quietly, and they stood for a few minutes without speaking. "Now, what had we better do? Shall we start to run home?"

"I can't," Frank laughed, for he had nothing on but his trousers. These he had slipped on after the return from his first trip, pushing the rest of his things into a crevice in the rocks as high up as he could reach. "You had better take off your things, Ruthven, and lay them out to dry in the sun. The boat will be here in half an hour. I wonder how Childers is getting on!"

"I think he will be safe," Ruthven said. "The tide will not rise high enough for there to be much danger of his being washed off."

"I don't think so either," Frank agreed, "or I would try and swim back again; but I really don't think I could get round the point against the tide again."

In half an hour a boat rowing four oars was seen approaching. "They are laying out well," Ruthven said. "They couldn't row harder if they were rowing a race. But had it not been for you, old fellow, they would have been too late, as far as I am concerned." As the boat approached, the coxswain waved his hat to the boys. Frank motioned with his arm for them to row on round the point. The boat swept along at a short distance from the shore. The boys watched them breathlessly. Presently as it reached the point they saw the coxswain stand up and say something to the men, who glanced over their shoulders as they rowed. Then the coxswain gave a loud shout. "Hold on! We'll be with you directly."

"Thank God!" Frank exclaimed, "Childers is all right." It was well, however, that the boat arrived when it did, for Childers was utterly exhausted when it reached him. The sea had risen so high that the waves broke against his feet, throwing the spray far above his head, and often nearly washing him from the ledge on which he stood. Had it not been, indeed, for the hold which he obtained of the cliff, it would several times have swept him away. About eighteen inches above his head he had found a ledge sufficiently wide to give a grip for his hands, and hanging by these he managed to retain his place when three times his feet were swept off the rock by the rush of water. The tide was just on the turn when the boat arrived, and so exhausted was he that he certainly would not have been able to hold out for the half hour's buffeting to which he would have been exposed before the water fell sufficiently to leave him. After helping him into the boat the men gathered the clothes jammed in fissures of the cliffs. These were, of course, drenched with water, but had for the most part remained firm in their places. They now pulled round to the spot where Frank and Ruthven were awaiting them.

"Childers must have been pretty nearly done," Frank said. "He must be lying in the bottom of the boat." Childers gave a smile of pleasure as his school-fellows jumped on board. He had, glancing over his shoulder, seen them drift out of sight round the point, and had felt certain that they had reached shore. It was, however, a great pleasure to be assured of the fact.

"You have made quite a stir upon the beach, young gentlemen," the coxswain of the boat said. "When they two came running up without their shoes or coats and said there were three of you cut off in the bay under the foreland, there didn't seem much chance for you. It didn't take us two minutes to launch the boat, for there were a score of hands helping to run her down; and my mates bent to it well, I can tell you, though we didn't think it would be of any use. We were glad when we made you two out on this side of the point. Look, there's half Deal and Walmer coming along the shore."

It was as the boatman said. Numbers of persons were streaming along the beach, and loud were the cheers which rose as the coxswain stood up and shouted in a stentorian voice, "All saved!"

Frank put on his things as they approached Walmer. His shoes were lost, as were those of Ruthven, and he had difficulty in getting his arms into his wet and shrunken jacket. Quite a crowd were gathered near the castle as the boat rowed to shore, and a hearty cheer arose as it was run up on the shingle and the boys were helped out. Frank and Ruthven, indeed, required no assistance. They were in no way the worse for the adventure, but Childers was so weak that he was unable to stand. He was carried up and laid in a fly, the others sitting opposite, the driver having first taken the precaution of removing the cushions.

There were among the crowd most of the boys from Dr. Parker's. Goodall and Jackson had arrived nearly an hour and a half before, and the news had spread like wildfire. Bats and balls had been thrown down and everyone had hurried to the beach. Goodall and his companion had already related the circumstance of their being cut off by the water and taken round the point by Frank; as Ruthven on jumping out had explained to his comrades who flocked round to shake his hand, "I owe my life to Hargate," the enthusiasm reached boiling-point, and Frank had difficulty in taking his place in the fly, so anxious were all to shake his hand and pat him on the shoulder. Had it not been for his anxiety to get home as soon as possible, and his urgent entreaties, they would have carried him on their shoulders in triumph through the town. They drove first to the school, where Childers was at once carried up to a bed, which had been prepared with warm blankets in readiness; Ruthven needed only to change his clothes.

The moment they left the fly Frank drove straight home, and was delighted at finding, from his mother's exclamation of surprise as he alighted from the cab, that she had not been suffering any anxiety, no one, in the general excitement, having thought of taking the news to her. In answer to her anxious inquiries he made light of the affair, saying only that they had stupidly allowed themselves to be cut off by the sea and had got a ducking. It was not, indeed, till the next morning, when the other four boys came around to tell Mrs. Hargate that they were indebted to Frank for their lives, that she had any notion that he had been in danger. Frank was quite oppressed by what he called the fuss which was made over the affair. A thrilling description of it appeared in the local papers. A subscription was got up in the school, and a gold watch, with an inscription, was presented to him; he received letters of heart-felt thanks from the parents of his four school-fellows, for Childers maintained that it was entirely to Frank's coolness and thoughtfulness that his preservation was also due.

On the following Wednesday the school broke up. Frank had several invitations from the boys to spend his holidays with them; but he knew how lonely his mother would feel in his absence, and he declined all the invitations. Mrs. Hargate was far from strong, and had had several fits of fainting. These, however, had taken place at times when Frank was at school, and she had strictly charged her little servant to say nothing about it.

One day, on returning from a long walk, he saw the doctor's carriage standing at the door. Just as he arrived the door opened and the doctor came out. Upon seeing Frank he turned. "Come in here, my boy," he said.

Frank followed him, and seeing that the blinds were down, went to draw them up. The doctor laid his hand on his arm. "Never mind that," he said gently. "My boy," he said, "do you know that your mother has been for some time ailing?"

"No, indeed," Frank said with a gasp of pain and surprise.

"It is so, my boy. I have been attending her for some time. She has been suffering from fainting fits brought on by weakness of the heart's action. Two hours since I was sent for and found her unconscious. My poor boy, you must compose yourself. God is good and merciful, though His decrees are hard to bear. Your mother passed away quietly half an hour since, without recovering consciousness." Frank gave a short cry, and then sat stunned by the suddenness of the blow. The doctor drew out a small case from his pocket and poured a few drops from a phial into a glass, added some water, and held it to Frank's lips. "Drink this, my boy," he said.

Frank turned his head from the offered glass. He could not speak.

"Drink this, my boy," the doctor said again; "it will do you good. Try and be strong for the sake of your little sister, who has only you in the world now."

The thought of Lucy touched the right chord in the boy's heart, and he burst into a passionate fit of crying. The doctor allowed his tears to flow unchecked. "You will be better now," he said presently. "Now drink this, then lie down on the sofa. We must not be having you ill, you know."

Frank gulped down the contents of the glass, and, passive as a child, allowed the doctor to place him upon the sofa. "God help and strengthen you, my poor boy," he said; "ask help from Him." For an hour Frank lay sobbing on the sofa, and then, remembering the doctor's last words, he knelt beside it and prayed for strength.

A week had passed. The blinds were up again. Mrs. Hargate had been laid in her last home, and Frank was sitting alone again in the little parlour thinking over what had best be done. The outlook was a dark one, enough to shake the courage of one much older than Frank. His mother's pension, he knew, died with her. He had, on the doctor's advice, written to the War Office on the day following his mother's death, to inform the authorities of the circumstances, and to ask if any pension could be granted to his sister. The reply had arrived that morning and had relieved him of the greatest of his cares. It stated that as he was now just fifteen years old he was not eligible for a pension, but that twenty-five pounds a year would be paid to his sister until she married or attained the age of twenty-one.

He had spoken to the doctor that morning, and the latter said that he knew a lady who kept a small school, and who would, he doubted not, be willing to receive Lucy and to board and clothe her for that sum. She was a very kind and motherly person, and he was sure that Lucy would be most kindly treated and cared for by her. It was then of his own future only that Frank had to think. There were but a few pounds in the house, but the letter from the War Office inclosed a cheque for twenty pounds, as his mother's quarterly pension was just due. The furniture of the little house would fetch but a small sum, not more, Frank thought, than thirty or forty pounds. There were a few debts to pay, and after all was settled up there would remain about fifty pounds. Of this he determined to place half in the doctor's hands for the use of Lucy. "She will want," he said to himself, "a little pocket-money. It is hard on a girl having no money to spend of her own. Then, as she gets on, she may need lessons in something or other. Besides, half the money rightly belongs to her. The question is, What am I to do?"

CHAPTER V

ALONE IN THE WORLD

"WHAT am I to do?" A difficult question, indeed, for a boy of fifteen, with but twenty-five pounds, and without a friend in the world. Was he, indeed, without a friend? he asked himself. There was Dr. Parker. Should he apply to him? But the doctor had started for a trip on the Continent the day after the school had broken up, and would not return for six weeks. It was possible that, had he been at home, he might have offered to keep Frank for a while; but the boys seldom stayed at his school past the age of fifteen, going elsewhere to have their education completed. What possible claim had he to quarter himself upon the doctor for the next four years, even were the offer made? No, Frank felt; he could not live upon the doctor's charity. Then there were the parents of the boys he had saved from drowning. But even as he sat alone Frank's face flushed at the thought of trading upon services so rendered. The boy's chief fault was pride. It was no petty feeling, and he had felt no shame at being poorer than the rest of his school-fellows. It was rather a pride which led him unduly to rely upon himself, and to shrink from accepting favours from anyone. Frank might well, without any derogation, have written to his friends, telling them of the loss he had suffered and the necessity there was for him to earn his living, and asking them to beg their fathers to use their interest to procure him a situation as a boy clerk, or any other position in which he could earn his livelihood. Frank, however, shrunk from making any such appeal, and determined to fight his battle without asking for help. He knew nothing of his parents' relations. His father was an only son, who had been left early an orphan. His mother, too, had, he was aware, lost both her parents, and he had never heard her speak of other relations. There was no one, therefore, so far as he knew, to whom he could appeal on the ground of

44

ties of blood. It must be said for him that he had no idea how hard was the task which he was undertaking. It seemed to him that it must be easy for a strong, active lad to find employment of some sort in London. What the employment might be he cared little for. He had no pride of that kind, and so that he could earn his bread he cared not much in what capacity he might do it.

Already preparations had been made for the sale of the furniture, which was to take place next day. Everything was to be sold except the scientific books which had belonged to his father. These had been packed in a great box until the time when he might place them in a library of his own, and the doctor kindly offered to keep it for him until such time should arrive. Frank wrote a long letter to Ruthven, telling him of his loss, and his reasons for leaving Deal, and promising to write some day and tell him how he was getting on in London. This letter he did not intend to post until the last thing before leaving Deal. Lucy had already gone to her new home, and Frank felt confident that she would be happy there. His friend, the doctor, who had tried strongly, but without avail, to dissuade Frank from going up to London to seek his fortune there, had promised that if the lad referred any inquiries to him he would answer for his character.

He went down to the beach the last evening and said good-bye to his friends among the fishermen, and he walked over in the afternoon and took his last meal with Farmer Gregson.

"Look ye here, my lad," the farmer said as they parted. "I tell ye, from what I've heerd, this London be a hard nut to crack. There be plenty of kernel, no doubt, when you can get at it, but it be hard work to open the shell. Now, if so be as at any time you run short of money, just drop me a line, and there's ten pound at your service whenever you like. Don't you think it's an obligation. Quite the other way. It would be a real pleasure to me to lend you a helping hand."

Two days after the sale Frank started for London. On getting out of the train he felt strange and lonely amid the bustle and confusion which was going on on the platform. The doctor had advised him to ask one of the porters, or a policeman, if he could

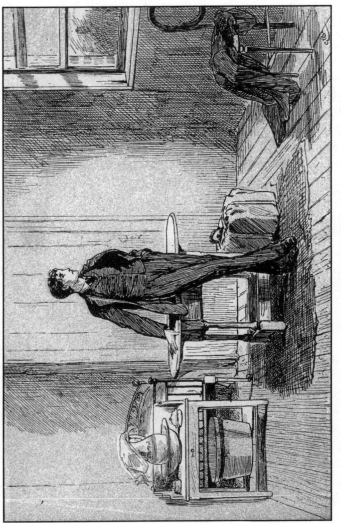

ALONE IN THE WORLD.

recommend him to a quiet and respectable lodging, as expenses at an hotel would soon make a deep hole in his money. He, therefore, as soon as the crowd cleared away, addressed himself to one of the porters.

"What sort of lodgings do you want, sir?" the man said, looking at him rather suspiciously, with, as Frank saw, a strong idea in his mind that he was a runaway schoolboy.

"I only want one room," he said, "and I don't care how small it is, so that it is clean and quiet. I shall be out all day, and should not give much trouble."

The porter went away and spoke to some of his mates, and presently returned with one of them.

"You're wanting a room I hear, sir," the man said. "I have a little house down the Old Kent Road, and my missus lets a room or two. It's quiet and clean, I'll warrant you. We have one room vacant at present."

"I'm sure that would suit me very well," Frank said. "How much do you charge a week?"

"Three and sixpence, sir, if you don't want any cooking done."

Frank took the address, and leaving his portmanteau in charge of the porter, who promised, unless he heard to the contrary, that he would bring it home with him when he had done his work, he set off from the station.

Deal is one of the quietest and most dreary places on the coast of England, and Frank was perfectly astounded at the crowd and bustle which filled the street, when he issued from the railway approach, at the foot of London Bridge. The porter had told him that he was to turn to his left, and keep straight along until he reached the "Elephant and Castle." He had, therefore no trouble about his road, and was able to give his whole attention to the sights which met his eye. For a time the stream of omnibuses, cabs, heavy waggons, and light carts, completely bewildered him, as did the throng of people who hastened along the footway. He was depressed rather than exhilarated at the sight of this busy multitude. He seemed such a solitary atom in the midst of this great moving crowd. Presently, however, the thought that where so many millions gained their living there must be room for one boy more, somewhat cheered him. He was a long time making his way to his place of destination, for he stared into every shop window, and being, although he was perfectly ignorant of the fact, on the wrong side of the pavement, he was bumped and hustled continually, and was not long in arriving at the conclusion that the people of London must be the roughest and rudest in the world. It was not until he ran against a gentleman, and was greeted with the angry, "Now then, boy. Where are you going? Why the deuce don't you keep on your own side of the pavement?" that he perceived that the moving throng was divided into two currents, that on the inside meeting him, while the outside stream was proceeding in the same direction as himself. After this he got on better, and arrived without adventure at the house of the porter, in the Old Kent Road.

It was a small house, but was clean and respectable, and Frank found that the room would suit him well.

"I do not wait upon the lodgers," the landlady said, "except to make the beds and tidy the rooms in the morning. So if you want breakfast and tea at home you will have to get them yourself. There is a separate place down-stairs for your coals. There are some tea things, plates and dishes, in this cupboard. You will want to buy a small tea-kettle, and a gridiron, and a frying-pan, in case you want a chop or a rasher. Do you think you can cook them yourself?"

Frank, amused at the thought of cooking and catering for himself, said boldly that he should soon learn.

"You are a very young gentleman," the landlady said, eyeing him doubtfully, "to be setting up on your own hook. I mean," she said, seeing Frank look puzzled, "setting up housekeeping on your own account. You will have to be particular careful with the frying-pan, because if you were to upset the fat in the fire you might have the house in a blaze in a jiffey."

Frank said that he would certainly be careful with the frying-pan.

"Well," she went on, "as you're a stranger to the place I don't know as you could do better than get your tea, and sugar, and things at the grocer's at the next corner. I deals there myself, and he gives every satisfaction. My baker will be round in a few minutes, and, if you likes, I can take in your bread for you. The same with milk."

These matters being arranged, and Frank agreeing at once to the proposition that as he was a stranger it would make things more comfortable were he to pay his rent in advance, found himself alone in his new apartment. It was a room about ten feet square. The bed occupied one corner, with the wash-stand at its foot. There was a small table in front of the fireplace, and two chairs; a piece of carpet half covered the floor, and these with the addition of the articles in the cupboard constituted the furniture of the room.

Feeling hungry after his journey Frank resolved to go in at once and get something to eat, and then to lay in a stock of provisions. After some hesitation regarding the character of the meal he decided upon two Bath-buns, determining to make a substantial tea. He laid in a supply of tea, sugar, butter, and salt, bought a little kettle, a frying-pan, and a gridiron. Then he hesitated as to whether he should venture upon a mutton chop or some bacon, deciding finally in favour of the latter, upon the reflection that any fellow could see whether bacon were properly frizzled up, while as to a chop there was no seeing anything about it till one cut it. He, therefore, invested in a pound of prime streaky Wiltshire bacon, the very best, as the shopman informed him, that could be bought. He returned carrying all his purchases, with the exception of the hardware. Then he inquired of his landlady where he could get coal.

"The green-grocer's round the corner," the landlady said. "Tell him to send in a hundredweight of the best, that's a shilling, and you'll want some firewood too."

The coal arrived in the course of the afternoon, and at half-past six the porter came in with Frank's trunk. He had by this time lit a fire, and while the water was boiling got some of his things out of the box, and by hanging some clothes on the pegs on the back of the door, and by putting the two or three favourite books he had brought with him on to the mantel-piece, he gave the room a more homelike appearance. He enjoyed his tea all the more from the novelty of having to prepare it himself, and succeeded very fairly for a first attempt with his bacon.

When tea was over he first washed up the things and then started for a ramble. He followed the broad straight road to Waterloo Bridge, stood for a long time looking at the river, and then crossed into the Strand. The lamps were now alight and the brightness and bustle of the scene greatly interested him. At nine o'clock he returned to his lodgings, but was again obliged to sally out, as he found he had forgotten candles.

After breakfast next morning he went out and bought a newspaper, and set himself to work to study the advertisements. He was dismayed to find how many more applicants there were for places than places requiring to be filled. All the persons advertising were older than himself, and seemed to possess various accomplishments in the way of languages; many too could be strongly recommended from their last situation. The prospect did not look hopeful. In the first place he had looked to see if any required boy clerks, but this species of assistant appeared little in demand; and then, although he hoped that it would not come to that, he ran his eye down the columns to see if any required errand-boys or lads in manufacturing businesses. He found, however, no such advertisements. However, as he said to himself, it could not be expected that he should find a place waiting for him on the very day after his arrival, and that he ought to be able to live for a year on his five-and-twenty pounds; at this reflection his spirits rose and he went out again for a walk.

For the first week, indeed, of his arrival in London Frank did not set himself very earnestly to work to look for a situation. In his walks about the streets he several times observed cards in the window indicating that an errand-boy was wanted. He resolved, however, that this should be the last resource which he would adopt, as he would much prefer to go to work as a common lad in a factory to serving in a shop. After the first week he answered many advertisements, but in no case received a reply. In one case, in which it was stated that a lad who could write a good fast hand was required in an office, wages to begin with eight shillings a week, he called two days after writing. It was a small office with a solitary clerk sitting in it. The latter, upon learning Frank's business, replied with some exasperation that his mind was being worried out by boys. "We have had four hundred and thirty letters," he said; "and I should think that a hundred boys must have called. We took the first who applied, and all the other letters were chucked into the fire as soon as we saw what they were about."

Frank returned to the street greatly disheartened. "Four hundred and thirty letters!" he said. "Four hundred and thirty other fellows on the look-out, just as I am, for a place as a boy clerk, and lots of them, no doubt, with friends and relations to recommend them! The look-out seems to be a bad one."

Two days later, when Frank was walking along the Strand he noticed the placards in front of a theatre. "Gallery one shilling!" he said to himself; "I will go. I have never seen a theatre yet." The play was *The Merchant of Venice*, and Frank sat in rapt attention and interest through it. When the performance was over he walked briskly homewards. When he had proceeded some distance he saw a glare in the sky ahead, and presently a steam-engine dashed past him at full speed. "That must be a house on fire," he said. "I have never seen a fire;" and he broke into a run.

Others were running in the same direction, and as he passed the "Elephant and Castle" the crowd became thicker, and when within fifty yards of the house he could no longer advance. He could see the flames now rising high in the air. A horrible fear seized him. "It must be," he exclaimed to himself, either our house or the one next door." It was in vain that he pressed forward to see more nearly. A line of policemen was drawn up across the road to keep a large space clear for the firemen. Behind the policemen the crowd were thickly packed. Frank inquired of many who stood near him if they could tell him the number of the house which was on fire; but none could inform him.

Presently the flames began to die away, and the crowd to disperse. At length Frank reached the first line of spectators.

"Can you tell me the number of the houses which are burned?" Frank said to a policeman.

"There are two of them," the policeman said; "a hundred and four and a hundred and five. A hundred and four caught first, and they say that a woman and two children have been burned to death."

"That is where I live!" Frank cried. "Oh, please let me pass!"

"I'll pass you in," the policeman said good-naturedly, and he led him forward to the spot where the engines were playing upon the burning houses. "Is it true, mate," he asked a fireman, "that a woman and two children have been burned?"

"It's true enough," the fireman said. "The landlady and her children. Her husband was a porter at the railway-station, and had been detained on overtime. He only came back a quarter of an hour ago, and he's been going on like a madman;" and he pointed to the porter, who was sitting down on the doorsteps of a house facing his own, with his face hidden in his hands.

Frank went and sat down beside him. "My poor fellow," he said, "I am sorry for you." Frank had had many chats with his landlord of an evening, and had become quite friendly with him and his wife.

"I can't believe it," the man said huskily. "Just to think! When I went out this morning there was Jane and the kids, as well and as happy as ever, and there, where are they now?"

"Happier still," Frank said gently. "I lost my mother just as suddenly only five weeks ago. I went out for a walk, leaving her as well as usual, and when I came back she was dead; so I can feel for you with all my heart."

"I would have given my life for them," the man said, wiping his eyes, "willing."

"I'm sure you would," Frank answered.

"There's the home gone," the man said, "with all the things that it took ten years' savings of Jane and me to buy; not that that matters one way or the other now. And your traps are gone, too, I suppose, sir."

"Yes," Frank replied quietly, "I have lost my clothes and twenty-three pounds in money; every penny I've got in the world except half a crown in my pocket."

"And you don't say nothing about it!" the man said, roused into animation. "But, there, perhaps you've friends as will make it up to you."

"I have no one in the world," Frank answered, "whom I could ask to give me a helping hand."

"Well, you are a plucky chap," the man said. "That would be a knock-down blow to a man, let alone a boy like you. What are you going to do now?" he asked, forgetting for the moment his own loss, in his interest in his companion.

"I don't know," Frank replied. "Perhaps," he added, seeing that the interest in his condition roused the poor fellow from the thought of his own deep sorrow, "you might give me some advice. I was thinking of getting a place in an office, but of course I must give that up now, and should be thankful to get anything by which I can earn my bread."

"You come along with me," the man said rising. "You've done me a heap of good. It's no use sitting here. I shall go back to the station, and turn in on some sacks. If you've nothing better to do, and nowhere to go to, you come along with me. We will talk it all over."

Pleased to have some one to talk to, and glad that he should not have to look for a place to sleep, Frank accompanied the porter to the station. With a word or two to the nightmen on duty, the porter led the way to a shed near the station, where a number of sacks were heaped in a corner.

"Now," the man said, "I will light a pipe. It's against the regulations, but that's neither here nor there now. Now, if you're not sleepy, would you mind talking to me? Tell me something about yourself, and how you come to be alone here in London. It does me good to talk. It prevents me from thinking."

"There is very little to tell," Frank said; and he related to him the circumstances of the deaths of his father and mother, and how it came that he was alone in London in search of a place.

"You're in a fix," the porter said. "Yes, I can see that. You see you're young for most work, and you never had no practice with horses, or you might have got a place to drive a light cart. Then, again, your knowing nothing of London is against you as an errand-boy; and what's worse than all this, anyone can see with half an eye that you're a gentleman, and not accustomed to hard work. However, we will think it over. The daylight's breaking now, and I has to be at work at six. But look ye here, young fellow, tomorrow I've got to look for a room, and when I gets it there's half of it for you, if you're not too proud to accept it. It will be doing me a real kindness, I can tell you, for what I am to do alone of an evening without Jane and the kids, God knows. I can't believe they're gone yet."

Then the man threw himself down upon the sacks, and broke into sobs. Frank listened for half an hour till these gradually died away, and he knew by the regular breathing that his companion was asleep. It was long after this before he himself closed his eyes. The position did, indeed, appear a dark one. Thanks to the offer of his companion, which he at once resolved to accept for a time, he would have a roof to sleep under. But this could not last; and what was he to do? Perhaps he had been wrong in not writing at once to Ruthven and his school-fellows. He even felt sure he had been wrong; but it would be ten times as hard to write now. He would rather starve than do this. How was he to earn his living? He would, he determined, at anyrate try for a few days to procure a place as an errand-boy. If that failed, he would sell his clothes, and get a rough working suit. He was sure that he should have more chance of obtaining work in such a dress than in his present attire.

Musing thus, Frank at last dropped off to sleep. When he woke he found himself alone, his companion having left without disturbing him. From the noises around him of trains coming in and out, Frank judged that the hour was late.

"I have done one wise thing," he said, "anyhow, and as far as I can see it's the only one, in leaving my watch with the doctor to keep. He pointed out that I might have it stolen if I carried it, and that there was no use in keeping it shut up in a box. Very possibly it might be stolen by the dishonesty of a servant. That's safe any-how, and it is my only worldly possession, except the books, and I would rather go into the workhouse than part with either of them." Rising, he made his way into the station, where he found the porter at his usual work.

"I would not wake you," the man said; "you were sleeping so quiet, and I knew 'twas no use your getting up early. I shall go out and settle for a room at dinner-time. If you will come here at six o'clock we'll go off together. The mates have all been very kind, and have been making a collection to bury my poor girl and the kids. They've found 'em, and the inquest is to be to-morrow, so I shall be off work. The governor has offered me a week; but there, I'd rather be here where there's no time for thinking, than hanging about with nothing to do but to drink."

CHAPTER VI

THE FIRST STEP

ALL that day Frank tramped the streets. He went into many shops where he saw notices that an errand-boy was required, but everywhere without success. He perceived at once that his appearance was against him, and he either received the abrupt answer of, "You're not the sort of chap for my place," or an equally decided refusal upon the grounds that he did not know the neighbourhood, or that they preferred one who had parents who lived close by and could speak for him. At six o'clock he joined the porter. He brought with him some bread and butter and a piece of bacon. When, on arriving at the lodging of his new friend, a neat room with two small beds in it, he produced and opened his parcel, the porter said angrily, "Don't you do that again, young fellow, or we shall have words. You're just coming to stop with me for a bit till you see your way, and I'm not going to have you bring things in here. My money is good for two mouths, and your living here with me won't cost three shillings a week. So don't you hurt my feelings by bringing things home again. There, don't say no more about it."

Frank, seeing that his companion was really in earnest, said no more, and was the less reluctant to accept the other's kindness as he saw that his society was really a great relief to him in his trouble. After the meal they sallied out to a second-hand clothes shop. Here Frank disposed of his things, and received in return a good suit of clothes fit for a working lad.

"I don't know how it is," the porter said as they sat together afterwards, "but a gentleman looks like a gentleman put him in what clothes you will. I could have sworn to your being that if I'd never seen you before. I can't make it out, I don't know what it is, but there's certainly something in gentle blood, whatever you may say about it. Some of my mates are for ever saying that one man's as good as another. Now I don't mean to say they ain't as good; but what I say is, as they ain't the same. One man ain't the same as another any more than a race-horse is the same as a cart-horse. They both sprang from the same stock, at least so they says; but breeding and feeding and care has made one into a slim-boned creature as can run like the wind, while the other has got big bones and weight and can drag his two ton after him without turning a hair. Now, I take it, it's the same thing with gentle folks and working men. It isn't that one's bigger than the other, for I don't see much difference that way; but a gentleman's lighter in the bone, and his hands and his feet are smaller, and he carries himself altogether different. His voice gets a different tone. Why, Lord bless you, when I hears two men coming along the platform at night, even when I can't see 'em, and can't hear what they says, only the tone of their voices, I knows just as well whether it's a first class or a third door as I've got to open as if I saw 'em in the daylight. Rum, ain't it?"

Frank had never thought the matter out, and could only give his general assent to his companion's proposition.

"Now," the porter went on, "if you go into a factory or workshop, I'll bet a crown to a penny that before you've been there a week you'll get called Gentleman Jack, or some such name. You see if you ain't."

"I don't care what they call me," Frank laughed, "so that they'll take me into the factory."

"All in good time," the porter said; "don't you hurry yourself. As long as you can stay here you'll be heartily welcome. Just look what a comfort it is to have you sitting here sociable and comfortable. You don't suppose I could have sat here alone in this room if you hadn't been here? I should have been in a public-house making a beast of myself, and spending as much money as would keep the pair of us."

Day after day Frank went out in search of work. In his tramps he visited scores of workshops and factories, but without success. Either they did not want boys, or they declined altogether to take one who had no experience in work, and had no references in the neighbourhood. Frank took his breakfast and tea with the porter, and was glad that the latter had his dinner at the station, as a penny loaf served his purposes. One day in his walks Frank entered Covent Garden and stood looking on at the bustle and flow of business, for it happened to be market-day. He leaned against one of the columns of the piazza, eating the bread he had just bought. Presently a sharp-faced lad, a year or two younger than himself, came up to him. "Give us a bit," he said, "I ain't tasted nothing today."

Frank broke the bread in half and gave a portion to him. "What a lot there is going on here!" Frank said.

"Law!" the boy answered, "that ain't nothing to what it is of a morning. That's the time, 'special on the mornings of the flower-market. It's hard lines if a chap can't pick up a tanner or even a bob then."

"How?" Frank asked eagerly.

"Why, by holding horses, helping to carry out plants, and such like. You seems a green 'un, you do. Up from the country, eh? Don't seem like one of our sort."

"Yes," Frank said, "I am just up from the country. I thought it would be easy to get a place in London, but I don't find it so."

"A place!" the boy repeated scornfully. "I should like anyone to see me in a place. It's better a hundred times to be your own master."

"Even if you do want a piece of bread sometimes?" Frank put in.

"Yes," the boy said. "When it ain't market-day and ye haven't saved enough to buy a few papers or boxes of matches, it does come hard. In winter the times is bad, but in summer we gets on fairish, and there ain't nothing to grumble about. Are you out of work yourself?"

"Yes," Frank answered, "I'm on the look-out for a job."

"You'd have a chance here in the morning," said the boy, looking at him. "You look decent, and might get a job unloading. They won't have us at no price, if they can help it."

"I will come and try anyhow," Frank said.

That evening Frank told his friend, the porter, that he thought of going out early next morning to try and pick up odd jobs at Covent Garden.

"Don't you think of it," the porter said. "There's nothing worse for a lad than taking to odd jobs. It gets him into bad ways and bad company. Don't you hurry. I have spoken to lots of my mates, and they're all on the look-out for you. We on the platform can't do much. It ain't in our line, you see; but in the goods department, where they are constant with vans and waggons and such like, they are likely enough to hear of something before long."

That night, thinking matters over in bed, Frank determined to go down to the docks and see if he could get a place as cabin-boy. He had had this idea in his mind ever since he lost his money, and had only put it aside in order that he might, if possible, get some berth on shore which might seem likely in the end to afford him a means of making his way up again. It was not that he was afraid of the roughness of a cabin-boy's life; it was only because he knew that it would be so very long before, working his way up from boy to able-bodied seaman, he could obtain a mate's certificate, and so make a first step up the ladder. However, he thought that even this would be better than going as a waggoner's boy, and he accordingly crossed London Bridge, turned down Eastcheap, and presently found himself in Ratcliff Highway. He was amused here at the nautical character of the shops, and presently found himself staring into a window full of foreign birds, for the most part alive in cages, among which, however, were a few cases of stuffed birds. "How stupid I have been!" he thought to himself. "I wonder I never thought of it before! I can stuff birds and beasts at anyrate a deal better than those wooden-looking things. I might have a chance of getting work at some naturalist's shop. I will get a directory and take down all the addresses in London, and then go around."

He now became conscious of a conversation going on between a little old man with a pair of thick horn-rimmed spectacles and a sailor who had a dead parrot and a cat in his hand.

"I really cannot undertake them," the old man said. "Since the death of my daughter I have had but little time to attend to that branch. What with buying and selling, and feeding and attending to the live ones, I have no time for stuffing. Besides, if the things were poisoned, they would not be worth stuffing."

"It isn't the question of worth, skipper," the sailor said; "and I don't say, mind ye, that these here critturs was pisoned, only if you looks at it that this was the noisiest bird and the worst-tempered thievingest cat in the neighbourhood—though, Lord bless you, my missus wouldn't allow it for worlds—why, you know, when they were both found stiff and cold this morning people does have a sort of a suspicion as how they've been pisoned;" and he winked one eye in a portentous manner, and grinned hugely. "The missus she's in a nice taking, screeching, and yelling, as you might hear her two cables' length away, and she turns round on me and will have it as I'd a hand in the matter. Well, just to show my innocence, I offers to get a glass case for 'em, and have 'em stuffed, if it cost me a couple of pounds. I wouldn't care if they fell all to pieces a week afterwards, so that it pacified the old woman just at present. If I can't get 'em done, I shall ship at once, for the place will be too hot to hold me. So you can't do it nohow?"

The old man shook his head, and the sailor was just turning off when Frank went up to him:

"Will you please wait a moment? Can I speak to you, sir, a minute?" he asked the old man.

The naturalist went into his shop, and Frank followed him.

"I can stuff birds and animals, sir," he said. "I think I really stuff them well, for some which I did for amusement were sold at ten shillings a case, and the man who bought them off me told me they would be worth four times as much in London. I am out of work, sir, and very very anxious to get my living. You will find me hard-working and honest. Do give me a chance. Let me stuff that cat and parrot for the sailor. If you are not satisfied then, I will go away and charge nothing for it."

The man looked at him keenly.

"I will at anyrate give you a trial," he said. Then he went to the door and called in the sailor. "This lad tells me he can stuff birds. I know nothing about him, but I believe he is speaking truthfully. If you like to intrust them to him he will do his best. If you're not satisfied he will make no charge."

Much pleased at seeing a way out of his dilemma, the sailor placed the dead animals on the counter.

"Now," the old man said to Frank, "you can take these out into the back-yard and skin them. Then you can go to work in that back-room. You will find arsenical soap, cotton-wool, wires, and everything else you require there. This has been a fine cat," he said, looking at the animal.

"Yes, it has been a splendid creature," Frank answered. "It is a magnificent macaw also."

"Ah! You know it is a macaw!" the old man said.

"Of course," Frank said simply; "it has a tail."

The old man then furnished Frank with two or three sharp knives and scissors. Taking the bird and cat, he went out into the yard and in the course of an hour had skinned them both. Then he returned to the shop and set to work in the room behind.

"May I make a group of them?" he asked.

"Do them just as you like," the old man said.

After settling upon his subject, Frank set to work, and, except that he went out for five minutes to buy and eat a penny loaf, continued his work till nightfall. The old man came in several times to look at him, but each time went out again without making a remark. At six o'clock Frank laid down his tools.

"I will come again tomorrow, sir," he said.

The old man nodded, and Frank went home in high spirits. There was a prospect at last of getting something to do, and that in a line most congenial to his own tastes.

The old man looked up when he entered next morning.

"I shall not come in to-day," he remarked. "I will wait to see them finished."

Working without interruption till the evening, Frank finished them to his satisfaction, and enveloped them with many wrappings of thread to keep them in precisely the attitudes in which he had placed them.

61

"They are ready for drying now, sir," he said. "If I might place them in an oven they would be dried by morning."

The old man led the way to the kitchen, where a small fire was burning.

"I shall put no more coals on the fire," he said, "and it will be out in a quarter of an hour. Put them in there and leave the door open. I will close it in an hour when the oven cools."

The next day Frank was again at work. It took him all day to get fur and feather to lie exactly as he wished them. In the afternoon he asked the naturalist for a piece of flat board, three feet long, and a perch, but said that instead of the piece of board he should prefer mounting them in a case at once. The old man had not one in the shop large enough, and therefore Frank arranged his group temporarily on the table. On the board lay the cat. At first sight she seemed asleep, but it was clearly only seeming. Her eyes were half open, the upper lip was curled up, and the sharp teeth showed. The hind-feet were drawn somewhat under her as in readiness for an instant spring. Her front-paws were before her, the talons were somewhat stretched, and one paw was curved. Her ears lay slightly back. She was evidently on the point of springing. The macaw perch, which had been cut down to a height of two feet, stood behind her. The bird hung by its feet, and, head downwards, stretched with open beak towards the tip of the cat's tail, which was slightly uplifted. On a piece of paper Frank wrote, "Dangerous Play." It was evening before he had finished perfectly to his satisfaction. Then he called the naturalist in. The old man stopped at the door, surveying the group. Then he entered and examined it carefully.

"Wonderful!" he said. "Wonderful! I should have thought them alive. There is not a shop in the west end where it could have been turned out better, if so well. Lad, you are a wonder! Tell me now who and what are you? I saw when you first addressed me that you were not what you seemed to be, a working lad."

"I have been well educated," Frank said, "and was taught to preserve and stuff by my father, who was a great naturalist. My parents died suddenly, and I was left on my own resources, which," he said, smiling faintly, "have hitherto proved of very small avail. I am glad you are pleased. If you will take me into your service I will work hard and make myself useful in every way. If you require references I can refer you to the doctor who attended us in the country; but I have not a single friend in London except a railway porter, who has most kindly and generously taken me in and sheltered me for the last two months."

"I need no references," the old man said; "your work speaks for itself as to your skill, and your face for your character. But I can offer you nothing fit for you. With such a genius as you have for setting up animals, you ought to be able to earn a good income. Not one man in a thousand can make a dead animal look like a live one. You have the knack or the art."

"I shall be very content with anything you can give me," Frank said; "for the present I only ask to earn my living. If later on I can, as you say, do more, all the better."

The old man stood for some time thinking, and presently said, "I do but little except in live stock. When I had my daughter with me I did a good deal of stuffing, for there is a considerable trade here about. The sailors bring home skins of foreign birds, and want them stuffed and put in cases, as presents for their wives and sweethearts. You work fast as well as skilfully. I have known men who would take a fortnight to do such a group as that, and then it would be a failure. It will be quite a new branch for my trade. I do not know how it will act yet, but to begin with I will give you twelve shillings a week, and a room upstairs. If it succeeds we will make other arrangements. I am an old man, and a very lonely one. I shall be glad to have such a companion."

Frank joyfully embraced the offer, and ran all the way home to tell his friend, the porter, of the engagement.

"I am very glad," the man said; "heartily glad. I shall miss you sorely. I do not know what I should have done without you when I first lost poor Jane and the kids. But now I can go back to my old ways again."

"Perhaps," Frank suggested, "you might arrange to have a room also in the house. It would not be a very long walk, not above

"LAD, YOU ARE A WONDER !"

twenty or five-and-twenty minutes, and I should be so glad to have you with me."

The man sat silent for a time. "No," he said at last; "I thank you all the same. I should like it too, but I don't think it would be best in the end. Here all my mates live near, and I shall get on in time. The Christmas holiday season will soon be coming on and we shall be up working late. If you were always going to stop at the place you are going to, it would be different; but you will rise, never fear. I shall be seeing you in gentleman's clothes again some of these days. I've heard you say you were longing to get your books and to be studying again, and you'll soon fall into your own ways; but if you will let me, I'll come over sometimes and have a cup of tea and a chat with you. Now, look here, I'm going out with you now, and I'm going to buy you a suit of clothes, something like what you had on when I first saw you. They won't be altogether unsuitable in a shop. This is a loan, mind, and you may pay me off as you get flush."

Frank saw he should hurt the good fellow's feelings by refusing, and accordingly went out with him, and next morning presented himself at the shop in a quiet suit of dark-gray tweed, and with his other clothes in a bundle.

"Aha!" said the old man; "you look more as you ought to do now, though you're a cut above an assistant in a naturalist's shop in Ratcliff Highway. Now, let me tell you the names of some of these birds. They are, every one of them, foreigners; some of them I don't know myself."

"I can tell all the family names," Frank said quietly, "and the species, but I do not know the varieties."

"Can you!" the old man said in surprise. "What is this now?"

"That is a mocking-bird, the great black-capped mocking-bird, I think. The one next to it is a golden lory." So Frank went round all the cages and perches in the shop.

"Right in every case," the old man said enthusiastically; "I shall have nothing to teach you. The sailor has been here this morning. I offered him two pounds for the cat and bird to put in my front window, but he would not take it, and has paid me that sum for your work. Here it is. This is yours, you know. You were not in my employment then, and you will want some things to start with, no doubt. Now come upstairs, I will show you your room. I had intended at first to give you the one at the back, but I have decided now on giving you my daughter's. I think you will like it."

Frank did like it greatly. It was the front room on the second floor. The old man's daughter had evidently been a woman of taste and refinement. The room was prettily papered, a quiet carpet covered the floor, and the furniture was neat and in good keeping. Two pairs of spotless muslin curtains hung across the windows.

"I put them up this morning," the old man said, nodding. "I have got the sheets and bedding airing in the kitchen. They have not been out of the press for the last three years. You can cook in the kitchen. There is always a fire there. Now, the first thing to do," he went on when they returned to the shop, "will be for you to mount a dozen cases for the windows. These drawers are full of skins of birds and small animals. I get them for next to nothing from the sailors, and sell them to furriers and feather preparers, who supply ladies' hat and bonnet makers. In future, I propose that you shall mount them and sell them direct. We shall get far higher prices than we do now. I seem to be putting most of the work on your shoulders, but I do not want you to help me in the shop. I will look after the birds and buy and sell as I used to do; you will have the back-room private to yourself for stuffing and mounting."

Frank was delighted at this allotment of labour, and was soon at work rummaging the drawers and picking out specimens for mounting, and made a selection sufficient to keep him employed for weeks. That evening he sallied out and expended his two pounds in underlinen, of which he was sorely in need. As he required them his employer ordered show-cases for the window, of various sizes, getting the backgrounds painted and fitted up as Frank suggested. Frank did not get on so fast with his work as he had hoped, for the fame of the sailor's cat and macaw spread rapidly in the neighbourhood, and there was a perfect rush of sailors and their wives anxious to have birds and skins, which had been brought from abroad, mounted. The sailor himself looked in one day. "If you like another two pounds for that 'ere cat, governor, I'm game to pay you. It's the best thing that ever happened to me. Every one's wanting to see 'em, and there's the old woman dressed up in her Sunday clothes asitting in the parlour as proud as a peacock ashowing of 'em off. The house ain't been so quiet since I married. Them animals would be cheap to me at a ten pound note. They'll get you no end of orders, I can tell you."

The orders, indeed, came in much faster than Frank could fulfil them, although he worked twelve hours a day; laying aside all other work, however, for three hours in order to devote himself to the shop-cases, which were to be *chef-d'œuvres*.

CHAPTER VII

AN OLD FRIEND

FOR three months Frank passed a quiet and not unpleasant life with the old naturalist in Ratcliff Highway. The latter took a great liking to him, and treated him like a son rather than an assistant. The two took their meals together now, and Frank's salary had been raised from twelve to eighteen shillings a week. So attractive had the cases in the windows proved that quite a little crowd was generally collected round them, and the business had greatly augmented. The old naturalist was less pleased at this change than most men would have been in his position. He had got into a groove and did not care to get out of it. He had no relatives or any one dependent on him, and he had been well content to go on in a jog-trot way, just paying his expenses of shop and living. The extra bustle and push worried rather than pleased him. "I am an old man," he said to Frank one day, as after the shop was closed they sat over their tea. "I have no motive in laying by money, and had enough for my wants. I was influenced more by my liking for your face and my appreciation of your talent, than by any desire of increasing my business. I am taking now three times as much as I did before. Now I should not mind, indeed, I should be glad, if I thought that you would succeed me here as a son would do. I would gladly take you into partnership with me, and you would have the whole business after my death. But I know, my boy, that it wouldn't do. I know that the time will come when you will not be content with so dull a life here. You will either get an offer from some West End house which would open higher prospects to you, or you will be wandering away as a collector. In any case you would not stop here, of that I am quite sure, and therefore do not care, as I should have done, had you been my son, for the increase of the business. As it is, lad, I could not even wish to see you waste your life here."

Frank, after he was once fairly settled at his new work, had written to his friend the doctor, at Deal, telling him of the position he had taken, and that he was in a fair way to make at least a comfortable living, and that at a pursuit of which he was passionately fond. He asked him, however, while writing to him from time to time to give him news of his sister, not to tell anyone his address, as although he was not ashamed of his berth, still he would rather that, until he had made another step up in life, his old school-fellows should not know of his whereabouts. He had also written to his friend Ruthven a bright chatty letter, telling him somewhat of his adventures in London and the loss of his money, and saying that he had now got employment at a naturalist's, with every chance of making his way. "When I mount a bit higher," he concluded, "I shall be awfully glad to see you again, and will let you know what my address may then be. For the present I had rather keep it dark. If you will write to me, addressed to the General Post Office, telling me all about yourself and the fellows at school, I shall be very very glad to get your letter. I suppose you will be breaking up for Christmas in a few days."

Christmas came and went. It was signalized to Frank only by the despatch of a pretty present to Lucy, and the receipt of a letter from her written in a round childish hand. A week afterwards he heard somebody come into the shop. His employer was out, and he therefore went into the shop.

"I knew it was!" shouted a voice. "My dear old Frank, how are you?" and his hand was warmly clasped in that of Ruthven.

"My dear Ruthven," was all Frank could say.

"I had intended," Ruthven exclaimed, "to punch your head directly I found you; but I am too glad to do it, though you deserve it fifty times over. What a fellow you are! I wouldn't have believed it of you, running away in that secret sort of way and letting none of us know anything about you. Wasn't I angry, and sorry too, when I got the letter you wrote me from Deal! When I went back to school and found that not even Dr. Parker, not even your sister, knew where you were, I was mad. So were all the other fellows. However, I said I would find you wherever you had hidden yourself."

"But how did you find me?" Frank asked, greatly moved at the warmth of his school-fellow's greeting.

"Oh, it wasn't so very difficult to find you when once I got your letter saying what you were doing. The very day I came up to town I began to hunt about. I found from the Directory there were not such a great number of shops where they stuffed birds and that sort of thing. I tried the places in Bond Street, and Piccadilly, and Wigmore Street, and so on to begin with. Then I began to work east, and directly I saw the things in the window here I felt sure I had found you at last. You tiresome fellow! Here I have wasted nearly half my holidays looking for you."

"I am so sorry, Ruthven."

"Sorry! You ought to be more than sorry. You ought to be ashamed of yourself, downright ashamed. But, there, I won't say any more now. Now, can't you come out with me?"

"No, I can't come out now, Ruthven; but come into this room with me."

There for the next hour they chatted, Frank giving a full account of all he had gone through since he came up to town, while Ruthven gave him the gossip of the half-year at school.

"Well," Ruthven said at last, "this old Horton of yours must be a brick. Still, you know, you can't stop here all your life. You must come and talk it over with my governor."

"Oh, no, indeed, Ruthven! I am getting on very well here, and am very contented with my lot, and I could not think of troubling your father in the matter."

"Well, you will trouble him a great deal," Ruthven said, "if you don't come, for you will trouble him to come all the way down here. He was quite worried when he first heard of your disappearance, and has been almost as excited as I have over the search for you. You are really a foolish fellow, Frank," he went on more seriously; "I really didn't think it of you. Here you save the lives of four or five fellows and put all their friends under a tremendous obligation, and then you run away and hide yourself as if you were ashamed. I tell you you can't do it. A fellow has no more right to get rid of obligations than he has to run away without paying his debts.

It would be a burden on your mind if you had a heavy debt you couldn't pay, and you would have a right to be angry if, when you were perfectly able to pay, your creditor refused to take the money. That's just the position in which you've placed my father. Well, anyhow, you've got to come and see him, or he's got to come and see you. I know he has something in his mind's eye which will just suit you, though he did not tell me what it was. For the last day or two he has been particularly anxious about finding you. Only yesterday when I came back and reported that I had been to half a dozen places without success, he said, 'Confound the young rascal, where can he be hiding? Here are the days slipping by and it will be too late. If you don't find him in a day or two, Dick, I will set the police after him—say he has committed a murder or broken into a bank, and offer a reward for his apprehension.' So you must either come home with me this afternoon, or you will be having my father down here tonight."

"Of course, Ruthven," Frank said, "I would not put your father to such trouble. He is very kind to have taken so much interest in me, only I hate—"

"Oh, nonsense! I hate to see such beastly stuck-up pride, putting your own dignity above the affection of your friends; for that's really what it comes to, old boy, if you look it fairly in the face."

Frank flushed a little and was silent for a minute or two.

"I suppose you are right, Ruthven; but it is a little hard for a fellow—"

"Oh, no, it isn't," Ruthven said. "If you'd got into a scrape from some fault of your own one could understand it, although even then there would be no reason for you to cut your old friends till they cut you. Young Goodall, who lives over at Bayswater, has been over four or five times to ask me if I have succeeded in finding you, and I have had letters from Handcock, and Childers, and Jackson. Just as if a fellow had got nothing to do but to write letters. How long will you be before you can come out?"

"There is Mr. Horton just come in," Frank said. "I have no doubt he will let me go at once."

The old naturalist at once assented upon Frank's telling him that a friend had come who wished him to go out.

"Certainly, my dear boy. Why, working the hours and hours of overtime that you do, of course you can take a holiday whenever you're disposed."

"He will not be back till late," Ruthven said, as they went out. "I shall keep him all the evening."

"Oh, indeed, Ruthven, I have no clothes!"

"Clothes be bothered," Ruthven said. "I certainly shall end by punching your head, Frank, before the day's out."

Frank remonstrated no more, but committed himself entirely to his friend's guidance. At the Mansion House they mounted on the roof of an omnibus going west, and at Knightsbridge got off and walked to Eaton Square, where Ruthven's father resided. The latter was out, so Frank accompanied his friend to what he called his sanctum, a small room littered up with books, bats, insect-boxes, and a great variety of rubbish of all kinds. Here they chatted until the servant came up and said that Sir James had returned.

"Come on, Frank," Ruthven said, running downstairs. "There's nothing of the ogre about the governor."

They entered the study, and Ruthven introduced his friend.

"I've caught him, father, at last. This is the culprit."

Sir James Ruthven was a pleasant-looking man, with a kindly face.

"Well, you troublesome boy," he said, holding out his hand, "where have you been hiding all this time?"

"I don't know that I've been hiding, sir," Frank said.

"Not exactly hiding," Sir James smiled, "only keeping away from those who wanted to find you. Well, and how are you getting on?"

"I am getting on very well, sir. I am earning eighteen shillings a week and my board and lodging, and my employer says he will take me into partnership as soon as I come of age."

"Ah, indeed!" Sir James said. "I am glad to hear that, as it shows you must be clever and industrious."

"Yes, father, and the place was full of the most lovely cases of things Frank had stuffed. There was quite a crowd looking in at the window."

"That is very satisfactory. Now, Frank, do you sit down and write a note to your employer, asking him to send down half a dozen of the best cases. I want to show them to a gentleman who will dine with me here today, and who is greatly interested in such matters. When you have written the note I will send a servant off at once in a cab to fetch them."

"And, father," Dick continued, "if you don't mind, might Frank and I have our dinner quietly together in my room? You've got a dinner party on, and Frank won't enjoy it half as much as he would dining quietly with me."

"By all means," Sir James said. "But mind he is not to run away without seeing me. You are a foolish lad," he went on in a kind voice to Frank; "and it was wrong as well as foolish to hide yourself from your friends. However independent we may be in this world, all must, to a certain extent, rely upon others. There is scarcely a man who can stand aloof from the rest and say, 'I want nothing of you.' I can understand your feeling in shrinking from asking a favour of me, or of the fathers of the other boys who are, like myself, deeply indebted to you for the great service you have rendered their sons. I can admire the feeling if not carried too far; but you should have let your school-fellows know exactly how you were placed, and so have given us the opportunity of repaying the obligation if we were disposed, not to have run away and hidden yourself from us."

"I am sorry, sir," Frank said simply. "I did not like to seem to trade upon the slight service I rendered some of my school-fellows. Dr. Bateman told me I was wrong, but I did not see it then. Now I think, perhaps he was right, although I am afraid that if it happened again I should do the same."

Sir James smiled.

"I fear you are a stiff-necked one, Master Frank. However, I will not scold you any further. Now, what will you do with yourselves till dinner-time?"

"Oh, we'll just sit and chat, father. We have got lots more things to tell each other."

The afternoon passed in pleasant talk. Frank learned that Ruthven had now left Dr. Parker's for good, and that he was going down after the holidays to a clergyman who prepared six or eight boys for the army. Before dinner the footman returned with half a dozen of the best cases from the shop, which were brought up to Dick's room, and the latter was delighted with them. They greatly enjoyed their dinner together. At nine o'clock a servant came up and took down the cases. Five minutes later he returned again with a message, saying that Sir James wished Mr. Richard and his friend to go down into the dining-room. Frank was not shy, but he felt it rather a trial when he entered the room, where seven or eight gentlemen were sitting round the table, the ladies having already withdrawn. The gentlemen were engaged in examining and admiring the cases of stuffed birds and animals.

"This is my young friend," Sir James said, "of whom I have been speaking to you, and whose work you are all admiring. This, Frank, is Mr. Goodenough, the traveller and naturalist, of whom you may have heard."

"Yes, indeed," Frank said, looking at the gentleman indicated. "I have Mr. Goodenough's book on *The Passerine Family* at home."

"It is rather an expensive book too," the gentleman said.

"Yes, sir. My father bought it, not I. He was very fond of natural history and taught me all I know. He had a capital library of books on the subject, which Dr. Bateman is keeping for me, at Deal, till I have some place where I can put them. I was thinking of getting them up soon."

Mr. Goodenough asked him a few questions as to the books in the library, and then put him through what Frank felt was a sort of examination, as to his knowledge of their contents.

"Very good indeed!" Mr. Goodenough said. "I can see from your work here that you are not only a very clever preparer, but a close student of the habits and ways of wild creatures. But I was hardly prepared to find your scientific knowledge so accurate and extensive. I was at first rather inclined to hesitate when Sir James

Ruthven made me a proposal just now. I do so no longer. I am on the point of starting on an expedition into the centre of Africa in search of specimens of natural history. He has proposed that you should accompany me, and has offered to defray the cost of your outfit, and of your passage out and home. I may be away for two years. Of course you would act as my assistant, and have every opportunity of acquiring such knowledge as I possess. It will be no pleasure trip, you know, but hard work, with all sorts of hardships and, perhaps, some dangers. At the same time it would be a fine opening in a career as a naturalist. Well, what do you say?"

"Oh, sir!" Frank exclaimed, clasping his hands. "It is of all things in the world what I should like most. How can I thank you enough? And you, Sir James, it is indeed kind and thoughtful of you."

"We are not quits yet by any means, Frank," Sir James said kindly. "I am glad indeed to be able to forward your wishes; and now you must go upstairs and be introduced to my wife. She is most anxious to see you. She only returned home just before dinner."

Frank was taken upstairs, where he and his cases of birds were made much of by Lady Ruthven and the ladies assembled in the drawing-room. He himself was so filled with delight at the prospect opened to him that all thought of his dark tweed suit being out of place among the evening dresses of the ladies and gentlemen, which had troubled him while he was awaiting the summons to the dining-room, quite passed out of his mind, and he was able to do the honours of his cases naturally and without embarrassment. At eleven o'clock he took his leave, promising to call upon Mr. Goodenough, who was in lodgings in Jermyn Street, upon the following morning, that gentleman having at Sir James' request undertaken to procure all the necessary outfit.

"I feel really obliged to you, Sir James," Mr. Goodenough said when Frank had left. "The lad has a genius for natural history, and he is modest and self-possessed. From what you tell me he has done rather than apply for assistance to anyone, he must have plenty of pluck and resolution, and will make a capital travelling companion. I feel quite relieved, for it is so difficult to procure a companion who will exactly suit. Clever naturalists are rare, and one can never tell how one will get on with a man when you are thrown together. He may want to have his own way, may be irritable and bad-tempered, may in many respects be a disagreeable companion. With that lad I feel sure of my ground. We shall get on capitally together."

On his return to the shop Frank told his employer, whom he found sitting up for him, the change which had taken place in his life, and the opening which presented itself.

Mr. Horton expressed himself as sincerely glad. "I shall miss you sadly," he said, "shall feel very dull for a time in my solitary house here; but it is better for you that you should go, and I never expected to keep you long. You were made for better things than this shop, and I have no doubt that a brilliant career will be open before you. You may not become a rich man, for natural history is scarcely a lucrative profession, but you may become a famous one. Now, my lad, go off to bed and dream of your future."

The next morning Frank went over, the first thing after breakfast, to see his friend the porter. He, too, was very pleased to hear of Frank's good fortune, but he was too busy to talk much to him, and promised that he would come over that evening and hear all about it. Then Frank took his way to Jermyn Street, and went with Mr. Goodenough to Silver's, where an outfit suited for the climate of Central Africa was ordered. The clothes were simple. Shirts made of thin soft flannel, knickerbockers and Norfolk jackets of tough New Zealand flax, with gaiters of the same material.

"There is nothing like it," Mr. Goodenough said; "it is the only stuff which has a chance with the thorns of an African forest. Now you will want a revolver, a Winchester repeating carbine, and a shotgun. My outfit of boxes and cases is ready, so beyond two or three extra nets and collecting-boxes there is nothing farther to do in that way. For your head you'd better have a very soft felt hat with a wide brim; with a leaf or two inside they are as cool as anything, and are far lighter and more comfortable than the helmets which many people use in the tropics."

"As far as shooting goes," Frank said, "I think that I shall do much better with my blow-gun than with a regular one. I can hit a small bird sitting nineteen times out of twenty."

"That is a good thing," Mr. Goodenough answered. "For shooting sitting there is nothing better than a blow-gun in skilful hands. They have the advantage too of not breaking the skin; but for flying a shot-gun is infinitely more accurate. You will have little difficulty in learning to shoot well, as your eye is already trained by the use of your blow-pipe. Will you want any knives for skinning?"

"No, sir. I have a plentiful stock of them."

"Are you going back to Eaton Square? I heard Sir James ask you to stop there until we start."

"No," Frank replied; "I asked his permission to stay where I am till tomorrow. I did not like to seem in a hurry to run away from Mr. Horton, who has been extremely kind to me."

"Mind, you must come here in three days to have your things tried on," Mr. Goodenough said. "I particularly ordered that they are to be made easy and comfortable, larger, indeed, than you absolutely require, but we must allow for growing, and two years may make a difference of some inches to you. Now, we have only to go to a bootmaker's and then we have done."

When the orders were completed they separated, as Mr. Goodenough was going down that afternoon to the country, and was not to return until the day preceding that on which they were to sail. That evening Frank had a long chat with his two friends, and was much pleased when the old naturalist, who had taken a great fancy to the honest porter, offered him the use of a room at his house, saying that he should be more than paid by the pleasure of his company of an evening. The offer was accepted, and Frank was glad to think that his two friends would be sitting smoking their pipes together of an evening instead of being in their solitary rooms. The next day he took up his residence in Eaton Square.

CHAPTER VIII

TO THE DARK CONTINENT

AFTER spending two or three days going about London and enjoying himself with his friend Dick, Frank started for Deal, where he was pleased to find his sister well and happy. He bade good-bye to her, to the doctor, and such of his school-fellows as lived in Deal, to whom his start for Central Africa was quite an event. Dr. Bateman handed over to him his watch and chain and his blow-gun, which he had taken care of for him, also his skinning knives and instruments. The same evening he returned to town, and spent the days very pleasantly until the afternoon came when he was to depart. Then he bade farewell to his kind friends Sir James and Lady Ruthven. Dick accompanied him in the cab to Euston station, where a minute or two later Mr. Goodenough arrived. The luggage was placed in a carriage, and Frank stood chatting with Dick at the door, until the guard's cry, "Take your places!" caused him to jump into the carriage. There was one more hearty hand-shake with his friend, and then the train steamed out of the station.

It was midnight when they arrived at Liverpool, and at once went to bed at the Station Hotel. On coming down in the morning Frank was astonished at the huge heap of baggage piled up in the hall, but he was told that this was of daily occurrence, as six or eight large steamers went out from Liverpool every week for America alone, and that the great proportion of the passengers came down, as they had done, on the previous night, and slept at the Station Hotel. Their own share of the baggage was not large, consisting only of a portmanteau each, Mr. Goodenough having sent down all his boxes two days previously. At twelve o'clock they went on board the *Niger*, bound for the west coast of Africa. This would carry them as far as Sierra Leone, whence Mr. Goodenough intended to take passage in a sailing ship to his starting-point for the interior.

Frank enjoyed the voyage out intensely, and three days after sailing they had left winter behind; four days later they were lying in the harbour of Funchal.

"What a glorious place that would be to ramble about!" he said to Mr. Goodenough.

"Yes, indeed. It would be difficult to imagine a greater contrast than between this mountainous island of Madeira and the country which we are about to penetrate. This is one of the most delightful climates in the world, the west coast of Africa one of the worst. Once well in the interior, the swamp fevers, which are the curse of the shores, disappear, but African travellers are seldom long free from attacks of fever of one kind or the other. However, quinine does wonders, and we shall be far in the interior before the bad season comes on."

"You have been there before, you said, Mr. Goodenough?"

"Yes, I have been there twice, and have made excursions for short distances from the coast. But this time we are going into a country which may be said to be altogether unknown. One or two explorers have made their way there, but these have done little towards examining the natural productions of the country, and have been rather led by inducements of sport than by those of research."

"Did you have fever, sir?"

"Two or three little attacks. A touch of African fever, during what is called the good season, is of little more importance than a feverish cold at home. It lasts two or three days, and then there is an end of it. In the bad season the attacks are extremely violent, sometimes carrying men off in a few hours. I consider, however, that dysentery is a more formidable enemy than fever. However, even that, when properly treated, should be combated successfully."

"Do you mean to hire the men to go with you at Sierra Leone?"

"Certainly not, Frank. The natives of Sierra Leone are the most indolent, the most worthless, and the most insolent in all Africa. It is the last place in the world at which to hire followers. We must get them at the Gaboon itself, and at each place we arrive at afterwards we take on others, merely retaining one of the old lot to act as interpreter. The natives, although they may allow white men to pass safely, are exceedingly jealous of men of other tribes. I shall, however, take with me, if possible, a body of, say six Houssas, who are the best fighting negroes on the coast. These I shall take as a body-guard; the carriers we shall obtain from the different tribes we visit. The Kroomen, whom you will see at Cape Palmas, are a magnificent set of men. They furnish sailors and boatmen to all the ships trading on these shores. They are strong, willing, and faithful, but they do not like going up into the interior. Now we will land here and get a few hours' run on shore. There are one or two peculiarities about Madeira which distinguish it from other places. To begin with we will go for a ride in a bullock-cart without wheels."

"But surely it must jolt about terribly," Frank said.

"Not at all. The roads are paved with round knubbly stones, such as you see sometimes in narrow lanes and courts in seaside places at home. These would not make smooth roads for wheeled vehicles; but here, as you will see, the carts are placed on long runners like those of sledges. These are greased, and the driver always has a pound of candles or so hanging to the cart. When he thinks that the runners want greasing he takes a candle, lays it down on the road in front of one of the runners, and lets this pass over it. This greases it sufficiently, and it glides along over the stones almost as smoothly as if passing over ice."

Frank thoroughly enjoyed his run on shore, but was surprised at the air of listlessness which pervaded the inhabitants. Every one moved about in the most dawdling fashion. The shopkeepers looked out from their doors as if 'twere a matter of perfect indifference to them whether customers called or not. The few soldiers in Portuguese uniform looked as if they had never done a day's drill since they left home. Groups sat in chairs under the trees and sipped cooling drinks or coffee. The very bullocks which drew the gliding waggons seemed to move more slowly than bullocks in other places. Frank and his friend drove in a waggon to the monastery, high up on the mountain, and then took their places on a little hand-sledge, which was drawn by two men with ropes, who took them down the sharp descent at a run, dashing round corners at a pace which made Frank hold his breath. It took them but a quarter of an hour to regain the town, while an hour and a half had been occupied in the journey out.

"I shall buy a couple of hammocks here," Mr. Goodenough said. "They are made of knotted string, and are lighter and more comfortable than those to be met with on the coast. I will get a couple of their cane-chairs, too; they are very light and comfortable."

In the afternoon they again embarked, and then steamed away for Sierra Leone. After several days' passage, they arrived there at daylight, and Frank was soon on deck.

"What a beautiful place!" he exclaimed. "It is not a bit what I expected."

"No," Mr. Goodenough said; "no one looking at it could suppose that bright pretty town had earned for itself the name of the white man's grave."

Sierra Leone is built on a somewhat steep ascent about a mile up the river. Freetown, as the capital is properly called, stands some fifty feet or so above the sea, and the barracks upon a green hill three hundred feet above it, a quarter of a mile back. The town, as seen from the sea, consists entirely of the houses of the merchants and shopkeepers, the government buildings, churches, and other public and European buildings. The houses are all large and bright with yellow-tinged whitewash, and the place is completely embowered in palms and other tropical trees. The native town lies hidden from sight among trees on low ground to the left of the town. Everywhere around the town the hills rise steep and high, wooded to the summit. Altogether there are few more prettily situated towns than the capital of Sierra Leone.

"It is wonderful," Mr. Goodenough said, "that generations and generations of Europeans have been content to live and die in that wretchedly unhealthy place, when they might have established themselves on those lofty hills but a mile away. There they would be far above the malarious mists which rise from the low ground. The walk up, and down to their warehouses and offices here would be good for them, and there is no reason why Sierra Leone should be an unhealthy residence. Unfortunately the European in Africa speedily loses his vigour and enterprise. When he first lands he exclaims, 'I certainly shall have a bungalow built upon those hills;' but in a short time his energy leaves him. He falls into the ways of the place, drinks a great deal more spirits than is good for him, stops down near the water, and at the end of a year or so, if he lives so long, is obliged to go back to Europe to recruit. Look at the boats coming out."

A score of boats, each containing from ten to twelve men, approached the ship. They remained at a short distance until the harbour-master came on board and pronounced the ship free from quarantine. Then the boats made a rush to the side, and with shouts, yells, and screams of laughter scrambled on board. Frank was at once astonished and amused at the noise and confusion.

"What on earth do they all want?" he asked Mr. Goodenough.

"The great proportion of them don't want anything at all," Mr. Goodenough answered, "but have merely come off for amusement. Some of them come to be hired, some to carry luggage, others to tout for the boatmen below. Look at those respectable negresses coming up the gangway now. They are washerwomen, and will take our clothes ashore and bring them on board again this afternoon before we start."

"It seems running rather a risk," Frank said.

"No, you will see they all have testimonials, and I believe it is perfectly safe to intrust things to them."

Mr. Goodenough and Frank now prepared to go on shore, but this was not easily accomplished, for there was a battle royal among the boatmen whose craft thronged at the foot of the ladder. Each boat had about four hands, three of whom remained on board her, while the fourth stood upon the ladder and hauled at the painter to keep the boat to which he belonged alongside. As out of the twenty boats lying there not more than two could be at the foot of the ladder together, the conflict was a desperate one. All the boatmen shouted, "Here, sar. This good boat, sar. You come wid me, sar," at the top of their voices, while at the same time they were hard at work pulling each other's boats back and pushing their own forward. So great was the struggle as Frank and Mr. Goodenough approached the gangway, so great the crowd upon the ladder, that one side of the iron bar from which the ladder chains depend broke in two, causing the ladder to drop some inches and giving a ducking to those on the lower step, causing shouts of laughter and confusion. These rose into perfect yells of amusement when one of the sailors suddenly loosed the ladder rope, letting five or six of the negroes into the water up to their necks. So intense was the appreciation by the sable mind of this joke that the boatmen rolled about with laughter, and even the victims, when they had once scrambled into their boats, yelled like people possessed.

On landing, Frank was delighted with the greenness of everything. The trees were heavy with luxuriant foliage, the streets were green with grass as long and bright as that in a country lane in England. The hill on which the barracks stand was as bright a green as you would see on English slopes after a wet April, while down the streets clear streams were running. The town was alive with a chattering, laughing, good-natured, excitable population, all black, but with some slight variation in the dinginess of the hue. Never was there such a place for fun as Sierra Leone. Every one was brimful of it. Every one laughed when he or she spoke, and every one standing near joined freely in the conversation and laughed too. Frank was delighted with the display of fruit in the market, which is probably unequalled in the world. Great piles there were of delicious big oranges, green but perfectly sweet, and of equally refreshing little green limes; pine-apples and bananas, green, yellow, and red, guava, and custard-apples, alligator-pears, melons, and sour-sops, and many other native fruits.

Mr. Goodenough purchased a large basket of fruit, which they took with them on board the ship. The next morning they started down the coast. They passed Liberia, the republic formed of liberated slaves, and of negroes from America, and brought up a mile or two off Monrovia, its capital. The next day they anchored off Cape Palmas, the headquarters of the Kroomen. A number of these men came off in their canoes, and caused great amusement to Frank and the other passengers by their fun and dexterity in the management of their little craft. These boats are extremely light, being hollowed out until little thicker than paste-board, and even with two Kroomen paddling it is difficult for a European to sit in them, so extremely crank are they. Light as they are the Krooboy can stand up and dive from his boat without upsetting it, if he takes time; but in the hurry and excitement of diving for coppers, when half a dozen men would leap overboard together, the canoes were frequently capsized. The divers, however, thought nothing of these mishaps, righting the boats and getting in again without difficulty. Splendidly muscular fellows they were. Indeed, except among the Turkish hamals it is doubtful whether such powerful figures could be found elsewhere.

"They would be grand fellows to take with us, Mr. Goodenough," Frank said.

"Yes, if they were as plucky as they are strong, one could wish for nothing better; but they are notorious cowards, and no offer would tempt them to penetrate into such a country as that into which we are going."

Stopping a few hours at Cape Coast Castle, Accra, and other ports, they at last arrived at Bonny.

"It is not tempting in appearance," Frank said, "certainly."

"No," Mr. Goodenough replied, "this is one of the most horribly unhealthy spots in Africa. As you see, the white traders do not dare to live on shore, but take up their residence in those old floating hulks which are thatched over, and serve as residences and storehouses. I have a letter from one of the African merchants in London, and we shall take up our abode on board his hulk until we get one of the coasting steamers to carry us down. I hope it will not be many days."

The very bulky luggage was soon transferred to the hulk, where Frank and Mr. Goodenough took up their residence. The agent in charge was very glad to receive them, as any break in the terrible monotony of such a life is eagerly welcomed. He was a pale, unhealthy-looking man, and had just recovered from an unusually bad attack of fever. Like most of the traders on the coast, he had an immense faith in the power of spirits.

"It is the ruin of them," Mr. Goodenough said to Frank when they were alone. "Five out of six of the men here ruin their constitutions with spirits, and then fall an easy prey to the fever."

"But you have brought spirits with you, Mr. Goodenough. I saw some of the cases were labelled 'Brandy.'"

"Brandy is useful when taken as a medicine, and in moderation. A little mixed with water at the end of a long day of exhausting work acts as a restorative, and frequently enables a worn-out man to sleep. But I have brought the brandy you see for the use of others rather than myself. One case is of the very best spirits for our own use. The rest is common stuff and is intended as presents. Our main drink will be tea and chocolate. These are invaluable for the traveller. I have, besides, large quantities of calico, brass stair-rods, beads, and powder. These are the money of Africa, and pass current everywhere. With these we shall pay our carriers and boatmen, with these purchase the right of way through the various tribes we shall meet. Moreover, it is almost necessary in Africa to pass as traders. The people perfectly understand that white men come here to trade; but if we said that our object was to shoot birds and beasts, and to catch butterflies and insects, they would not believe us in the slightest degree, but would suspect us of all sorts of hidden designs. Now we will go ashore and pay our respects to the king."

"Do you mean to say that there is a king in that wretched-looking village?" Frank asked in surprise.

"Kings are as plentiful as peas in Africa," Mr. Goodenough said, "but you will not see much royal state."

Frank was disappointed indeed upon landing. Sierra Leone had given him an exalted idea of African civilization, but this was at once dispelled by the appearance of Bonny. The houses were constructed entirely of black mud, and the streets were narrow and filthy beyond description. The palace was composed of two or three hovels, surrounded by a mud wall. In one of these huts the king was seated. Mr. Goodenough and Frank were introduced by the agent, who had gone ashore with them, and His Majesty, who was an almost naked negro, at once invited them to join him in the meal of which he was partaking. As a matter of courtesy they consented, and plates were placed before them, heaped with a stew consisting of meat, vegetables, and hot peppers. While the meal went on the king asked Mr. Goodenough what he had come to the coast for, and was disappointed to find that he was not going to set up as a trader at Bonny, as it was the custom for each newcomer to make a handsome present to him. When the meal was over they took their leave.

"Do you know what you have been eating?" the agent asked Frank.

"Not in the least," Frank said. "It was not bad; what was it?"

"It was dog flesh," the agent answered.

"Not really!" Frank exclaimed, with an uncomfortable sensation of sickness.

"Yes, indeed," the agent replied. "Dog's meat is considered a luxury in Bonny, and dogs are bred specially for the table."

"You'll eat stranger things than that before you've done, Frank," Mr. Goodenough continued, "and will find them just as good, and in many cases better, than those to which you are accustomed. It is a strange thing why in Europe certain animals should be considered fit to eat and certain animals altogether rejected, and this without the slightest reason. Horses and donkeys are as clean feeders as oxen and sheep. Dogs, cats, and rats are far cleaner than pigs and ducks. The flesh of the one set is every bit as good as that of the other, and yet the poorest peasant would turn up his nose at them. Here sheep and oxen, horses and donkeys, will not live, and the natives very wisely make the most of the animals which can do so."

Frank was soon tired of Bonny, and was glad to hear that they would start the next day for Fernando Po in a little steamer called the *Retriever*. The island of Fernando Po is a very beautiful one, the peak rising ten thousand feet above the sea, and wooded to the very summit. Were the trees to some extent cleared away the island might be very healthy. As it is, it is little better than the mainland.

There was not much to see in the town of Clarence, whose population consists entirely of traders from Sierra Leone, Kroomen, &c. The natives, whose tribal name is Adiza, live in little villages in the interior. They are an extremely primitive people, and for the most part dispense altogether with clothing. The island belongs to Spain, and is used as a prison, the convicts being kept in guardships in the harbour. After a stay of three days there Mr. Goodenough and Frank took passage in a sailing-ship for the Gaboon.

CHAPTER IX

THE START INLAND

AFTER the comforts of a fine steamer the accommodation on board the little trader was poor indeed. The vessel smelt horribly of palm-oil and was alive with cockroaches. These, however, Mr. Goodenough and Frank cared little for, as they brought up their mattresses and slept on deck. Upon their voyage out from England Frank, as well as several of the other passengers, had amused himself by practising with his rifle at empty bottles thrown overboard, and other objects, and having nothing else to do now, he resumed the practice, accustoming himself also to the use of his revolver, the mark being a small log of wood swung from the end of a yard.

"I told you," Mr. Goodenough said, "that your skill with the blow-gun would prove useful to you in shooting. You are as good a shot as I am, and I am considered a fair one. I have no doubt that with a little practice you will succeed as well with your double-barrel. The shooting of birds on the wing is a knack which seems to come naturally to some people, while others, practise as they will, never become good shots."

The ship touched twice upon its way down to the Gaboon. Once at the Malimba river, the second time at Botauga, the latter being the principal ivory port in equatorial Africa.

"Shall we meet with any elephants, do you think?" Frank asked his friend.

"In all probability," Mr. Goodenough said. "Elephant shooting, of course, does not come within our line of action, and I should not go at all out of my way for them. Still, if we meet them we will shoot them. The ivory is valuable and will help to pay our expenses, while the meat is much prized by the natives, who will gladly assist us in consideration of the flesh."

On the sixteenth day after leaving Fernando Po they entered the Gaboon. On the right-hand bank were the fort and dwellings of the French. A little farther up stood the English factories; and upon a green hill behind, the church, school, and houses of an American mission. On the left bank was the wattle town of King William, the sable monarch of the Gaboon. Mr. Goodenough at once landed and made inquiries for a house. He succeeded in finding one, consisting of three rooms, built on piles, an important point in a country in which disease rises from the soil. At Bonny Mr. Goodenough had, with the assistance of the agent, enlisted six Houssas. These people live much higher up on the coast, but they wander a good deal and may be met with in most of the ports. The men had formed a guard in one of the hulks, but trade having been bad the agent had gone home, and they were glad to take service with Mr. Goodenough. They spoke a few words of English, and, like the Kroomen, rejoiced in names which had been given them by sailors. They were called Moses, Firewater, Ugly Tom, Bacon, Tatters, and King John. They were now for the first time set to work, and the goods were soon transported from the brig to the house.

"Is anything the matter with you, Frank?" Mr. Goodenough asked that evening.

"I don't know, sir. My head feels heavy, somehow, and I am giddy."

Mr. Goodenough felt his pulse.

"You have got your first touch of fever," he said. "I wonder you've been so long without it. You had better lie down at once."

A quarter of an hour afterwards Frank was seized with an overpowering heat, every vein appearing to be filled with liquid fire; but his skin, instead of being, as usual, in a state of perspiration, was dry and hard.

"Now, Frank, sit up and drink this. It's only some mustard and salt and water. I have immense faith in an emetic."

The draught soon took its effect. Frank was violently sick, and the perspiration broke in streams from him.

"Here is a cup of tea," Mr. Goodenough said; "drink that

and you will find that there will be little the matter with you in the morning."

Frank awoke feeling weak, but otherwise perfectly well. Mr. Goodenough administered a strong dose of quinine, and after he had had his breakfast, he felt quite himself again.

"Now," Mr. Goodenough said, "we will go up to the factories and mission and try and find a really good servant. Everything depends upon that."

In a short time an engagement was made with a native of the name of Ostik. He was a Mpongwe man, that being the name of the tribe on the coast. He spoke English fairly, as well as two or three of the native languages. He had before made a journey some distance into the interior with a white traveller. He was tall and powerfully built, very ugly, but with a pleasant and honest face. Frank felt at once that he should like him.

"You quite understand," Mr. Goodenough explained, "we are going through the Fan country, far into the interior. We may be away from the coast for many months."

"Me ready, sar," the man answered with a grin. "Mak no odds to Ostik. He got no wife, no child. Ostik very good cook. Master find good grub; he catch plenty of beasts."

"You're not afraid, Ostik, because it is possible we may have trouble on the way?"

"Me not very much afraid, massa. You good massa to Ostik he no run away if fightee come; but no good fight whole tribe."

"I hope not to have any fighting at all, Ostik; but as I have got six Houssas with me who will all carry breech-loading guns, I think we should be a match for a good-sized tribe, if necessary."

Ostik looked thoughtful. "More easy, massa, go without Houssas," he said. "Black man not often touch white traveller."

"No, Ostik, that is true; but I must take with me trade goods for paying my way and hiring carriers, and if alone I should be at the mercy of every petty chief who chose to plunder and delay me. I am going as a peaceful traveller, ready to pay my way, and to make presents to the different kings through whose territories I may pass. But I do not choose to put myself at the mercy of any of them. I do not say that eight men armed with breech-loaders could defeat a whole tribe; but they would be so formidable, that any of these kings would probably prefer taking presents and letting us pass peacefully to trying to rob us. The first thing to do, will be to hire one large canoe, or two if necessary. The men must agree to take us up into the Fan country, as far as the rapids on the Gaboon. Then we shall take carriers there, and the boat can return by itself. These are the things which will have to go."

The baggage consisted of ten large tin cases, each weighing about eighty pounds. These contained cotton cloths, powder, beads, tea, chocolate, sugar, and biscuits. There were in addition three bundles of stair-rods, each about the same weight as the boxes. These were done up in canvas. There was also a tent made of double canvas weighing fifty pounds, and two light folding tressel beds weighing fifteen pounds apiece. Thus fourteen men would be required as carriers, besides some for plantains and other provisions, together with the portmanteaus, rugs, and water-proof sheets of the travellers. There were besides six great chests made of light iron. Four of these were fitted with trays with cork bottoms, for insects. The other two were for the skins of birds. All the boxes and cases had strips of india-rubber where the lids fitted down, in order to keep out both damp and the tiny ants which are the plague of naturalists in Africa.

Four or five days were occupied in getting together a crew, for the natives had an abject fear of entering the country of the cannibal Fans. Mr. Goodenough promised that they should not be obliged to proceed unless a safe-conduct for their return was obtained from the King of the Fans. A large canoe was procured, sufficient to convey the whole party. Twelve paddlers were hired, and the goods taken down and arranged in the boat. The Houssas had been, on landing, furnished with their guns, which were Snider rifles, had been instructed in the breech-loading arrangement, and had been set to work to practise at a mark at a hundred and fifty yards distance—the stump of an old tree, some five feet in height, serving for the purpose. The men were delighted with the accuracy of their pieces and the rapidity at which they could be fired.

Mr. Goodenough impressed upon them that unless attacked at close quarters, and specially ordered to fire fast, they must aim just as slowly and deliberately as if using their old guns, for that in so long a journey ammunition would be precious, and must, therefore, on no account whatever, be wasted. In the boxes were six thousand rounds of ammunition, a thousand for each gun, besides the ammunition for the rifles and fowling-pieces of Mr. Goodenough and Frank.

In order to render the appearance of his followers as imposing as possible, Mr. Goodenough furnished each of the Houssas with a pair of trousers made of New Zealand flax, reaching to their knees. These he had brought from England with him. They were all found to be too large, but the men soon set to work with rough needles and thread and took them in. In addition to these, each man was furnished with a red sash, which went several times round the waist, and served to keep the trousers up and to give a gay aspect to the dress. The Houssas were much pleased with their appearance. All of them carried swords in addition to the guns, as in their own country they are accustomed to fight with these weapons.

They started early in the morning, and after four hours' paddling passed Konig Island, an abandoned Dutch settlement. Here they stopped for an hour or two, and then the sea-breeze sprang up, a sail was hoisted, and late at night they passed a French guard-ship placed to mark the boundary of that settlement at a point where a large tributary called the Boqui runs into it. Here is a little island called Nenge-Nenge, formerly a missionary station, where the natives are still Christians. At this place the canoe was hauled ashore. The Houssas had already been instructed in the method of pitching the tent, and in a very few minutes this was erected. It was a double-poled tent, some ten feet square, and there was a waterproof sheet large enough to cover the whole of the interior, thus preventing the miasma from arising from the ground within it. The beds were soon opened and fixed, two of the large cases formed a table and two smaller ones did service as chairs. A lamp was lit, and Frank was charmed with the comfort and snugness of the abode. The men's weapons were fastened round one of the poles to keep them from the damp night air. Ostik had at once set to work on landing, leaving the Houssas to pitch the tent. A fire was soon blazing and a kettle and saucepans suspended over it. Rice was served out to the men, with the addition of some salt meat, of which sufficient had been purchased from the captain of the brig to last throughout the journey in the canoe. The men were all in high spirits at this addition to their fare, which was more than had been bargained for, and their songs rose merrily round the fire in the night air.

In the morning, after breakfast, they again took their places in the canoe. For twelve miles they paddled, the tide at first assisting them, but after this the water from the mountains ahead overpowered it. Presently they arrived at the first Fan village, called Olenga, which they reached six hours after starting. The natives crowded round as the canoe approached, full of curiosity and excitement, for never but once had a white man passed up the river. These Fans differed widely from the coastal Africans. Their hair was longer and thicker, their figures were slight, their complexion coffee-coloured, and their projecting upper jaws gave them a rabbit-mouthed appearance. They wore coronets on their heads adorned with the red tail-feathers of the common gray parrot. Most of the men had beards, which were divided in the middle, red and white beads being strung up the tips. Some wore only a strip of goatskin hanging from the waist, or the skin of a tiger-cat, while others had short petticoats made of cloth woven from the inner bark of a tree. The travellers were led to the hut of the chief, where they were surrounded by a mob of the cannibals. The Houssas had been strictly enjoined to leave their guns in the bottom of the canoe, as Mr. Goodenough desired to avoid all appearance of armed force. The chief demanded of Ostik what these two white men wanted here, and whether they had come to trade. Ostik replied that the white men were going up the river into the country beyond to shoot elephants and buy ivory, that they did not want to trade for logwood or oil, but that they would give presents to the chiefs of the Fan villages. A score of cheap Birmingham muskets had been brought from England by Mr. Goodenough for this purpose. One of these was now bestowed upon the chief, together with some powder and ball, three bright cotton handkerchiefs, some gaudy glass beads, and two looking-glasses for his wives. This was considered perfectly satisfactory.

The crowd was very great, and at Mr. Goodenough's dictation Ostik informed the chief that if the white men were left quiet until the evening, they would show his people many strange things. On the receipt of this information the crowd dispersed. But when at sunset the two travellers took a turn through the village, the excitement was again very great. The men stood their ground and stared at them, but the women and children ran screaming away to hide themselves. The idea of the people of Central Africa of the whites is that they are few in number, that they live at the bottom of the sea and are possessed of great wealth, but that they have no palm-oil or logwood, and are, therefore, compelled to come to land to trade for these articles. They believe that the strange clothes they wear are manufactured from the skins of sea-beasts. When night fell Mr. Goodenough fastened a sheet against the outside of the chief's hut, and then placed a magic lantern in position ten paces from it. The Fans were then invited to gather round and take their seats upon the ground. A cry of astonishment greeted the appearance of the bright disc. This was followed by a wilder yell when this was darkened, and an elephant bearing some men sitting on his back was seen to cross the house. The men leaped to their feet and seized their spears. The women screamed, and Ostik, who was himself somewhat alarmed, had great difficulty in calming their fears and persuading them to sit down again, assuring them that they would see many wonderful things, but that nothing would hurt them.

The next view was at first incomprehensible to many of them. It was a ship tossing in a stormy sea; but some of those present had been down to the mouth of the river, and these explained to the others the nature of the phenomenon. In all there were twenty slides, all of which were provided with movable figures; the last two being chromatropes, whose dancing colours elicited screams of delight from the astonished natives. This concluded the performance, but for hours after it was over the village rang with a perfect babel of shouts, screams, and chatter. The whole thing was to the Fans absolutely incomprehensible, and their astonishment was equalled by their awe at the powers of the white men.

The next two days they remained at Olenga, as word was sent up to Itchongué, the next town, asking the chief there for leave to come forward. The people had now begun to get over their first timidity, and when Frank went out for a walk after breakfast he was somewhat embarrassed by the women and girls crowding round him, feeling his clothes and touching his hands and face to assure themselves that these felt like those of human beings. He afforded them huge delight by taking off his Norfolk jacket and pulling up the sleeves of his shirt to show them that his arms were the same colour as his hands, and so elated were they with this exhibition that it was with great difficulty that he withstood their entreaties that he would disrobe entirely. Indeed, Ostik had at last to come to his rescue and carry him off from the laughing crowd by which he was surrounded. After dinner Mr. Goodenough invited the people to sit down in a vast circle holding each other's hands. He then told them that he should at a word make them all jump to their feet. Then taking out a small but powerful galvanic battery, he arranged it and placed wires into the hands of the two men nearest to him in the great circle.

"Now," he said, "when I clap my hands you will find that you are all obliged to jump up." He gave the signal. Frank turned on the battery, and in an instant the two hundred men and women, with a wild shriek, either leapt to their feet or rolled backward on the ground. In another minute not a native was to be seen, with the exception of the chief, who had not been included in the circle. The latter, at Mr. Goodenough's request, shouted loudly to his subjects to return, for that the white men would do them no harm; but it was a long time before, slowly and cautiously, they crept back again. When they had reassembled Mr. Goodenough showed them several simple but astonishing chemical experiments, which stupefied them with wonder; and concluded with three or four conjuring tricks, which completed their amazement.

A long day's paddling took them to Itchongué, where they were as well received as at Olenga. Here they stopped for two days, and the magic lantern was again brought out, and the other tricks repeated with a success equal to that which they had before obtained. As another day's paddling would take them to the rapids Mr. Goodenough now set up a negotiation for obtaining a sufficient number of carriers. After great palaver, and the presentation of three guns to the chief to obtain his assistance, thirty men were engaged. These were each to receive a yard of calico or one brass stair-rod a day, and were to proceed with the party until such time as they could procure carriers from another tribe.

The new recruits were taken up in another canoe. Several villages were passed on the way. The river became a mere rapid, against which the canoes with difficulty made their way. They had now entered the mountains which rose steeply above them, embowered in wood. Two days of severe work took them to the foot of the falls. Here the canoes were unloaded. The men hired on the coast received their pay, and turned the boat's head down stream. The other canoe accompanied it, and the travellers remained with their body-guard of Houssas and their carriers.

"Now," Mr. Goodenough said, "we are fairly embarked on our journey, and we will commence operations at once. I have heard the cries of a great many birds which are strange to me today, and I expect that we shall have a good harvest. We may remain here for some time. The first thing to do is to find food for our followers. We have got six sacks of rice, but it will never do to let our men depend solely upon these. They would soon come to an end."

"But how are we to feed forty people?" Frank asked in astonishment.

"I pointed out to you today," Mr. Goodenough said, "the tracks of hippopotami in various places. One of these beasts will feed the men for nearly a week. There were, too, numbers of alligators' eggs on the banks, and these creatures make by no means bad eating. Your rifle will be of no use against such animals as these. You had better take one of the Sniders. I have some explosive shells which will fit them. My own double-barrelled rifle is of the same bore."

After dinner Mr. Goodenough told two of the Houssas to accompany them with their rifles, together with three or four of the Fans. He made his way down the stream to a point where the hills receded, and where he had observed a great many marks of the river-horses. As they approached the spot they heard several loud snorts, and making their way along as quietly as possible they saw two of the great beasts standing in the stream. At this point it widened a good deal and was shallow and quiet near the bank. The Fans had been told to stay behind directly the snorting was heard, and Mr. Goodenough and Frank, rifle in hand, crept forward, with the Houssas as still and noiseless as cats close behind them.

CHAPTER X

LOST IN THE FOREST

THE hippopotami were playing together, floundering in the shallow water, and the noise they made prevented their hearing the stealthy approach of their enemies.

"You take the one nearest shore, Frank, I will take the other. Aim at the forehead between the eyes. I will make a slight sound to attract their attention." Frank knelt on one knee and took steady aim. Mr. Goodenough then gave a shout, and the two animals turning their heads, stood staring at the foliage, scarce a dozen yards away, in which the travellers were concealed. The guns flashed at the same moment, and as if struck by lightning the hippopotami fell in the stream. The explosive balls had both flown true to the mark, invariably a fatal one in the case of the river-horse. Frank as he fired had taken another rifle which the Houssas held in readiness for him, but there was no occasion for its use. The Fans came running up, and on seeing the great beasts lying in the stream, gave a shout of joy.

"That will do for this evening," Mr. Goodenough said. "They are large beasts, and will give food enough for a week or ten days."

They then returned to the camp, which, at the news brought by one of the Fans, had already been deserted. Before the natives retired to sleep the hippopotami had been cut up and carried to the camp. Portions were already frizzling over the fires, other parts set aside for the consumption of the next two days, and the rest cut up in strips to be dried in the sun. The tongue of one was cut up and fried as a great luxury for the white men's supper by Ostik. It is not often that the natives of equatorial Africa are able to indulge in meat, and the joy of the Fans at this abundant supply, and the prospect afforded them of further good eating, raised their spirits to the highest extent.

Next morning at daybreak Mr. Goodenough and Frank set out from the camp. Each carried a double-barrelled gun, and was accompanied by one of the Houssas carrying his rifle and a butter-fly-net, and when three hours later they returned to the camp for breakfast and compared their spoils they found that an excellent beginning had been made. Nearly a score of birds, of which several were very rare, and five were pronounced by Mr. Goodenough to be entirely new, had been shot, and many butterflies captured. Frank had been most successful in this respect, as he had come across a small clearing in which were several deserted huts. This was just the place in which butterflies delight, for, although many kinds prefer the deep shades of the forest, by far the greater portion love the bright sunlight.

After breakfast they again set out, Frank this time keeping along the edge of the stream, where he had observed many butter-flies as he came up, and where many birds of the kingfisher family had also been seen. He had been very successful, and was walking along by the edge of the water with his eyes fixed upon the trees above, where he had a minute before heard the call of a bird, when he was startled by a shout from the Houssa behind him. He invol-untarily sprang back, and it was well he did so; for on the instant something swept by within an inch or two of his head. Looking round he saw, at the edge of the stream below him, a huge alliga-tor. This had struck at him with its tail—the usual manner in which the alligator supplies itself with food—and had it not been for the warning cry of the Houssa, would have knocked him into the stream. Its mouth was open, and Frank, as if by instinct, fired the contents of both barrels into its throat. The animal rolled over on to its back in the water, and then turned as if to struggle to regain the bank. The Houssa, however, had run up, and, placing the muzzle of his gun within a foot of its eye, fired, and the creature rolled over dead, and was swept away by the stream.

The Houssa gave a loud shout which was answered in the dis-tance. He then shouted two or three words and turning to Frank, said: "Men get alligator;" and proceeded on his way without con-cerning himself further in the matter. On his return to camp in the evening Frank found that the alligator had been discovered and fished out, and that its steaks were by no means bad eating. Frank told Mr. Goodenough of the narrow escape he had had, and the latter pointed out to him the necessity of always keeping his eyes on the watch.

"Alligators frequently carry off the native women when engaged in washing," he said, "and almost invariably strike them, in the first place, into the river with a blow of their tails. Once in the water they are carried off, drowned, and eaten at leisure. Sometimes, indeed, a woman may escape with the loss of a foot or arm, but this is the exception."

"What is the best thing to do when so attacked?" Frank asked. "I don't mean to be caught napping again, still it is as well to know what to do if I am."

"Men when so attacked have been known frequently to escape by thrusting their thumbs or fingers into the creature's eyes. If it can be done, the alligator is sure to lose his hold, but it demands quickness and great presence of mind. When a reptile is tearing at one's leg, and hurrying one along under water, you can see that the nerve required to keep perfectly cool, to feel for the creature's eyes, and to thrust your finger into them is very great. The best plan, Frank, distinctly is to keep out of their reach altogether."

After remaining for a fortnight at their camp they prepared for a move. Another hippopotamus was killed, cut up and dried, and the flesh added to the burdens. Then the tent was struck and they proceeded farther into the mountains. Two days later they halted again, the site being chosen beside a little mountain rivulet. They were now very high up in the hills, Mr. Goodenough expecting to meet with new varieties of butterflies and insects at this elevation. They had scarcely pitched their camp when Frank exclaimed:

"Surely, Mr. Goodenough, I can hear some dogs barking! I did not know that the native dogs barked."

"Nor do they. They may yelp and howl, but they never bark like European dogs. What you hear is the bark of some sort of monkey or baboon."

This opinion was at once confirmed by the Fans.

"We will sally out with our guns at once," Mr. Goodenough said.

"I don't like the thought of shooting monkeys," Frank muttered, as he took up his Winchester carbine.

"They are very excellent eating," Mr. Goodenough continued, "superior in my opinion, and, indeed, in that of most travellers, to any other meat. We shall meet with no other kind of creature fit for food up here. The birds, indeed, supply us amply, but for the men it is desirable that we should obtain fresh meat when we have the chance. These baboons are very mischievous creatures, and are not to be attacked with impunity. Let four of the Houssas with their guns come with us."

Following the direction of the sounds they had heard the travellers came upon a troupe of great baboons. It was a curious sight. The males were as big as large dogs some were sitting sunning themselves on rocks, others were being scratched by the females. Many of these had a baby monkey clinging on their necks, while others were playing about in all directions.

"I'd rather not shoot at them, Mr. Goodenough," Frank said.

"You will be glad enough to eat them," Mr. Goodenough answered, and, selecting a big male, he fired. The creature fell dead. The others all sprang to their feet. The females and little ones scampered off. The males, with angry gestures, rushed upon their assailants, barking, showing their teeth, and making menacing gestures. Mr. Goodenough fired again, and Frank now, seeing that they were likely to be attacked, also opened fire. Six of the baboons were killed before the others abstained from the attack and went screaming after the females. The dead baboons were brought down, skinned, and two were at once roasted, the others hung up to trees. It required a great effort on Frank's part to overcome his repugnance to tasting these creatures, but, when he did so, he admitted that the meat was excellent.

That night they were disturbed by a cry of terror from the men. Seizing their rifles they ran out.

"There are two leopards, sar," Ostik said; "they have smelt the monkeys."

The shouts scared the creatures away, and the natives kept up a great fire till morning.

"We must get the skins if we can," Mr. Goodenough said. "The skins of the equatorial leopard are rare. If we can get them both they will make a fine group for you to stuff when you get back, Frank."

"Are you thinking of following their trail?" Frank asked.

"That would be useless," Mr. Goodenough answered. "In soft swampy ground, we might do so, but up here it would be out of the question. We must set a bait for them tonight, but be careful while you are out today. They have probably not gone far from the camp, and they are very formidable beasts. They not unfrequently attack and kill the natives."

The Fans were much alarmed at the neighbourhood of the leopards, and none would leave the camp during the day. Two of the Houssas were left on guard, although Mr. Goodenough felt sure that the animals would not attempt to carry off any meat in the daylight, and two Houssas accompanied each of the travellers while out in search of butterflies. Nothing was heard of the leopards during the day. At nightfall a portion of one of the monkeys was roasted and hung up, so as to swing within four feet of the ground, from the arm of a tree, a hundred yards from the camp. Mr. Goodenough and Frank took their seats in another tree a short distance off. The night was fine and the stars clear and bright. The tree on which the meat hung stood somewhat alone, so that sufficient light penetrated from above to enable any creatures approaching the bait to be seen. Instead of his little Winchester, Frank had one of the Sniders with explosive bullets. The Houssas were told to keep a sharp watch in camp, in case the leopards, approaching from the other side, might be attracted by the smell of meat there, rather than by the bait. The Fans needed no telling to induce them to keep up great fires all night.

Soon after dark the watchers heard a roaring in the forest. It came from the other side of the camp. "That is unlucky," Mr. Goodenough said. "We have pitched on the wrong side. However, they will probably be deterred by the fire from approaching the camp, and will wander round and round; so we may hope to hear of them before long." In answer to the roar of the leopards the natives kept up a continued shouting. For some hours the roaring continued at intervals, sometimes close at hand, sometimes at a considerable distance. Frank had some difficulty in keeping awake, and was beginning to wish that the leopards would move off altogether. Two or three times he had nearly dosed off, and his rifle had almost slipped from his hold. All at once he was aroused by a sharp nudge from his companion. Fixing his eyes on the bait he made out something immediately below it. Directly afterwards another creature stole forward. They were far less distinct than he had expected.

"You take the one to the left," Mr. Goodenough whispered. "Now!"

They fired together. Two tremendous roars were heard. One of the leopards immediately bounded away. The other rolled over and over, and then, recovering its feet, followed its companion, Mr. Goodenough firing his second barrel after him. "I'm afraid you missed altogether, Frank," he said.

"I don't think so, sir. I fancied I saw the flash of the shell as it struck him, but where, I have not the remotest idea. I could not make him out clear enough. It was merely a dim shape, and I fired as well as I could at the middle of it. Shall we go back to the camp now?" Frank asked.

"Yes, we can safely do so. You can tell by the sound of the roars that they are already some distance away. There is little chance of their returning tonight. In the morning we will follow them. There is sure to be blood, and the natives will have no difficulty in tracking them." The rest of the night passed quietly, although roars and howling could be heard from time to time in the distance.

Early in the morning they started with the Houssas. "We must be careful today," Mr. Goodenough said, "for a wounded leopard is a really formidable beast." There was no difficulty in taking up the traces. "One of them at least must be hard hit," Mr. Goodenough remarked; "there are traces of blood every yard." They had gone but a short distance when one of the Houssas gave a sudden exclamation, and pointed to something lying at the edge of a clump of bushes, "Leopard," he said.

"Yes, there is one of them, sure enough. I think it's dead, but we cannot be too cautious. Advance very carefully, Frank, keeping ready to fire instantly."

They moved forward slowly in a body, but their precaution was unnecessary. There was no movement in the spotted, tawny skin as they advanced, and when they came close they could see that the leopard was really dead. He had been hit by two bullets. The first had struck his shoulder and exploded there, inflicting so terrible a wound that it was wonderful he had been able to move afterwards. The other had struck him on the back, near the tail, and had burst inside him. Frank on seeing the nature of the wounds was astonished at the tenacity of life shown by the animal. "I wonder whether I hit the other," he said.

"I have no doubt at all about it," Mr. Goodenough answered, "although I did not think so before. It seemed to me that I only heard the howls of one animal in the night, and thought it was the one I had hit. But as this fellow must have died at once, it is clear that the cries were made by the other."

A sharp search was now set up for the tracks of the other leopard, the Houssas going back to the tree and taking it up anew. They soon found traces of blood in a line diverging from that followed by the other animal. For an hour they followed this, great care being required, as at times no spots of blood could be seen for a considerable distance. At last they seemed to lose it altogether. Mr. Goodenough and Frank stood together, while the Houssas, scattered round, were hunting like well-trained dogs for a sign. Suddenly there was a sharp roar, and from the bough of a tree close by, a great body sprang through the air and alighted within a yard of Frank. The latter, in his surprise, sprang back, stumbled and fell, but in an instant the report of the two barrels of Mr. Goodenough's rifle rang out. In a moment Frank was on his feet again ready to fire. The leopard, however, lay dead, its skull almost blown off.

"You have had another narrow escape," Mr. Goodenough said. "I see that your ball last night broke one of his hind-legs. That spoilt his spring. Had it not been for that he would undoubtedly have reached you, and a blow with his paw, given with all his weight and impetus, would probably have killed you on the spot. We ought not to have stood near a tree strong enough to bear him when in pursuit of a wounded leopard. They will always take to trees if they can, and you see this was a very suitable one for him. This bough on which he was lying, starts from the trunk only about four feet from the ground, so that even with his broken leg he was able to get upon it without difficulty. Well, thank God, you've not been hurt, my boy. It will teach us both to be more careful in future."

That afternoon Frank was down with his second attack of fever, a much more severe one than the first had been. Mr. Goodenough's favourite remedy had its effect of producing profuse perspiration, but two or three hours afterwards the hot fit again came on, and for the next four days Frank lay half delirious, at one time consumed with heat, and the next shivering as if plunged into ice-water. Copious doses of quinine, however, gradually overcame the fever, and on the fifth day he was convalescent. It was, nevertheless, another week before he was sufficiently recovered to be able to resume his hunting expeditions. They again shifted their camp, and this time travelled for three weeks, making short journeys, and halting early so as to give half a day from each camping place for their work.

Frank was one day out as usual with one of the Houssas. He had killed several birds when he saw a butterfly, of a species which he had not before met with, flitting across a gleam of sunshine which streamed in through a rift in the trees. He told his Houssa to wait where he was in charge of the two guns and birds, and started off with his net in pursuit of the butterfly. The creature fluttered away with Frank in full pursuit. Hither and thither it flitted, seemingly taking an impish delight in tantalizing Frank, settling on a spot where a gleam of sunlight streamed upon the bark of a tree, till Frank had stolen up within a couple of paces of it, and then darting away again at a pace which defied Frank's best attempts to keep up with it until it chose to play with him again. Intent only upon his chase, Frank thought of nothing else. At last, with a shout

LOST IN THE FOREST.

of triumph, he inclosed the creature in his net, shook it into the wide pickle bottle, containing a sponge soaked with chloroform, and then, after tightly fitting in the stopper, he looked around. He uttered an exclamation of dismay as he did so. He saw by the bands of light the sun was already setting, and knew that he must have been for upwards of an hour in chase of the butterfly. He had not the slightest idea of the direction in which he had come. He had, he knew, run up hill and down, but whether he had been travelling in a circle or going straight in one direction, he had not the least idea. He might be within a hundred yards of the spot where he had left the Houssa. He might be three or four miles away.

He at once drew out his revolver, which he always carried strapped to his belt, and discharged the six chambers, waiting for half a minute between each shot, and listening intently for an answer to his signal. None came. The stillness of the wood was unbroken, and Frank felt that he must have wandered far indeed from his starting place, and that he was completely lost. His first impulse was to start off instantly at the top of his speed, but a moment's thought convinced him that this would be useless. He had not an idea of the direction which he should pursue. Besides the sun was sinking twilight is short in the tropics, and in half an hour it would be as dark as midnight in the forest. Remembering his adventure with the leopard, he determined to climb into a tree and pass the night there. He knew that an active search would be set on foot by his friends next morning, and that, as every step he took was as likely to lead him from as towards the camp, it was better to stay where he was. He soon found a tree with a branch which would suit his purpose, and, climbing up into it, lit his pipe and prepared for an uncomfortable night. Frank had never smoked until he reached Africa, but he had then taken to it on the advice of Mr. Goodenough, who told him that smoking was certainly a preventive, to some extent, of fever in malarious countries, and, although he had not liked it at first, he had now taken kindly to his pipe, and smoked from the time when the evening mists began to rise until he went to bed.

The time passed very slowly. The cries of wild creatures could be heard in the woods, and although Frank did not expect to be attacked, it was impossible to sleep with these calls of leopards, with which the forest seemed to abound, in his ears. He had reloaded his revolver immediately after discharging it, and had replaced it in his pouch, and felt confident that nothing could climb the tree. Besides, he had heard that leopards seldom attack men unless themselves attacked. Sleep, however, was out of the question, for when he slept he might have fallen from his seat in the crutch of the tree. Occasionally, however, he dosed off, waking up always with an uncomfortable start, and a feeling that he had just saved himself from falling. With the earliest dawn of morn he descended, stiff and weary, from the tree. Directly the sun rose he set off walking. He knew at least that he was to the south of the camp, and that by keeping the sun on his right hand till it reached the zenith he must get in time to the little stream on which it was pitched. As he walked he listened intently for the sound of guns. Once or twice he fancied that he heard them, but he was quite unable to judge of the direction. He had been out with the Houssa about six hours before he strayed from him in the pursuit of the butterfly, and they had for some time been walking towards the camp, in order to reach it by nightfall. Thus he thought, that at that time, he could only have been some three or four miles distant from it. Supposing that he had run due south, he could still be but eight miles from the stream, and he thought that in three hours walking he might arrive there. In point of fact, after leaving the Houssa the butterfly had led him towards the south-east, and as the stream took a sharp bend to the north a little distance above the camp, he was many miles farther from it than he expected. This stream was one of the upper tributaries of the Gaboon.

After walking for two hours the character of the forest changed. The high trees were farther apart, and a thick undergrowth began to make its appearance, frequently causing him to make long detours and preventing his following the line he had marked out for himself. This caused him much uneasiness, for he knew that he had passed across no such country on his way from the camp, and the thought that he might experience great difficulties in recovering it, now began to press upon him.

CHAPTER XI

A HOSTILE TRIBE

EVERY step that he went the ground grew softer and more swampy, and he at length determined to push on no farther in this direction, but turning to his left to try and gain higher ground, and then to continue on the line he had marked out for himself. His progress was now very slow. The bush was thick and close, thorny plants and innumerable creepers continually barred his way, and the necessity for constantly looking up through the trees to catch a glimpse of the sun, which was his only guide, added to his difficulty. At length, when his watch told him it was eleven o'clock, he came to a standstill, the sun being too high overhead to serve him as a reliable guide. He had now been walking for nearly six hours, and he was utterly worn out and exhausted, having had no food since his mid-day meal on the previous day. He was devoured with thirst, having merely rinsed his mouth in the black and poisonous water of the swamps he had crossed. His sleepless night, too, had told on him. He was bathed in perspiration, and for the last hour had scarcely been able to drag his feet along.

He now lay down at the foot of a great tree, and for three or four hours slept heavily. When he awoke he pursued his journey, the sun serving as a guide again. In two hours' time he had got upon higher ground. The brushwood was less dense, and he again turned his face to the north, and stepped forward with renewed hopes. It was late in the afternoon when he came upon a native path. Here he sat down to think. He did not remember having crossed such a path on the day before. Probably it crossed the stream at some point above the encampment. Therefore it would serve as a guide, and he might, too, come upon some native village where he could procure food. By following it far enough he must arrive somewhere. He sat for a quarter of an hour to rest himself, and then proceeded along the path, whose direction seemed to be the north-west.

For an hour he proceeded and then paused, hearing a sudden outcry ahead. Scampering along the path came a number of great baboons, and Frank at once stepped aside into the bush to avoid them, as these are formidable creatures when disturbed. They were of a very large species, and several of the females had little ones clinging around their necks. In the distance Frank could hear the shouts of some natives, and supposed that the monkeys had been plundering their plantations, and that they were driving them away. The baboons passed without paying any attention to him, but Frank observed that the last of the troop was carrying a little one in one of its forearms.

Frank glanced at the baby-monkey and saw that it had round its waist a string of blue beads. As a string of beads is the only attire which a native child wears until it reaches the age of ten or eleven years old, the truth at once flashed upon Frank that the baboons were carrying off a native baby, which had probably been set down by its mother while she worked in the plantation. Instantly he drew his pistol, leaped into the road, and fired at the retreating ape. It gave a cry, dropped the baby, and turned to attack its aggressor.

Frank waited till it was within six feet, and then shot it through the head. He sprang forward and seized the baby, but in a moment he was attacked by the whole party of baboons, who, barking like dogs, and uttering angry cries, rushed at him. Frank stood his ground, and discharged the four remaining barrels of his revolver at the foremost animals. Two of these dropped, but the others who were only wounded sprang upon him. Frank struck out with the butt-end of his pistol, but in a minute he was overpowered. One monkey seized him by the leg with his teeth, while another bit his arm. Others struck and scratched at him, and he was at once thrown down. He tried to defend his face with his arms, kicking and struggling to the best of his power. With one hand he drew the long knife for skinning animals, which he wore at his belt, and struck out fiercely, but a baboon seized his wrist in its teeth, and Frank felt that all was over, when suddenly his assailants left him, and the instant afterwards he was lifted to his feet by some Africans. He had, when attacked by the apes, thrown the baby into a clump of ferns close by, in order to have the use of both his hands, and when he looked round he found that a woman had already picked it up, and was crying and fondling it. The tribe appeared intensely astonished at Frank's colour, and he judged by their exclamations of surprise that, not only had they not seen a white man before, but that they had not heard of one being in the neighbourhood.

Frank had been too severely bitten and mauled by the baboons to be able to walk, and the natives, seeing this, raised him, and four of them carried him to their village, which was but a quarter of a mile distant. Here he was taken to the principal hut, and laid on a bed. His wounds were dressed with poultices formed of bruised leaves of some plant, the natives evincing the utmost astonishment as Frank removed his clothes to enable these operations to be performed. By pointing to his lips he indicated that he was hungry and thirsty. Water was brought to him, and cakes made from pounded yams pressed and baked. Having eaten and drunk, he closed his eyes and lay back, and the natives, who had before been all noisily chattering together, now became suddenly silent, and stealing away, left the strange white visitor to sleep.

When Frank woke he could see by the light that it was early morning. A woman with a child in her lap, whom Frank recognized as the female who had picked up the baby, was sitting on a low stool by his side. On seeing him open his eyes she came to the bed, took his hand and put it to her lips, and then raised the baby triumphantly and turned it round and round to show that it had escaped without damage. Then when Frank pointed again to his lips, she brought him a pine-apple, roughly cut off the skin, and sliced it. Frank ate the juicy fruit, and felt immensely refreshed, for the West Coast pine-apple is even more delicious than that found in the West Indies. Then the woman removed the bandages and applied fresh poultices to his wounds,

talking in low soft tones, and, as Frank had no doubt, expressing sorrow at their cause.

Frank now endeavoured to explain to her that he had a
white companion in the woods, but the woman, not under-
standing, brought in two or three other natives, who stood
round the couch and endeavoured to gather what he wished to
say. Frank held up two fingers. Then he pointed to himself and
shut down one finger, keeping the other erect, and then pointed
all round to signify that he had a friend somewhere in the wood.
A grin of comprehension stole over the faces of the tribesmen,
and Frank saw that he was understood.

Then he again held up his two fingers, and taking the hands
of the woman raised all her fingers by the side of the white ones to
signify that there were many natives with them. Then he took aim,
with an imaginary gun, up at the roof of the hut, and said "Bang"
very loud, and a chorus of approving laughter from the natives
showed that he was understood. Then one of them pointed towards
the various points of the compass, and looked interrogatively at
Frank. The sun was streaming in through the doorway, and he was
thus able to judge of the direction in which the camp must lie. He
made a sweep with his hand towards the north-west, signifying that
they were somewhere in that direction.

That afternoon fever set in, and for the two next days Frank
was delirious. When he recovered consciousness he found Mr.
Goodenough sitting beside him. The latter would not suffer him to
talk, but gave him a strong dose of quinine and told him to lie quiet
and go to sleep. It was not till the next day that Frank learned what
had happened in his absence. The Houssa had not returned until
long after nightfall. He reported that Frank had told him to wait
with the guns, and that he had waited until it grew nearly dark.
Then he had fired several times and had walked about, firing his
gun at intervals. Obtaining no responses he had made his way back
to the camp, where his arrival alone caused great consternation.

It was impossible to do anything that night, and the next
morning Mr. Goodenough, accompanied by five of the Houssas,
one only remaining to keep guard over the camp, had gone to the

place where Frank had last been seen. Then they scattered in various directions, shouting and firing their guns. The search had been continued all day without success, and at nightfall, disheartened and worn out, they had returned to the camp. The next day the search had been continued with an equal want of success, and the fears that a leopard had attacked and killed Frank became stronger and stronger. On the third day the whole of the carriers were sent out with instructions to search the woods for native paths, to follow these to villages, and to enlist the natives in the search. One of these men had met one of the villagers on the search for the party of the white man.

It was another ten days before Frank was sufficiently recovered from his fever and wounds to march back to the camp. After a stay there of two or three more days, to enable him completely to regain his strength, the party started again on their journey.

In another three weeks they had descended the hills, and the Fans announced their unwillingness to travel farther. Mr. Goodenough, however, told them quietly that they had promised to go on until he could obtain other carriers, and that if they deserted him he should pay them nothing. They might now expect every day to meet people of another tribe, and as soon as they should do so, they would be allowed to depart. Finding that he was firm, and having no desire to forfeit the wages they had earned, the Fans agreed to go forward, although they were now in a country entirely unknown to them, where the people would presumably be hostile. They had, however, such faith in the arms carried by the white men and Houssas, that they felt comparatively easy as to the result of any attack which might be made upon them.

The very day after this little mutiny, smoke was seen curling up from the woods. Mr. Goodenough deemed it inexpedient to show himself at once with so large a number of men. He, therefore, sent forward Ostik with two of the Fans, each of whom could speak several native dialects, to announce his coming. They returned in an hour, saying that the village was a very large one, and that the news of the coming of two white men had created great excitement. The people spoke of sending at once to their king, whom they called Malembe, whose place, it seemed, was a day's march off.

They now prepared to enter the village. Ostik went first carrying himself with the dignity of a beadle at the head of a school procession. Two of the Houssas walked next. Mr. Goodenough and Frank followed, their guns being carried by two Fans behind them. Then came the long line of bearers, two of the Houssas walking on each side as a baggage guard. The villagers assembled in great numbers as they entered. The head man conducted the whites to his hut. No women or children were to be seen, and the expression of the men was that of fear rather than curiosity.

"They are afraid of the Fans," Mr. Goodenough said. "The other tribes all have a species of terror of these cannibals. We must reassure them as soon as possible."

A long palaver then took place with the chief, with whose language one of the Fans was sufficiently acquainted to make himself understood. It was rather a tedious business, as each speech had to be translated twice, through Ostik and the Fan.

Mr. Goodenough informed the chief that the white men were friends of his people, that they had come to see the country and give presents to the chiefs, that they only wished to pass quietly through and to journey unmolested, and that they would pay handsomely for food and all that they required. They wished to obtain bearers for their baggage, and these they would pay in cloth and brass rods, and as soon as they procured carriers, the Fans would return to their own country. The chief answered expressing his gratification at seeing white men in his village, and saying that the king would, no doubt, carry out all their wishes. One of the boxes was opened and he was presented with five yards of bright-coloured calico, a gaudy silk handkerchief, and several strings of bright beads. In return a large number of plantains were presented to the white men. These were soon distributed among the Fans.

"Me no like dat man," Ostik said. "Me think we hab trouble. You see all women and children gone, dat bad. Wait till see what do when king come."

That day and the next passed quietly. The baggage had been piled in a circle, as usual, in an open space outside the village, the tent being pitched in the centre, and Ostik advised Mr. Goodenough to sleep here instead of in the village. The day after their arrival passed but heavily. The natives showed but little curiosity as to the new-comers, although these must have been far more strange to them than to the people nearer the coast. Still no women or children made their appearance. Towards evening a great drumming was heard in the distance.

"Here is his majesty at last," Mr. Goodenough said, "we shall soon see what is his disposition."

In a short time the village was filled with a crowd of men, all carrying spears and bows and arrows. The drumming came nearer and nearer, and then, carried in a chair on the shoulders of four strong warriors, while ten others armed with guns marched beside him, the king made his appearance.

Mr. Goodenough and Frank advanced to meet him. The king was a tall man with a savage expression of countenance. Behind Mr. Goodenough, Ostik and the Fan who spoke the language advanced. The king's chair was lowered under the shade of a tree, and two attendants with palm-leaf fans at once began to fan his majesty.

"Tell the king," Mr. Goodenough said, "that we are white men who have come to see his country, and to pass through to the countries beyond. We have many presents for him, and wish to buy food and to hire carriers in place of those who have brought our things thus far."

The king listened in silence. "Why do the white men bring our enemies into our land?" he asked angrily.

"We have come up from the coast," Mr. Goodenough said; "and as we passed through the Fan country we hired men there to carry our goods, just as we wish to hire men here to go on into the country beyond. There were none of the king's men in that country or we would have hired them."

"Let me see the white men's presents," the king said.

A box was opened, a bright scarlet shirt and a smoking-cap of the same colour, worked with beads, a blue silk handkerchief and twenty yards of bright calico, were taken out. To these were added twelve stair-rods, five pounds of powder, and two pounds of shot.

The king's eye sparkled greedily as he looked at the treasures. "The white men must be very rich," he said, pointing to the pile of baggage.

"Most of the boxes are empty," Mr. Goodenough said. "We have brought them to take home the things of the country and show them to the white men beyond the sea;" and to prove the truth of his words, Mr. Goodenough had two of the empty cases opened, as also one already half filled with bird skins, and another with trays of butterflies and beetles.

The king looked at them with surprise, "And the others?" he asked, pointing to them.

"The others," Mr. Goodenough said, "contain, some of them, food such as white men are accustomed to eat in their own country, the others, presents for the other kings and chiefs I shall meet when we have passed on. The fellow is not satisfied," he said to Ostik, "give him two of the trade-guns and a bottle of brandy."

The king appeared mollified by these additional presents, and saying that he would talk to the white men in the morning, he retired into the village.

"I don't like the look of things," Mr. Goodenough said. "I fear that the presents we have given the king will only stimulate his desire for more. However, we shall see in the morning."

When night fell, two of the Houssas were placed on guard. The Fans slept inside the circle formed by the baggage. Several times in the night the Houssas challenged bodies of men whom they heard approaching, but these at once retired. In the morning a messenger presented himself from the king, saying that he required many more presents, that the things which had been given were only fit for the chief of a village, and not for a great king. Mr. Goodenough answered, that he had given the best he had, that the presents were fit for a great king, and that he should give no more.

"If we are to have trouble," he said to Frank, "it is far better to have it at once while the Fans are with us, than when we are alone with no one but the Houssas and the subjects of this man. The Fans will fight, and we could hold this encampment against any number of warriors."

A quarter of an hour later the drums began beating furiously again. Loud shouts and yells arose in the village, and the natives could be seen moving excitedly about. Presently these all disappeared.

"Fight come now," Ostik said.

"You'd better lower the tent at once, Ostik. It will only be in our way."

The tent was speedily lowered. The Fans grasped their spears and lay down behind the circle of boxes and bales, and the six Houssas, the two white men and Ostik, to whom a trade-musket had been entrusted, took their places at regular intervals round the circle, which was some eight yards in diameter. Presently the beat of the drums again broke the silence, and a shower of arrows, coming apparently from all points of the compass, fell in and around the circle.

"Open fire steadily and quietly," Mr. Goodenough said, "among the bushes, but don't fire fast. We must tempt them to show themselves."

A dropping fire commenced against the invisible foe, the firing being no more frequent than it would have been had they been armed with muzzle-loading weapons. Presently musketry was heard on the enemy's side, the king's body-guard having opened fire. This was disastrous to them, for, whereas the arrows had afforded but slight index as to the position of those who shot them, the puffs of smoke from the muskets at once showed the lurking-places of those who used them, and Mr. Goodenough and Frank replied so truly that in a very short time the musketry fire of the enemy ceased altogether. The rain of arrows continued, the yells of the natives rose louder and louder, and the drums beat more furiously.

"They will be out directly," Mr. Goodenough said. "Fire as quickly as you can when they show, but be sure and take good aim."

Presently the sound of a war-horn was heard, and from the wood all round a crowd of dark figures dashed forward, uttering appalling yells. On the instant the dropping fire of the defenders changed into an almost continuous fusillade, as the Sniders of the Houssas, the breech-loading rifle of Mr. Goodenough, and the repeating Winchester of Frank were brought into play at their full speed. Yells of astonishment broke from the natives, and a minute later, leaving nearly a score of their comrades on the ground, the rest dashed back into the forest. There was silence for a time and then the war-drums began again.

"Dey try again hard dis time," Ostik said. "King tell 'em he cut off deir heads dey not win battle."

This time the natives rushed forward with reckless bravery, in spite of the execution made among them by the rapid fire of the defenders, and rushed up to the circle of boxes. Then the Fans leaped to their feet, and, spear in hand, dashed over the defences and fell upon the enemy. The attack was decisive. Uttering yells of terror, the natives fled, and two minutes later not a sound was to be heard in the forest.

"I tink dey run away for good dis time, sar," Ostik said. "Dey hav' 'nuf of him. Dey fight very brave, much more brave than people down near coast. Dere in great battle only three, four men killed. Here as many men killed as we got altogether."

This was so, nearly fifty of the natives having fallen between the trees and the encampment. When an hour passed and all was still, it became nearly certain that the enemy had retreated, and the Houssas, who are splendid scouts, divested themselves of their clothing and crawled away into the wood to reconnoitre. They returned in half an hour in high glee, bearing the king's chair.

"Dey all run away, sar, ebery one, de king an' all, and leab his chair behind. Dat great disgrace for him."

A council was now held. The Fans were so delighted with the victory they had won, that they expressed their readiness to remain with their white companions as long as they chose, providing these would guarantee that they should be sent home on the expiration of their service. This Mr. Goodenough readily promised. After discussing the question with Frank, he determined to abstain from pushing farther into the interior, but to keep along northward, and then turning west with the sweep of the coast to travel slowly along, keeping at about the same distance as at present from the sea, and finally to come down either upon Cape Coast or Sierra Leone.

This journey would occupy a considerable time. They would cross countries but little known, and would have an ample opportunity for the collection of specimens, which they might, from time to time, send down by the various rivers they would cross, to the trading stations at their mouths.

It was felt that after this encounter with the natives it would be imprudent in the extreme to push further into the interior. They would have continual battles to fight, large numbers of the natives would be killed, and their collecting operations would be greatly interfered with. As a lesson to the natives the village was burnt to the ground; the presents, which the king in the hurry of his flight had left behind him, being recovered. A liberal allowance of tobacco was served out as a "dash" or present to the Fans, and a bright silk handkerchief given to each. Then they turned off at right angles to the line they had before been pursuing and continued their journey.

Two days later Mr. Goodenough was prostrated by fever, and for several days lay between life and death. When he became convalescent he recovered strength very slowly. The heat was prodigious and the mosquitoes rendered sleep almost impossible at night. The country at this place was low and swampy, and, weak as he was, Mr. Goodenough determined to push forward. He was, however, unable to walk, and, for the first time, a hammock was got out and mounted.

There is no more comfortable conveyance in the world than a hammock in Africa. It is slung from a long bamboo pole, overhead, a thick awning keeps the sun from the hammock. Across the ends of the pole boards of some three feet long are fastened. The natives wrap a piece of cloth into the shape of a muffin and place it on their heads, and then take their places, two at each end of the pole, with the ends of the board on their heads. They can trot along at the rate of six miles an hour, for great distances, often keeping up a monotonous song. Their action is perfectly smooth and easy, and the traveller in the hammock, by shutting his eyes, might imagine himself swinging in a cot on board ship on an almost waveless sea.

After two days travelling they got on to higher ground, and here they camped for some time, Mr. Goodenough slowly recovering strength, and Frank busy in adding to their collections. In this he was in no slight degree assisted by the Fans, who, having nothing else to do, had now come to enter into the occupation of their employers. A good supply of muslin had been brought, and nets having been made, the Fans captured large quantities of butterflies, the great difficulty being in convincing them that only a few of each species were required. They were still more valuable in grubbing about in the decaying trunks of fallen trees, under loose bark and in broken ground, for beetles and larvae, a task which suited them better than running about after butterflies, which, moreover, they often spoilt irreparably by their rough handling. Thus Frank was able to devote himself entirely to the pursuit of birds, and although all the varieties more usually met with had been obtained, the collection steadily increased in size.

Frank himself had several attacks of fever, but none of these were so severe as that which he had had on the day of the death of the leopards.

At the end of a month Mr. Goodenough had recovered his strength, and they again moved forward.

CHAPTER XII

THE CHIEF'S STORY

ON arriving at a large village one day, they were struck as they approached by the far greater appearance of comfort and neatness than generally distinguish African villages. The plots of plantations were neatly fenced the street was clean and well kept. As they entered the village they were met by the principal people, headed by an old white-haired man.

"Me berry glad to see you, white men," he said. "Long time me no see white men."

"And it is a long time," said Mr. Goodenough, shaking hands with him, "since I have heard the sound of my own tongue outside my party."

"Me berry glad to see you," repeated the man. "Me chief of dis village. Make you berry comfortable, sar. Great honour for dis village dat you come here. Plenty eberyting for you, fowl, and eggs, and plantain, and sometime a sheep."

"We have, indeed, fallen into the lap of luxury," Mr. Goodenough said to Frank; and they followed the chief to his hut. "I suppose the old man has been employed in one of the factories upon the coast."

The interior of the hut was comfortably furnished and very clean. A sort of divan covered with neatly-woven mats extended round three sides. In the centre was an attempt at a table. A double-barrelled gun and a rifle hung over the hearth. A small looking-glass and several coloured prints in cheap frames were suspended from the walls. A great chest stood at one end of the room, while on a shelf were a number of plates and dishes of English manufacture. The chief begged his guests to be seated, and presently a girl entered, bringing in a large calabash full of water for them to wash their hands and faces. In the meantime the old man had gone to his chest, and, to the immense surprise of the travellers, brought out a snow-white table-cloth, which he proceeded to lay on the table, and then to place knives, forks, and plates upon it.

"You must 'scuse deficiencies, sar," he said. "We bery long way from coast, and dese stupid natives dey break tings most ebery day."

"Don't talk about deficiencies," Mr. Goodenough answered, smiling. "All this is, indeed, astonishing to us here."

"You bery good to say dat, sar, but dis man know how tings ought to be done. He libed in good Melican family. He know bery well how tings ought to be done."

"Ah, you have travelled a good deal!" Mr. Goodenough said.

"Yes, sar, me trabel great deal. Me lib in Cuba long time. Den me lib slave states, what you call Confederate. Den me lib Northern state, also Canada under Queen Victoria. Me trabel bery much. Now, sar, dinner come. Time to eat, not to talk. After dinner white gentleman tell me what they came here for. Me tell dem if they like about my trabels, but dat bery long story."

The dinner consisted of two fowls cut in half and grilled over a fire, fried plantains, and, to the astonishment of the travellers, green peas, followed by cold boiled rice over which honey had been poured. Their host had placed plates, only for two, but they would not sit down until he had consented to join them. Two girls waited, both neatly dressed in cotton, in a fashion which was a compromise between European and African notions.

After dinner the chief presented them with two large and excellent cigars, made, as he said, from tobacco grown in his own garden, and the astonishment of the travellers was heightened by the reappearance of one of the girls bearing a tray with three small cups of excellent black coffee.

Their host now asked them for the story of their journey from the coast, and the object with which they had penetrated Africa. Mr. Goodenough related their adventures, and said that they were naturalists in search of objects of natural history. When he had finished, Ostik, in obedience to a whisper from him, brought in a bottle of brandy, at the sight of which the chief broke into a chuckle.

"Me tree months widout taste dat. Once ebery year me send down to coast, get coffee, tea, sugar, calico, beads, and rum. Dis time de rum am finish too soon. One of de cases get broke and half de bottles smash. Dat bery bad job. Dis man calculate dat six dozen last for a year, dat give him one bottle each week and twenty bottles for presents to oder chiefs. Eighteen bottles go smash, and as de oder chiefs expec' deir present all de same, Sam hab to go widout. De men start three weeks ago for coast. Me hope dey come back in six weeks more."

"Well," Mr. Goodenough said, "you need not go without it till they come back, for I can give you eight bottles which will last you for two months. I have got a good supply, and as I never use it for trade unless a chief particularly wants it, I can very well spare it."

The old chief was greatly pleased, and when he had drunk his glass of brandy and water, he responded to Mr. Goodenough's request, and, lighting a fresh cigar, he began the story of his adventures.

"I was born in dis bery village somewhere about seventy years ago. I not know for sure widin two or three year, for when I young man I no keep account. My fader was de chief of dis village, just as I am now, but de village was not like dis. It was not so big, and was bery dirty and bery poor, just like the oder native villages. Well, sar, dere am nothing perticlar to tell about de first years of my life. I jus' dirty little naked boy like de rest. Dose were bery bad times. Ebery one fight against ebery one else. Ebery one take slabes and send dem down de river, and sell to white men dere to carry ober sea. When I grow up to seventeen, I spose, I take spear and go out wid de people of dis village and de oder villages of dis part ob country under king, and fight against oder villages and carry the people away as slabes. All bery bad business dat. But Sam he tink nothing, and jus' do the same as oder people. Sometimes oder tribes come and fight against our villages and carry our people away. So it happened to Sam.

"Jus' when he about twenty year old we had come back from a long 'spedition. Dis village got its share ob slabes, and we drink and sing and make merry wid de palm tree wine and tink ourselves bery grand fellows. Well, sar, dat night great hullyballoo in de village. De dogs bark, de men shout and seize deir arms and run out to fight, but it no good. Anoder tribe fall on us ten times as many as we. We fight hard but no use. All de ole men and de ole women and de little babies dat no good to sell dey killed, and de rest ob us, de men and de woman and de boys and girls, we tied together and march away wid de people dat had taken us.

"Bery bad time dat, sar. De season was dry and de water scarce. We make long march ebery day, and bery little food given. Dey beat us wid sticks and prod us wid spear to make us go. A good many ob de weak ones dey die, but de most ob us arribe at mouth ob riber; me neber know what riber dat was, but we were bery nigh two months in getting dere. By dis time Sam arribe at the conclusion bery strong, dat de burning ob villages and carrying off ob slabes bery bad affair altogether. Sam hab changed his mind about a great many things, but about dat he am fixed right up to dis time.

"Well, at de mouth ob dat riber Sam saw de white man for de first time; and me tell you fair, sar, Sam not like him no way. Dey were Spanish men, and de way dey treat us poor Africans was someting awful. We huddle up night and day in a big shed dey call a barracoon. Dey gabe us bery little food, bery little water. Dey flog us if we grumble. Dese men belong to ships, and had bought us from dose who brought us down from up country. Deir ship not come yet, and for a long time we wait in the barracoon wishing dat we could die. At last de ship came, and we were taken on board and huddled down below. Law, what a place dat was to be sure! Not more than tree feet high, just high enough to sit up, and dere we chained to deck. De heat, sar, was someting terrible. Some ob us yell out and scream for air, but dey only come down and beat us wid whips.

"De day after we got on board de ship set sail. Tree hours after dat we hear a great running about on deck, and a shouting by the white men. Den we hear big gun fire ober head, almost make us jump out of skin wid de noise. Den more guns. Den dere was a crash, and before we knew what was de matter dere was a big hole in de side, and six Africans was killed dead. Ebery one yelled bery loud. We tink for sure that de last day come. For a long time de guns keep firing, and den everyting quiet again. At de time no one could tink what de matter, but I s'pose dat British cruiser chase us and dat de slaber sail away.

"Dat was an awful voyage, sar. At first de sea smoove, and de ship go along straight. Den de ship begin to toss about, jus' as a man does when he has taken too much palm-wine, and we all feel bery bad. Ebery one groan and cry and tink dat dey must have been poisoned. For tree days it was a terrible time. De hatches were shut down and no air could come to us, and dere we was all alone in de dark, and no one could make out why de great house on de water roll and tumble so much. We cry and shout till all breaff gone, and den lie quiet and moan, till jus' when ebery one tink he dead, dey take off de hatch and come down and undo de padlocks and tell us to go up on deck. Dat bery easy to say, not at all easy to do. Most of us too weak to walk, and say dat we dead and cannot move. Den dey whip all about, and it was astonishing, sar, to see what life dat whip put into dead men. Somehow people feel dat dey could crawl after all, and when dey get up on deck and see de blessed sun again and de blue sky dey feel better. But not all. In spite ob de whip many hab to be carried up on deck, and dere de sailor men lay 'em down and trow cold water ober dem till dey open dere eyes and come to life. Some neber come to life. Dere were about six hundred when we start, and ob dese, pretty nigh a hundred die in dose tree days.

"After dat tings not so bad. De weather was fine and no more English cruisers seen, so dey let half ob us up on deck at once for tree or four hours ebery day. Dey give us more food, too, and fatten us up. We talk dis ober among ourselves, and s'pose dat dey going to eat us when we get to land again. Some propose not eat food, but when dey try dat on they get de whip, and conclude dat if dey must be eaten, dey might as well be eaten fat as lean.

"At last we come in sight of land. Den we all sent below and stay dere till night. Den we brought on deck, and find de vessel lying in a little creek. Den we all land in boats, and march up country all night. In de morning we halt. Tree or four white men come on horses and look at us. Dey separate us into parties, and each march away into country again. Den we separate again, till at last me and twenty oders arribe at a plantation up in de hills. Here we range along in line before a white man. He speak in bery fierce tones, and a black man by his side tell us dat dis man our master, dat he say if we work well he gib us plenty of food and treat us well, but dat if we not work wid all our might he whip us to death. After dis it was ebident that de best ting to do was to work hard.

"I was young and bery strong, sar, and soon got de name of a willing hard-working man. De massa he keep his word. Dose who work well not bad treated, plenty ob food and a piece of ground to plant vegetables and to raise fowls for ourselves. So we passed two or tree year, plenty ob hard work, but not bery much to grumble at. Den me and a gal of my own village, who had been bought in de same batch wid me, we go to massa and say we want to marry. Massa say, bery well. I fine strong man and work well, so he gib de gal four yards ob bright cotton for wedding dress, and a bottle ob rum to me, and we married.

"Two or tree years pass, and my wife hab two children. Den de massa go home to Spain, and leab overseer in plantation. Bery bad man dat. Before, if slave work well he not beaten. Now he beaten wheder he work or not. For two or tree months we 'tand it, but tings get worse and worse. De oberseer he always drunk and go on like wild beast. One day he passed by my wife hoeing de sugar-cane and he gib her cut wid whip, jus' out of 'musement. She turn round and ask, 'What dat for?' He get mad, cut her wid whip, knock her down wid de handle, and den seizing de chile dat she had fastened to her back, he catch him by de leg and smash him skull against a tree. Den, sar, I seize my hoe, I rush at him, and I chop him down wid all my strength, cut his skull clean in sunder, and he drop down dead.

"Den I knew dat dat was no place for Sam, so I take my hoe and I run away as fast as I could. No one try to stop me. De oder workersß dance and sing when dey saw de oberseer fall dead. I ran all dat day up among de hills, skirting round de different planta- tions till I get quite into de wild part. Wheneber I came to stream

127

I walk a long way in him till I get to tree hanging ober. Den pull myself up into de branches, climb along and drop at de farthest end, and den run again, for I knew dat dey would set de bloodhounds after me.

"At last I tink dat it am quite safe, and when de night came on lie down to sleep for a few hours. Before morning me off again, and by night get to de centre of de wild country. Here I light a fire, and sit down, and, just as I 'spected, in two or tree hours five or six men come down to me. Dese were slaves who had run away from plantations. I tell dem my story, dey agree dat I did bery right in killing oberseer. Dey take me away to place where dey hab little huts and patches of yams. Two or tree days pass and no one come, so we s'pose dat dey hab lost de scent. Me waited a month and den determined to go down and see about wife. I journey at night, and reach plantation in two days. Dere I hide till I see a slave come along close to bush. I call him and he come. I tell him to tell my wife to steal away when night come, and to meet me dere. He nod and go away. Dat night my wife come wid de oder chile. We not talk much but start away for mountains. Me bery much afraid now because my wife not bery strong, she hurt by de blow and fretting after me. Howeber, we follow the way I had gone before. I make shift to help her up into trees from the streams, and dis time after tree days travel we get back to hut in the mountain.

"Dere we lib bery happy for a year. Sometimes some ob us go down to plantation and take down baskets and oder tings dat we had made and chop dem for cotton. We had tobacco of our own, and some fowls which we got from the plantations in de fust place. Altogether we did bery well. Sometimes band of soldiers come and march trough the country, but we hab plenty hiding-places and dey never find us. More and more runaway slabes come, and at last we hear dat great 'spedition going to start to search all de mountains. Dey come, two tree thousand ob dem. Dey form long skirmishing line, five or six mile long, and dey go ober mountain. Ebery slave dey find who not surrender when dey call to him dey shoot. When I heard ob deir coming I had long talk wid wife. We agree that it better to leave de mountains altogether and go down and live in the bushes close to the old plantation. Nobody look for us dere. So we make our way down and lib there quiet. We get the yams out ob de plantations and lib very comfortable. When we tink all ober in the mountain we go back.

"Well, sar, when we tink it all safe, and we get widin a mile of de huts whar we had libed, all at once we came upon a lot of soldiers in camp. Dey see us and make shout. I call to my wife to run, when dey fire. A bullet hit de baby, which she hab at her back, and pass through both deir bodies. I did not run any more, but jus' stood looking at my wife and chile as if my senses had gone. Dere I stood till the soldiers came up. Dey put a cord round my arms and led me away. After a time I was taken down the country. Dere I was chained, and when it was known I had killed a white oberseer I was tried. But de new oberseer did not want me to be hung, for I was a strong slave and worth money, so he told a story about how it happen, and after dey had flogged me very hard dey sent me back to plantation. Dere I work for a long time wid a great log of wood chained to my ankle to prevent me from running away again.

"For a time I not care whether I lib or die, but at last I made up my mind to 'scape again. After six months dey took off de log, tinking dat I had had enuf of de mountains and would not try to 'scape, and de log prevented my doing so much work. De bery next night I ran away again, but dis time I determined to make for de town in hopes ob getting on board an English ship, for I had heard from de oder slabes dat de English did not keep black men as slabes, but dat, on de contry, dey did what dey could to stop de Spanish from getting dem away from Africa, and I understood now dat de dreful noise we had heard on de first day we were on board ship was an attack upon our vessel by an English cruiser.

"It was four days journey down to de town by de sea. Dere was no difficulty in finding de way, for de road was good, and I s'pose dat dey only looked for me towards de hills. Anyhow I got dar safe, walking at night and sleeping in the bushes by day. I got as near de town as I dar, and could see seberal vessels lying near de shore. I could see dat some ob dem had de Spanish flag—I knew dat flag—de oders had flags which I did not know. When it was dark I walked boldly into the town; no one asked me any question, and I make my way through de streets down to de shore. Dere I get into a boat and lay quiet till all de town was asleep. Den I get into water and swim off to a ship—one dat I had noticed had a flag which was not Spanish. Dere was a boat alongside. I climb into it and pull myself up by the rope on to de deck. Den some white men seize me and say someting in a language which I not understand. Den dey take me into cabin and say someting to captain; me not know what it was, but de captain laugh, and me not like his laugh at all. Howeber, dey give me someting to eat, and den take me down into hold of ship and tell me to go to sleep on some sacks of sugar, and throw some empty sacks ober me to cover me. Den dey close up hatch and leab me alone.

"When I come on deck, de land was gone and de vessel sailing along. I speak to no one, for I only understand little Spanish, and dese people not speak dat. We sail along for some time, and at last we come in sight of land again. Den dey hoist flag and I see dat it a flag wid lots of red stars and stripes upon him. I know now dat it was a 'Merican ship. Den I know noting. We get to port and I want to land, but dey shake deir heads.

"De next day de captain he make sign to me to come wid him. I go along to shore and he take me to a open space in town, where a man was standing on a raised platform. He had a black woman by de side ob him. Seberal men come up and look at her. De man he shout bery loud. Oder men say something short. At last he knock on de table; a man tell de woman to come after him and she walk away. Den a boy was put up, and den two more women, and ebery time just de same ting was done. Den de man call out, and de captain push his way through the crowd wid me, and tell me to climb up on platform. I get up and look round quite surprised. Eberybody laugh. Den de man began to holloa again. Den seberal men come up and feel my arms and my legs. Dey point to de marks which de whip had left on my back, and dey laugh again. Presently de man who was shouting bang his hand on the table again, and a white man in the crowd, who had seberal times called out loud, come up to me, take me by de arm, and sign to me to go wid him.

"I begin to understand now; dat rascally captain had sold me for a slabe, and dat flag I had seen was not de English flag. However, it was no use to say anyting, and I went along wid my new massa. He was a nice-looking man, and I thought it might not be so bery bad after all. He took me to a high carriage wid two wheels and a fine horse. A black man, who was dressed up like a white man, was holding de horse. He showed me to climb up behind, de oders climb up in front, and we dribe away.

CHAPTER XIII

A FUGITIVE SLAVE

"WELL, sar, work bery much de same on plantation in Virginia and Cuba, but de slabe much merrier in 'Merica, when de master am good. My new massa bery good man. Slabes all treat bery kind, work not too hard. At night dance and sing bery much. Den I marry again, dis time to one ob de girls in de house. She favourite ob missy, and so when we marry, missy hab me taken off de fields and put to garden. Bery fine garden dat was. Tree, four of us work dar. Sam jus' as happy as man could be. Sometime, when der am party, Sam come into the house to help at de table, dat how Sam know how to do tings proper. De little massas dey bery fond ob me, and when dey want to go out hunting de coon or fishing in de riber, dey always cry for Sam.

"So fifteen years passed by, bery happy years, sar, den de ole massa die, missy, too, soon after. De young massa not like him father. Me tink de ole gentleman make mistake wid him when him chile, let him hab too much his own way. I bery fond ob him because I had been wid him so much, but I often shake my head when I tink de time come dat he be massa ob de plantation. It was not dat his nature was bad; he get in rage sometime, but dat all ober in no time, but he lub pleasure too much; go away to de races and 'top at de town weeks together, and play too much wid de cards. Dere were two boys and two girls; de second boy, he go to West Point and become officer in de army.

"After de death ob de ole people de house change bery much. Before dat time we keep good company, gib sometimes grand balls, and all de fust families ob Virginia in dat part visit dar. After dat always people in de house. De young massa, when he go to Richmond, bring back six or eight young men wid him, and dey laugh and drink and play cards half de night. I tink de young missus speak to him about his ways. Anyhow, one day dere great row, and dey off to lib wid an aunt in de city. After dat tings get worse. One day missy come back from town and she gib my wife her papers of freedom. You see, my wife was giben by de ole man to missy when her war a little girl, and fortunate it was dat he had made out de papers all right and presented dem to her. When missy gib her de papers ob freedom, she cry bery much. 'Me 'fraid bad time coming, Sally,' she said. 'Me tink dat it better for a time dat you clar out ob dis. Now you got de paper you free woman, but you wife ob slabe; might be difficulty about it. Me fear dat broder Dick ruined—de plantation and slabes to be sold;' and wid dat she bu'st out crying wus dan eber. Ob course my wife she cry too.

"'Better you go norf, Sally,' missy say presently. 'I gib you letter to friends dar, and tell dem you bery good nurse. Den if Sam get good master you can come back to him again. If not, as you tell me dat when he slabe before he run away, it jus' possible he do de same again.'

"'Don't you tink, missy,' de wife said, 'dat de young massa gib freedom to Sam too. Sam wait on him a great many years, sabe him life when he tumbled into water.'

"'I bery much afraid,' missy said, shaking her head, 'dat my broder not able to do so if he wish. He borrow money on de plantation and de slabes, and dat prevent him from making any ob dem free. De sale soon come now. You go tell Sam; tell him not to say word to nobody. Den you pack up and come right away wid me to de city. It bery much better you clar out ob dis before dey come down and seize eberybody.'

"Well, sar, you guess when Sam heard dis he in fine taking. He often grieve bery much dat he and Sally hab no children. Now he tank de Lord wid all his heart dat dere no children, for dey would hab been sold, one one way and one another, and we should neber hab seen dem again. Hows'ever, I make great effort, and tell Sally she do jus' what missy say. I tell her to go norf while she can, and promise dat some day or oder Sam join her dar. 'Better for to be parted for ten year, Sally, dan to hab de risk ob you being seize and sold to one master, me to anoder. You trus' Sam to break out some day. He do bery well here for a time. He bery good strong worker, good gardner, good at de horses, good carpenter. Sam sure to get good place, but, howeber good, when he see a chance, he run away. If no chance, he sabe up his money, and you sabe up your money, Sally, and buy him freedom.

"Well, sar, we bofe cry bery much, and den Sally go away wid de young missy. A week after dat de bust-up come. De officers dey come down and seize de place, and a little while after dey sell all de slabes. Dat was a terrible affair, to see de husbands and de wives and de children separated and sold to different masters. De young massa he not dere at sale. Dey say he pretty nigh break him heart, but he ought to hab thought ob dat before. Me sure dat de ole gentleman and de ole missy pretty nigh turn in deir grabe at de thought ob all de hands they was so kind to sold away.

"Dat de curse of slabery, sar. Me trabel a good deal, and me tink dat no working people in de world are so merry and happy as de slabe in a plantation wid a good massa and missy. Dey not work so hard as de white man. Dey have plenty to eat and drink, dey hab deir gardens and deir fowls. When dey are sick dey are taken care ob, when dey are ole they are looked after and hab noting to do. I have heard people talk a lot of nonsense about de hard life of de plantation slabe. Dat not true, sar, wid a good massa. De slabe hab no care and be bery happy. If all massas were good, and dere were a law dat if a plantation were broken up de slabes must be sold in families together, me tell you dat de life on a plantation a thousand times happier dan de life ob a black man in his own country. But all masters are not good. Some neber look after de slabes, and leabe all to overseers, and dese bery often bad, cruel men. But worst of all is when a sale comes. Dat terrible, sar. De husban' sold to Alabama, de wife to Carolina, de children scattered trough de States. Dis too bad, sar, dis make ob slabery a curse to de black men.

"Well, sar, we all sold. Me fetch high price and sold to a planter in Missouri. Sam no like dat. Dat a long way from the frontier. Tree years Sam work dar in plantation. Den he sold again to a man who hab boats on de riber at New Orleans. Dar Sam work discharging de ships and working de barges. Dar he come to learn for sure which de British flag. De times were slack, and my massa hire me out to be waiter in a saloon. Dat place dey hab dinners, and after dinner dey gamble. Dat war a bad place, mos' ebery night quarrels, and sometimes de pistols drawn, and de bullets flying about. Sam 'top dar six months; de place near de riber, and de captains ob de ships often come to dine.

"One young fellow come bery often, and one day Sam saw tree or four men he know to be Texas horse-dealers talking wid him. Now dis young captain had been bery friendly wid Sam; always speak cibil and gib him quarter for himself, and Sam sorry to see dese chaps get hold ob him. Dis went on for two or tree days, till one ebening de captain, instead of going away after dinner, stopped talking to dese fellows. De play begin at de table, and dey persuade him to join. He hab de debil's luck. Dey thought they going to cheat him, and if dey had got him by demselves dey would have cleaned him out sure. But dere were oder people playing and dey not able to cheat.

"Well, sar, he won all de money. Drinks had been flying about, and when at last de man dat kep' de table said, 'De bank will close for tonight,' de young fellow could scarce walk steady on his feet. His pockets were full ob notes. I went up to him and said, 'Will you hab a bed here, sar, bery good bed?' but he laugh and say, 'No, Sam, I may be a little fresh in de wind, but I tink I can make de boat.' I saw dose fellows scowl when I speak to him, and I make up my mind dey after no good. Well, sar, dey go out fust. Den he go out wid some oder people and stand laughing and talking at de door. Sam run up to him room, slip on his money belt, for he had had a good deal giben him while he was dar, and was sabing up to buy his freedom, and he didn't know what was going to happen. Den Sam look into de kitchen and caught up a heaby poker and a long knife, den he run down and turn out de lights ob de saloon and go out and lock de door after him.

"He was jus' in time, for he saw at de corner, where de street go down on to the wharves, de young captain separate from de men who had gone out wid him and walk away by hisself. Sam kicked off his shoes and ran as fast as he could to de end ob de street. De wharf was bery badly lighted, jus' a lamp here and dere. Sam ran along till he got widin about thirty yards ob de sailor, and den stole quiet along in de shadow ob de houses. Sudden he see five men run out. Den Sam he leap forward like tiger and gabe a shout to warn de captain. He turn round jus' in time. Sam saw an arm lifted and de captain fall, and den at de same moment almost him poker come down wid a crunch upon de top ob one ob deir head. Den they turn on Sam, but, law bless you, sar! what was de good ob dat? Bery strong man wid heavy poker in one hand and long knife in de oder more dan match for four men. He knock dem ober like nine-pin. Tree of dem he tink he kill straight, the poker fall on de top ob deir heads, de oder man give a dig in Sam's left shoulder wid his knife, and de sudden pain shake Sam's aim a little and de blow fall on him neck. He gib a shout and tumble down. None ob de oder four had shouted or made any remark when Sam hit dem. Den Sam caught up de captain and ran along de wharf. Presently he heard a hail. 'All right,' Sam said.

"'Am dat you, captain?' some one say.

"'Me got a captain here,' Sam say; 'you come and see wheder he yours.'

"De men came up and look in de captain's face.

"'Hullo,' dey say; 'de captain am dead.'

"'Me no tink him dead,' I say. 'He had a fight, and Sam come to him aid and beat de rascals off. You had better take him straight on board de ship.'

"Dey put him in boat and Sam go wid him to ship. Dey examine de wound and find it not bery serious. De captain was turning round when dey struck, and de blow had glanced off, but it had made an ugly gash; and what wid de surprise, and de loss ob blood, and knocking him head on de wharf, and de liquor, de captain had lost his consciousness. He soon come round, and Sam tell him all about it. De captain shake Sam's hand bery much and call him his preserber, and ask what he do for him.

"'You take me out ob dis country,' me said, 'and Sam be grateful all his life.'

"'Sartin, I will,' he said; 'and now what am de best ting to do?'

"'Me not stop on board now. Dey come and search de vessel for sure in de morning. When de four white men found dead, me hope five, den dere great rumpus. If five dead, no suspicion fall on Sam, but you sure to be asked questions. It would be known dat dey were gambling in de saloon, and it would be known dat you had broken de bank and had gone away wid your pockets stuffed full ob notes. People would suspec' dat likely enuf dey had made an attack on you. Dis you couldn't deny, for you will be bandaged up in de morning, and if you had killed dem no one would blame you. But it a different ting wid Sam. All dese rascals friends together, and you be bery sure dat some o' dem pay him off for it. If five men dead, all well and good. Den you say you knocked down and know nufing furder. You s'pose some people come up and take your side, and kill dese men, and carry you to de boat, and gib you ober to de sailors, and den go away; but dat you know nufing at all about it. If only four men killed, den de oder, who will be sure to go away and say nufing ob his share in de business, will tell all his mates dat dis slave intrude himself into de affair, and dat bad for Sam. So, sar, I propose dat I go ashore, and dat I go down de bank five or six mile, and dere hide in de bush. When your ship come down, you hoist little white flag, so Sam sure ob de right ship. If Sam tink de coast am clear, he swim off. If you no see Sam when you got fifteen mile down de riber, den you anchor, and at night send a boat ashore. Sam come down to it for sure.'

"So de matter was arranged. De captain say he tree more days fill up his ship, but dat no do for me to come on board by daylight because dere would be a pilot on board. Also he says little white flag no do, pilot tink him strange, but would tell one ob de men to hang a red shirt, as if to dry, up in de rigging. At night would show two lights ober de bow for me to know which was de ship.

"Fust dey bind up de wound on my shoulder, den dey gib me food for four days and a bottle of rum, and den row me ashore. Den Sam start, and before morning he hid in de swampy bush ten miles down de riber. He wait dere two days, den make him way down anoder four miles and dere stop. Late dat afternoon he see a ship come down de riber wid a red shirt in de rigging. He go on and on, and jus' as it get dark he anchor two miles furder down. Sam make his way along through de bush and at last get facing de ship. At twelbe o'clock boat come along bery quiet. Sam go down and get in. De men say, 'Hush, make no noise. De pilot am as watchful as a cat.' Dey had tied tings round de oars dat dey should make no noise, and when dey get to de side of de ship dey lay dem in very quiet, hook on de tackle and hoist her up. De hatchway were off, and de men beckon to Sam, and two ob dem go down wid him, and de hatchways closed down again.

"'I tink we hab tricked him,' one ob de sailors said. 'Dere great row at New Orleans about de four men found dead dar. Dey come off and inquire o' de captain ober and ober again. Dey know you missing, and dey find de kitchen poker lying by de men, and tink you must have had a hand in it. A thousand dollars reward have been offered, and dey searched de ship high and low, and turn ober all de cargo. A guard stop on board till de last ting to see no one come off. When de captain say he anchor, de pilot say no, but de captain say he in no hurry and not going to risk his ship by sailing at night. Me tink the pilot smell a rat, for ebery time he hear a noise on deck, he come out of his cabin and look round. We greased de falls to make dem run quiet, and took off our shoes so as to make no noise while we were lowering it. De men on deck was told to get de hatchway open when dey saw us coming, and so we hoped dat de pilot heard nufing. Now we must head you up in a cask. We hab bored some holes in it for do air. Den we shall pile oder casks on de top and leabe you. Dey are as likely as not to search de ship again when she goes past de forts, for de pilot will suspect dat it am possible dat you have come on board tonight.'

"Me take my place in a big sugar cask. Dey give me some water and some food, and den shut in de head ober me. Dere I remain two days. I heard some men come below and make a great noise, moving de cargo about near de hatchway, and dey hammered in all de casks ob de top tier to see if any ob dem was empty. I felt bery glad when it was all ober, and de hold was quiet again. I slept a great deal and did not know anything about time; but at last I heard a noise again, and de moving of casks, and den de head of de hogshead was taken out, and dere were de sailors and de captain. Dey shook Sam bery hearty by de hand, and told him dat de ship was safe out at sea, and dat he was a free man.

"All through dat voyage dey bery kind to Sam. He libed de life ob a gentleman; ate, and drink, and smoke plenty, and nuffng at all to do. At last we get to Liberpool, and dar de captain take Sam to a vessel bound to New York, pay him passage across, and gib Sam a present ob fifty pound. I had saved fifty beside, so I felt dat I was a rich man. Nuffng happen on passage, except great storm, and Sam thought dat de steamer go to de bottom, but she get through all right, and Sam land at New York. Den he journey to Philadelphia, dat the place where missy give Sam a card wid a name and address written on it, for him to go to ask where Sally was living. Well, sar, you could have knocked me down when I find a great bill in de window, saying dat de house were to let. Sam almost go out ob his mind. He ask a great many people, de servants at de doors, and de people in de shops, and at last find dat de family am gone to trabel in Europe, and dat dey might be away for years.

"For two months Sam searched about Philadelphia, and looked at ebery black woman he saw in de streets he could see no signs whatsomeber ob Sally. Den he took a place as waiter at an hotel, and he wrote to missy at Richmond, to ask if she knew Sally's address, but he neber got no answer to dat letter, and s'posed that missy was either dead or gone away. After he work dere for some months de idea come to Sam dat first-class hotel wasn't de best place in de world to look for black woman. Den Sam went to warehouse and bought a lot of books and started to peddle them trough de country. He walked thousands ob miles, and altogether saw thousands ob black men, but nothing like Sally. Ebery black woman he could he spoke to, and asked dem if dey knew her. It was a curious ting dat no one did. Me did not find Sally, but me made a good deal of money, and tree more years pass away at dis work. By dis time me was nigh forty-five years old, as well as me could tell. Ebery few months me go back to Philadelphia and search dere again.

"One day a woman, dressed bery plain, came up to me and

said, 'I hab been tole by my nurse dat you have been asking her if she had seen your wife.' I s'pose I looked hopeful like, for she said at once, 'Me know nothing o' her, but I was interested about you. You are an escaped slabe, are you not?'

"'Yes, ma'am,' me said. 'Dere is no law against me here.'

"'None at all,' she said. 'But I thought that you might, like me, be interested in freeing slabes.'

"'Dat I am,' I said, 'dough I had neber thought much about it.'

"'You hab heard, p'raps,' she said, 'ob de underground railway.'

"'Yes, ma'am,' said I. 'Dat is de blessed 'stitution which smuggles slaves across the frontier!'

"'Dat is it,' she said, 'and I belongs to it!'

"'Does you, missy?' me says. 'De Lord bless you.'

"'Now,' she said, 'we want two or three more earnest men, men not afraid to risk deir libes, or what is worse, deir freedom, to help deir fellow-creatures. I thought that you, habing suffered so much yourself, might be inclined to devote yourself to freeing oders from de horrors of slabery.'

"'Sam is ready, ma'am,' me says. 'It may be dat de Lord neber intends me see my Sally again, but if I can be de means ob helping to get oder men to join deir wives I shall be content.'

"'Very well,' she said. 'Come into my house now and we will talk about it.'

"Den she 'splained the whole business to me. Dere were, principally in lonely places, in swamps and woods, but sometimes libing in villages and towns in de south, people who had devoted deir libes to de carrying out of de purposes ob de underground railway. For de most part dese led libes differing no way from deir neighbours; dey tilled de land, or kept stores like oders, and none of dose around dem suspected in de slightest degree deir mission in de south. To deir houses at night fugitive slabes would come, guided by dose from de next post. De fugitives would be concealed for twenty-four hours or more, and den passed on at night again to de next station. Dese formed the larger portion ob de body.

"Dere were oders who lived a life in de swamps, scattered trough the country. Deir place of residence would be known to de slabes ob de neighbourhood, but de masters had no suspicion dat de emissaries ob de association were so near. To dese any slave, driben to desperation by harsh treatment, would resort, and from dem instructions would be received as to de route to be taken, and de places where aid could be obtained. Dese people held deir life in deir hands. Had any suspicion fallen upon dem ob belonging to do 'stitution dey would be lynched for sartin. De lady set before me all de dangers ob de venture. She said it war a case whar dere were no money to be earned, and only de chances of martyrdom. My mind quite made up. Me ready to undertake any work dey like to give me. My life ob no value to no one. De next day me saw some ob de oder people connected wid de affair, and tree days afterwards I started for de south.

CHAPTER XIV

A CHRISTIAN TOWN

"MY share ob de business was to make my way down south and settle in de swamps ob Carolina. I war to be taken down by trading schooner, to be landed on de coast, and to make my way to a place in de centre ob a big swamp whar an ole black man, named Joe, had been carrying on de work for four years. He had sent to say dat he war bery ill wid de swamp fever and like to die, dat he should not leabe de work as long as he libed, but hoped dat dey would send anoder man out to take on his work after his death.

"Well, sar, I was landed, and I made my way to de place. It war no easy matter. De folks all say dey know no such person, but I found de next post, and dere de man guided me to de path which led into de swamp. Dey told me dey thought de ole man dead, for dat no one had come along to dem from him for nigh two month. Well, sar, as I 'spected, I found him dead, and I buried him, and took up my place in de hut. Soon it became known through de plantations round dat de hut was occupied again, and dey began to come to me to ask for assistance. My 'structions war dat only to enable a husband to join his wife, or a wife her husband, or in cases where de masters were uncommon cruel, dat I was to send 'em along by de underground railway. De risks was too great to be run often. If we had tried to help eberyone to 'scape, we should mighty soon hab been hunted down.

"Well, sar, I libed dere for tree year. It was a lonesome life. I planted a few yams round de hut, and de plantation hands would bring me tings dat dey got hold of. It was my duty when I found dat a case was ob de proper description to arrange for de flight, de man or de woman would come to my hut, and I would guide dem through de swamps, twenty-five mile away, to de house ob a clergyman, which was de next station. I would jus' knock in a 'ticular

SAM ESCAPES FROM THE MAN-HUNTERS..

way at de door, and when dis was open leab de party dere and go straight away back to de swamp. More dan once de planters got up hunts and searched de swamp through and through for me wid dogs, and my hut was twice burnt to de ground, but de slabes always brought me notice in time, and I went away into de tickest part ob de swamp and lay dar tell dey had gone away.

"Well, sar, one time come, I bery busy, passed tree men away in two week. One night me hear barking of dogs, and jump up jus' in time to see party ob men coming out from de little path towards de hut. I ran for de swamp. Dey fire at me and one ball hit me. Den I ran in to de swamp, de dogs dey follow, but I get farder and farder away, and de swamp get deeper, and me tink dey lose me altogether. I sit quiet on a stump when I hear someting splashing in swamp, and all of a sudden a big hound sprang on me, and fix him teeth in my shoulder. I had no arms, for in de hurry I had not time to catch dem up. De beast he growl and bite, and hold on like death. I saw dere only one ting to do. I tumble forward into de swamp wid de dog underneath me, and dere I lay, wid my mouf sometimes above de water sometimes below, till de dog was drowned.

"Den I start for de next station. I was hit in de hip, and it took me tree days to crawl dat twenty-five miles. On de tird ebening I knock at de door ob de house, and when it was open I tumble down in faint inside. It war a long time before I come to myself, two weeks dey tell me, and den I tink I dream, for sitting by de side of de bed war dat woman Sally. Till she spoke, me couldn't believe dat it war true, but she told me dat it war her, sure enuf, and dat I war to ask no questions but to go off to sleep.

"Next day she told me all about it. She had stopped a year at Philadelphy. Den she heard ob de underground railway, and was tole dat a clergyman, who war just going down south to work a station, wanted a black nurse for his children, who would help in de work. Sally she volunteer, and dar she had been libing eber since, hoping all de time eider dat I should pass through dere or dat she should hear from Philadelphy dat I had got dere. She used to act as de guide ob de runaways to de next station, and ebery man who came along she asked if they knew me; but, law bless you, sar, de poor woman knew nuffing o' places, or she would hab known dat she war hundreds ob miles south of Virginia, and though she allowed she had heard I had gone to Missouri, she s'posed dat de way from dere might be by de sea coast. I hab observed, sar, dat de gography ob women am bery defective.

"I stopped thar till I was cured. The clergyman knew someting of surgery, and he managed to substract the ball from my hip. When I war quite well Sally and me started for the norf, whar we had helped so many oders to go, and, bress de Lord, we arribed dere safe. Den I told Sally dat I should like to libe under de British flag, so we went up to Canada and dere we libed bery comfortable for ten years together. Sally washed and I kep' a barber's shop, and we made plenty ob money. Den she die, sar, de tought come into my mind dat I would come back to Africa and teach dese poor natives here de ways ob de white men, and sar," and he pointed to a Bible standing on the chest, "de ways ob de Lord. So I came across the Atlantic, and stopped a little while on de coast, for I had pretty nigh forgotten de language ob de country. When I got it back again I started up for dis place, wid plenty ob goods and presents.

"I had hard work at fust to get de people to know me. It war nigh forty year since I had gone away, but at last some ob de ole people remember me, dat I was de son ob de chief. As I had plenty goods, and dey did not like de man dat was here, dey made me chief in my fader's place. I told dem dat I no accept de place unless dey promise to behave bery well, to mind what I said to dem, and to listen to my words; but dat if they do dat I gibe dem plenty goods, I make dem comfortable and happy, and I teach dem de way ob de Lord. Dey agree to all dis.

"I find de slave trade now all at an end, and dat de people not fight often now. Still, de twenty muskets dat I bring make de people of oder villages respec' us very much. Dey come ober to see de village. Dey see dat de houses are comfortable, dat de gardens are bery well cultivated, dat de people are well-dressed, not like common natives, dat dey are happy and contented. Dey see dat dey no believe in fetish any more, but dat ebery ebening when de work is ober, dey gadder under de big tree and listen for half an hour while I read to dem and den sing a hymn. Once a year I send down to de coast and get up plenty cloth, and hoes for de gardens, and eberyting dey want. When I land here ten year ago I hab eight hundred pound. I got five hundred ob him left here still. Dat more dan enuf to last Sam if he libe to be bery, bery ole man. Dar are some good men in de village, who, when I am gone, will carry on de work ob de Lord, and dat's all, sar, dat I hab to tell you about Sam, and I am sure dat you must be very tired and want to go to bed."

The hour was, indeed, for Africa, extremely late, but the time had passed unheeded, so interested were the listeners in the narrative of the fine old gentleman. They remained at the village for a week, and were greatly pleased with the industrious habits and happy appearance of the people, and with the earnestness and fervour in which every evening, and twice on Sunday, they joined in devotions under the great tree. At the end of that time they said good-bye to their kind host, giving him a large amount of cloth for distribution among his people. He was unable to furnish them with bearers, as a considerable tract of uninhabited country extended beyond his village, and the people on the other side were on bad terms with his villagers, on account of an outstanding feud which had existed long before his return from America, and which he had in vain attempted to settle since he assumed the headship of the village.

On approaching the Niger they again came upon an inhabited country, but the tribes here being accustomed to trade with the coast were friendly, and at the first large village they came to, no difficulty was experienced in obtaining a fresh relay of bearers. This was a matter of great satisfaction, for the Fans were regarded with extreme antipathy by the natives. As soon as arrangements had been made to supply their place the Fans were paid the four months' wages which they had earned. A large "dash" of beads and other presents were bestowed upon them, three of the remaining sacks of rice were given to them, and, greatly rejoicing, they started for their own country, which, by making long marches, they would regain in a fortnight's time. Although it was not probable that they would meet with any enemies, six trade muskets, with a supply of powder and ball, were given to them, as, although they would not be able to do much execution with these weapons, their possession would exercise a powerful influence over any natives they might meet.

In crossing the country to the Niger, the white men were the objects of lively curiosity, and the exhibition of the magic lantern, the chemical experiments, and conjuring tricks created an effect equal to that which they had produced among the Fans. On reaching the Niger, a canoe was hired with a crew of rowers. In this all the cases, filled with the objects they had collected, were placed, the whole being put in charge of the Houssas, Moses and King John, who had been seized with a fit of home-sickness. These were to deliver the cases to the charge of an English agent at Lagos or Bonny, to both of whom Mr. Goodenough wrote requesting him to pay the sum agreed to the boatmen on the safe arrival of the cases, and also to pay the Houssas, who preferred taking their wages there, as it was not considered advisable to tempt the cupidity of any of the native princes along the river. Should they be overhauled the Houssas were told to open the cases and show that these contained nothing but birds' skins and insects, which would be absolutely valueless in the eyes of a native.

When the precious freight had fairly started, the party crossed the Niger in a canoe, arrangements having already been made with the potentate of a village on the opposite side for a fresh relay of carriers, twenty men being now sufficient, owing to the gaps which had been made in the provisions, in the goods, by the payment of the carriers and presents, and, in the cases, by the despatch of eight of the largest of these to the coast. They had still, however, ample space for the collections they might still make. The cases of goods and provisions were utilized for this purpose as they were emptied.

For another two months they journeyed on, halting frequently and adding continually to their stores. The country was fairly populated, and there was no difficulty in buying plantains and fruit and in obtaining fresh sets of carriers through the territories of each petty chief. They were now approaching the Volta, when one day a native, covered with dust and bathed in perspiration, came up to their camp, and throwing himself on the ground before Mr. Goodenough poured out a stream of words.

"What does he say, Ostik?"

"Me not know, sar. P'r'aps Ugly Tom know. He been down near Volta country."

Ugly Tom was called, and after a conversation with the native, told Mr. Goodenough that he was a messenger from Abeokuta, that the people there were threatened by an attack by the King of Dahomey, and that they implored the white men, who, they heard, were in the neighbourhood, to come to their aid.

"What do you say, Frank?" Mr. Goodenough asked.

"I don't know anything about it, sir," Frank said. "I have heard of Dahomey, of course, and its horrible customs, but I don't know anything about Abeokuta."

"Abeokuta is a very singular town," Mr. Goodenough said. "Its people were christianized many years ago, and have faithfully retained the religion. The town lies not very far from Dahomey, and this power, which has conquered and enslaved all its other neighbours, has been unable to conquer Abeokuta, although it has several times besieged it. The Dahomey people have every advantage, being supplied with firearms, and even cannon, by the rascally white traders at Whydah, the port of Dahomey. Nevertheless, the Abeokuta people have opposed an heroic resistance, and so far successfully. Of course they know that every soul would be put to death did they fall into the hands of the King of Dahomey; but some natives do not always fight well, even under such circumstances, and every credit must be given to the people of Abeokuta. What do you say? It will be a perilous business, mind, for if Abeokuta is taken, we shall assuredly be put to death with the rest of the defenders."

"I think we ought to help them, sir," Frank said. "They must be a noble people, and with our guns and the four Houssas we might really be of material assistance. Of course there is a risk in it, but we have risked our lives from fever, and in other ways, every day since we've been in the country."

"Very well, my lad. I am glad that is your decision. Tell him, Ugly Tom, that we will at once move towards Abeokuta with all speed, and that they had better send out a party of carriers to meet us, as you may be sure that these men will not go far when they hear that the Dahomey people are on the war-path. Learn from him exactly the road we must move by, as, if our carriers desert us, we shall be detained till his people come up. How far is it to Abeokuta?"

Ugly Tom learned from the native that it was about forty-five miles.

"Very well," Mr. Goodenough said, "we will march twenty this afternoon. Where we halt they will most likely have heard the rumours of the war, and I expect the carriers will go no farther, so they must send out to that point."

The Houssa translated the message, and the native, saying, "I shall be at Abeokuta tonight," kissed the hands of the white men and started at a trot.

"Wonderful stamina some of these men have," Mr. Goodenough said. "That man has come forty-five miles at full speed, and is now going off again as fresh as when he started."

"What speed will he go at?" Frank asked.

"About six miles an hour. Of course he goes faster when he is running, but he will sometimes break into a walk. Five miles an hour may be taken as the ordinary pace of a native runner, but in cases which they consider of importance, like the present, you may calculate on six."

The camp was broken up at once, the carriers loaded, and they started on their way. It was late in the evening when they reached a village about twenty miles from their starting-place. They found the inhabitants in a great state of alarm. The news had come that a great army was marching to attack Abeokuta, and that the King of Dahomey had sworn on his father's skull that this time the place should be captured, and not a house or a wall left remaining. As Abeokuta was certain to make a strong resistance, and to hold out for some time, the villagers feared that the Dahomey people would be sending out parties to plunder and carry away captives all over the surrounding country. The panic at once extended to the bearers, who declared that they would not go a foot farther. As their fears were natural, and Mr. Goodenough was expecting a fresh relay from Abeokuta on the following evening, he consented to their demand to be allowed to leave immediately, and paying them their wages due, he allowed them to depart at once on the return journey. The tent was soon pitched and supper prepared, of fried plantains, rice, a tin of sardines, and tea. Later on they had a cup of chocolate, and then turned in for the night.

In the morning they were awakened just at daylight by great talking.

"Men come for baggage, sar," Ugly Tom said, putting his head in the tent door.

"They have lost no time about it, Frank!" Mr. Goodenough exclaimed. "It was mid-day yesterday when the messenger left us. He had forty-five miles to run, and could not have been in till pretty nearly eight o'clock, and these men must have started at once."

There was no time lost. While the Houssas were pulling down and packing up the tent, Ostik prepared two bowls of chocolate with biscuit soaked in it. By the time that this was eaten the carriers had taken up their loads, and two minutes later the whole party started almost at a trot. Ugly Tom soon explained the cause of the haste. The army of Dahomey was, the evening before, but eight miles from Abeokuta, and was expected to appear before the town by midday, although, of course, it might be later, for the movements of native troops are uncertain in the extreme, depending entirely upon the whims of their leader. So anxious were the bearers to get back to the town in time, that they frequently went at a trot. They were the better able to keep up the speed as a larger number than were required had been sent. Many of the cases, too, were light, consequently, the men were able to shift the heavy burdens from time to time. So great was the speed, that after an hour both Mr. Goodenough and Frank, weakened by the effect of fever and climate, could no longer keep up. The various effects carried in the hammocks were hastily taken out and lifted by men unprovided with loads. The white men entered and were soon carried along at a brisk trot by the side of the baggage. When they recovered from their exhaustion sufficiently to observe what was going on, they could not help admiring the manner in which the warriors, with perspiration streaming from every pore, hurried along with their burdens. So fast did they go, that in less than six hours they emerged from the forest into the clearing, and a shout proclaimed that Abeokuta was close at hand.

Ten minutes later the white men were carried through the gate, their arrival being hailed with shouts of joy by the inhabitants. They were carried in triumph to the principal building of the town, a large hut where the general councils of the people were held. Here they were received by the king and the leading inhabitants, who thanked them warmly for coming to their assistance in the time of their peril. The travellers were both struck with the appearance of the people. They were clad with far more decency and decorum than was usual among the tribes. Their bearing was quiet and dignified. An air of neatness and order pervaded everything, and it was clear that they were greatly superior to the people around.

Mr. Goodenough expressed to the king the willingness with which his friend and himself took part in the struggle of a brave people against a cruel and bloodthirsty foe, and he said that, as the four Houssa were also armed with fast-firing guns he hoped that their assistance would be of avail. He said that he would at once examine the defences of the town and see if anything could be done to strengthen them.

Accompanied by the king, Mr. Goodenough and Frank made a detour of the walls. These were about a mile in circumference, were built of clay, and were of considerable height and thickness, but they were not calculated to resist an attack by artillery. As, however, it was not probable that the Dahomey people possessed much skill in the management of their cannon, Mr. Goodenough had hopes that they should succeed in repelling the assault. They learnt that a large store of provisions had been brought into the town, and that many of the women and children had been sent far away.

The spies presently came in and reported that there was no movement on the part of the enemy, and that it was improbable that they would advance before the next day. Mr. Goodenough was unable to offer any suggestions for fresh defences until they knew upon which side the enemy would attack. He advised, however, that the whole population should be set to work throwing up an earthwork just outside each gate, in order to shelter these as far as possible from the effect of the enemy's cannon-balls. Orders were at once given to this effect, and in an hour the whole population were at work carrying earth in baskets and piling it in front of the gates. In order to economize labour, and to make the sides of the mounds as steep as possible, Mr. Goodenough directed them to cut stakes and to stick these in, with the interstices filled up with brush-wood, forming a sort of rough wattle-work. Not even when night set in did the people desist from their labour, and by the following morning the gates were protected from the effect of cannon shot, by mounds of earth twenty feet high, which rose before them. The king had, when Mr. Goodenough first suggested these defences, pointed out that much less earth would be required were it piled directly against the gates. Mr. Goodenough replied, that certainly this was so, but that it was essential to be able to open the gates to make a sortie if necessary against the enemy, and although the king shook his head, as if doubting the ability of his people to take such a desperate step as that of attacking the enemy outside their walls, he yielded to Mr. Goodenough's opinion.

CHAPTER XV

THE AMAZONS OF DAHOMEY

A SPACIOUS and comfortable hut was placed at the disposal of the white men, with a small one adjoining for the Houssas. That evening Frank asked Mr. Goodenough to tell him what he knew concerning the people of Dahomey.

"The word Dahomey, or more properly De-omi, means Da's belly. Da was, two hundred and fifty years ago, the king of the city of Abomey. It was attacked by Tacudona, the chief of the Fois. It resisted bravely, and Tacudona made a vow that if he took it he would sacrifice the king to the gods. When he captured the town he carried out his vow by ripping open the king, and then called the place Daomi. Gradually the conquerors extended their power until the kingdom reached to the very foot of the Atlas range, obtaining a port by the conquest of Whydah. The King of Dahomey is a despot, and even his nobility crawl on the ground in his presence. The taxes are heavy, every article sold in the market paying about one-eighteenth to the royal exchequer. There are besides many other taxes. Every slave is taxed, every article that enters the kingdom. If a cock crow it is forfeited, and, as it is the nature of cocks to crow, every bird in the kingdom is muzzled. The property of every one who dies goes to the king; and at the Annual Custom, a grand religious festival, every man has to bring a present in proportion to his rank and wealth. The royal pomp is kept up by receiving strangers who visit the country with much state, and by regaling the populace with spectacles of human sacrifices. The women stand high in Dahomey. Among other African nations they till the soil. In Dahomey they fight as soldiers, and perform all the offices of men. Dahomey is principally celebrated for its army of women, and its human sacrifices. These last take place annually, or even more often. Sometimes as many as a thousand captives are slain on these

153

occasions. In almost all the pagan nations of Africa, human sacrifices are perpetrated, just as they were by the Druids and Egyptians of old. Nowhere, however, are they carried to such a terrible extent as in Dahomey. Even Ashanti, where matters are bad enough, is inferior in this respect. The victims are mostly captives taken in war, and it is to keep up the supply necessary for these wholesale sacrifices that Dahomey is constantly at war with her neighbours."

"But are we going to fight against women, then?" Frank asked horrified.

"Assuredly we are," Mr. Goodenough answered. "The Amazons, as white men have christened the force, are the flower of the Dahomey army, and fight with extraordinary bravery and ferocity."

"But it will seem dreadful to fire at women!" Frank said.

"That is merely an idea of civilization, Frank. In countries where women are dependent upon men, leaving to them the work of providing for the family and home, while they employ themselves in domestic duties and in brightening the lives of the men, they are treated with respect. But as their work becomes rougher, so does the position which they occupy in men's esteem fall. Among the middle and upper classes throughout Europe, a man is considered a brute and a coward who lifts his hand against a woman. Among the lower classes, wife and woman beating is by no means uncommon, nor is such an assault regarded with much more reprobation than an attack upon a man. When women leave their proper sphere and put themselves forward to do man's work, they must expect man's treatment; and the foolish women at home who clamour for women's rights, that is to say, for an equality of work, would, if they had their way, inflict enormous damage upon their sex."

"Still," Frank said, "I sha'n't like having to fire at women."

"You won't see much difference between women and men when the fight begins, Frank. These female furies will slay all who fall into their hands, and therefore in self-defence you will have to assist in slaying them."

The following day the sound of beating of drums and firing of guns was heard, and soon afterwards the head of the army of

Dahomey was seen approaching. It moved with considerable order and regularity.

"Those must be the Amazons," Mr. Goodenough said. "They are proud of their drill and discipline. I do not think that any other African troops could march so regularly and solidly."

The main body of the army now came in view, marching as a loose and scattered mob. Then twelve objects were seen dragged by oxen. These were the cannon of the besiegers.

"How many do you think there are?" Frank asked.

"It is very difficult to judge accurately," Mr. Goodenough said. "But Dahomey is said to be able to put fifty thousand fighting men and women in the field, that is to say, her whole adult population, except those too old to bear arms. I should think that there are twenty or twenty-five thousand now in sight."

The enemy approached within musket shot of the walls, and, numbers of them running up, discharged their muskets. The Abeokuta people fired back; but Mr. Goodenough ordered the Houssas on no account to fire, as he did not wish the enemy to know the power of their rifles.

The first step of the besiegers was to cut down all the plantations round the town and to erect great numbers of little huts. A large central hut with several smaller ones surrounding it was erected for the king and his principal nobles. The Dahomans spread round the town, and by the gesticulation and pointing at the gates it was clear that the defences raised to cover these excited great surprise.

The wall was thick enough for men to walk along on the top, but being built of clay, it would withstand but little battering. Mr. Goodenough set a large number of people to work, making sacks from the rough cloth, of which there was an abundance in the place. These were filled with earth and piled in the centre of the town ready for conveyance to any point threatened. He likewise had a number of beams, used in construction of houses, sharpened at one end; stakes of five or six feet long were also prepared and sharpened at both ends. That day the enemy attempted nothing against the town. The next morning the twelve cannon were planted at a distance of about five hundred yards and opened fire on the walls. The shooting was wild in the extreme; many of the balls went over the place altogether; others topped the wall and fell in the town; some hit the wall and buried themselves in the clay.

"We will give them a lesson," Mr. Goodenough said, "in the modern rifle. Frank, you take my double-barrel rifle and I will take the heavy, large-bored one. Your Winchester will scarcely make accurate firing at five hundred yards."

The Houssas were already on the wall, anxious to open fire. Mr. Goodenough saw that their rifles were sighted to five hundred yards. The cannon offered an easy mark. They were ranged along side by side, surrounded by a crowd of warriors, who yelled and danced each time a shot struck the wall.

"Now," Mr. Goodenough said to the Houssas, "fire steadily, and, above all, fire straight. I want every shot to tell."

Mr. Goodenough gave the signal, and at once Frank and the Houssas opened fire. The triumphant yells of the Dahomans at once changed their character, and a cry of wrath and astonishment broke from them. Steadily Mr. Goodenough and his party kept up their fire. They could see that great execution was being done, a large proportion of the shots telling. Many wounded were carried to the rear, and black forms could be seen stretched everywhere on the ground. Still the enemy's fire continued with unabated vigour.

"They fight very pluckily," Frank said.

"They are plucky," Mr. Goodenough answered; "and as cowardice is punished with death, and human life has scarcely any value among them, they will be killed where they stand rather than retreat."

For three or four hours the fight continued. Several officers, evidently of authority, surrounded by groups of attendants, came down to the guns; but as Frank and Mr. Goodenough always selected these for their mark, and—firing with their guns resting on the parapet were able to make very accurate shooting, most of them were killed within a few minutes of their arriving on the spot.

At the end of four hours the firing ceased, and the Dahomans retired from their guns. The Abeokuta people raised a cry of triumph.

"I imagine they have only fallen back," Mr. Goodenough said, "to give the guns time to cool."

While the cannonade had been going on a brisk attack had been kept up on several other points of the wall, the enemy advancing within fifty yards of this and firing their muskets, loaded with heavy charges of slugs, at the defenders, who replied vigorously to them. Their cannonade was not resumed that afternoon, the Dahomans contenting themselves with skirmishing round the walls.

"They are disappointed with the result of their fire," Mr. Goodenough said. "No doubt they anticipated they should knock the wall down without difficulty. You will see some change in their tactics tomorrow."

That night Mr. Goodenough had a number of barrels of palm-oil carried on to the wall, with some of the great iron pots used for boiling down the oil, and a supply of fuel.

"If they try to storm," he said, "it will most likely be at the point which they have been firing at. The parapet is knocked down in several places, and the defenders there would be more exposed to their fire."

It was at this point, therefore, that the provision of oil was placed. Mr. Goodenough ordered fires to be lighted under the boilers an hour before daybreak, in order that all should be in readiness in case an attack should be made the first thing in the morning. The Abeokutans were in high spirits at the effect of the fire of their white allies, and at the comparative failure of the cannon, at whose power they had before been greatly alarmed. Soon after daylight the Dahomans were seen gathering near the guns. Their drums beat furiously, and presently they advanced in a solid mass against the wall.

"They have got ladders," Mr. Goodenough said. "I can see numbers of them carrying something."

The Houssas at once opened fire, and as the enemy approached closer, first the Abeokutans, who had muskets, then the great mass with bows and arrows, began to fire upon the enemy, while these answered with their musketry. The central body, however, advanced without firing a shot, moving like the rest at a quick run.

Mr. Goodenough and Frank were not firing now, as they were devoting themselves to superintending the defence. Ostik kept close to them, carrying Frank's Winchester carbine and a double-barrelled shot-gun.

"This is hot," Mr. Goodenough said, as the enemy's slugs and bullets whizzed in a storm over the edge of the parapet, killing many of the defenders, and rendering it difficult for the others to take accurate aim. This, however, the Abeokutans did not try to do; stooping below the parapet, they fitted their arrows to the string, or loaded their muskets, and then, standing up, fired hastily at the approaching throng.

The walls were about twenty-five feet high inside, but the parapet gave an additional height of some four feet outside. They were about three feet thick at the top, and but a limited number of men could take post there to oppose the storming party. Strong bodies were placed farther along on the wall to make a rush to sweep the enemy off should they gain a footing. Others were posted below to attack them should they leap down into the town, while men with muskets were on the roofs of the houses near the walls, in readiness to open fire should the enemy get a footing on the wall. The din was prodigious.

The Dahomans, having access to the sea-coast, were armed entirely with muskets, these being either cheap Birmingham trade guns or old converted muskets, bought by traders for a song at the sale of disused government stores. It is much to be regretted that the various governments of Europe do not insist that their old guns shall be used only as old iron. The price obtained for them is so trifling as to be immaterial, and the great proportion of them find their way to Africa to be used in the constant wars that are waged there, and to enable rich and powerful tribes to enslave and destroy their weaker neighbours. The Africans use very much heavier charges of powder than those in use in civilized nations, ramming down a handful of slugs, or half a dozen small bullets, upon the powder. This does not conduce to good shooting, but the noise made is prodigious. The Abeokutans, on the other hand, were principally armed with bows and arrows, as, having no direct access to the sea-coast, it was difficult for them to procure guns.

The Dahomans poured up in a mass to the foot of the wall, and then a score of rough ladders, constructed of bamboo, and each four feet wide, were placed against the walls. Directly the point to be attacked was indicated, Mr. Goodenough had distributed his cauldrons of boiling oil along the walls, and had set men to work to pierce holes through the parapet at distances of a couple of feet apart, and at a height of six inches from the ground. A line of men with long spears were told to lie down upon the ground, and to thrust through the holes at those climbing the ladders. Another line of holes was pierced two feet higher, through which those armed with muskets and bows were to fire, for when the enemy reached the foot of the walls their fire was so heavy that it was impossible to return it over the top of the parapet.

Immediately the ladders were placed, men with ladles began to throw the boiling oil over the parapet. Shrieks and yells from below at once testified to its effect, but it was only just where the cauldrons were placed that the besiegers were prevented by this means from mounting the ladders, and even here many, in spite of the agony of their burns, climbed desperately upwards.

When they neared the top the fight began in earnest. Those without were now obliged to cease firing, and the besieged were able to stand up and with sword and spear defend their position. The breech-loaders of Mr. Goodenough and the Houssas and Frank's repeating carbine now came into play. The Dahomans fought with extraordinary bravery, hundreds fell shot or cut down from above or pierced by the spears and arrows through the holes in the parapet. Fresh swarms of assailants took their places on the ladders. The drums kept up a ceaseless rattle, and the yells of the mass of warriors standing inactive were deafening. Their efforts, however, were in vain. Never did the Amazons fight with more reckless bravery; but the position was too strong for them, and at last, after upwards of a thousand of the assailants had fallen, the attack was given up, and the Dahomans retired from the wall followed by the exulting shouts of the men of Abeokuta.

The loss of the defenders was small. Some ten or twelve had been killed with slugs. Three or four times that number were more or less severely wounded about the head or shoulders with the same missiles. Frank had a nasty cut on the cheek, and Firewater and Bacon were both streaming with blood. There was no chance of a renewal of the attack that day. Sentries were placed on the walls, and a grand thanksgiving service was held in the open space in the centre of the town which the whole populace attended.

"What will be their next move, do you think?" Frank asked Mr. Goodenough.

"I cannot say," Mr. Goodenough said; "but these people know something of warfare, and finding that they cannot carry the place by assault, I think you will find that they will try some more cautious move next time."

For two days there was no renewal of the attack. At Mr. Goodenough's suggestion the Abeokutans on the wall shouted out that the Dahomans might come and carry off their dead, as he feared that a pestilence might arise from so great a number of decomposing bodies at the foot of the wall. The Dahomans paid no attention to the request, and, at Mr. Goodenough's suggestion, on the second day the whole populace set to work carrying earth in baskets to the top of the wall, and throwing this over so as to cover the mass of bodies at its foot. As to those lying farther off, nothing could be done. On the third morning it was seen that during the night a large number of sacks had been piled in a line upon the ground, two hundred yards away from the wall. The pile was eight feet in height and some fifty yards long.

"I thought they were up to something," Mr. Goodenough said. "They have been sending back to Dahomey for sacks." In a short time the enemy brought up their cannon, behind the shelter of the sacks, regardless of the execution done by the rifles of Mr. Goodenough's party during the movement. The place chosen was two or three hundred yards to the left of that on which the former attack had been made. Then a swarm of men set to work removing some of the sacks, and in a short time twelve rough embrasures were made just wide enough for the muzzles of the guns, the sacks removed being piled on the others, raising them to the height of ten feet and sheltering the men behind completely from the fire from the walls.

"They will make a breach now," Mr. Goodenough said. "We must prepare to receive them inside."

The populace were at once set to work digging holes and securely planting the beams already prepared in a semicircle a hundred feet across, behind the wall facing the battery. The beams when fixed projected eight feet above the ground, the spaces between being filled with bamboos twisted in and out between them. Earth was thrown up behind to the height of four feet for the defenders to stand upon. The space between the stockade and the wall was filled with sharp-pointed bamboos and stakes stuck firmly in the ground with their points projecting outwards. All day the townspeople laboured at these defences, while the wall crumbled fast under the fire of the Dahomey artillery, every shot of which, at so short a distance, struck it heavily. By five in the afternoon a great gap, fifty feet wide, was made in the walls, and the army of Dahomey again gathered for the assault. Mr. Goodenough with two of the Houssas took his place on the wall on one side of the gap, Frank with the other two faced him across the chasm. A large number of the Abeokuta warriors also lined the walls, while the rest gathered on the stockade.

With the usual tumult of drumming and yells the Dahomans rushed to the assault. The fire from the walls did not check the onset in the slightest, and with yells of anticipated victory they swarmed over the breach. A cry of astonishment broke from them as they saw the formidable defence within, the fire of whose defenders was concentrated upon them. Then, with scarce a pause, they leaped down and strove to remove the obstructions. Regardless of the fire poured upon them, they hewed away at the sharp stakes, or strove to pull them up with their hands. The riflemen on the walls directed their fire now exclusively upon the leaders of the column, the breech-loaders doing immense execution, and soon the Dahomans, in their efforts to advance, had to climb over lines of dead in their front. For half an hour the struggle continued, and then the Dahomans lost heart and retired, leaving fifteen hundred of their number piled deep in the space between the breach and the stockade.

"This is horrible work," Frank said, when he rejoined Mr. Goodenough.

"Horrible, Frank; but there is at least the consolation that by this fearful slaughter of their bravest warriors we are crippling the power of Dahomey as a curse and a scourge to its neighbours. After this crushing repulse the Abeokutans may hope that many years will elapse before they are again attacked by their savage neighbours, and the lessons which they have now learned in defence will enable them to make as good a stand on another occasion as they have done now."

"Do you think the attack will be renewed?"

"I should hardly think so. The flower of their army must have fallen, and the Amazon guard must have almost ceased to exist. I told you, Frank, you would soon get over your repugnance to firing at women."

"I did not think anything about women," Frank said. "We seemed to be fighting a body of demons with their wild screams and yells. Indeed, I could scarce distinguish the men from the women."

A strong guard was placed at night at the stockade, and Mr. Goodenough and Frank lay down close at hand in case the assault should be renewed. At daybreak the sound of a cannon caused them to start to their feet.

"They are not satisfied yet," Mr. Goodenough exclaimed, hurrying to the wall. In the night the Dahomans had either with sacks or earth raised their cannon some six feet, so that they were able to fire over the mound caused by the fallen wall at the stockade behind it, at which they were now directing their fire.

"Now for the sacks," Mr. Goodenough said. Running down, he directed the sacks laden with earth, to whose necks ropes had been attached, to be brought up. Five hundred willing hands seized them, and they were lowered in front of the centre of the stockade, which was alone exposed to the enemy's fire, until they hung two deep over the whole face. As fast as one bag was injured by a shot it was drawn up and another lowered to its place. In the meantime the rifles from the walls had again opened fire, and as the gunners were now more exposed, their shots did considerable execution. Seeing the uselessness of their efforts the Dahomans gradually slackened their fire.

When night came Mr. Goodenough gathered two hundred of the best troops of Abeokuta. He caused plugs to be made corresponding to the sizes of the various cannon-balls which were picked up within the stockade, which varied from six to eighteen pounders.

About midnight the gate nearest to the breach was thrown open, and the party sallied out and made their way towards the enemy's battery. The Dahomans had placed sentries in front facing the breach, but, anticipating no attack in any other direction, had left the flanks unguarded. Mr. Goodenough had enjoined the strictest silence on his followers, and their approach was unobserved until they swept round into the battery. Large numbers of the enemy were lying asleep here, but these, taken by surprise, could offer no resistance, and were cut down or driven away instantly by the assailants.

Mr. Goodenough and Frank, with a party who had been told off specially for the purpose, at once set to work at the cannon. These were filled nearly to the muzzle with powder, and the plugs were driven with mallets tight into the muzzles. Slow matches, composed of strips of calico dipped in saltpetre, were placed in the touch-holes. Then the word was given, and the whole party fell back to the gate just as the Dahomans in great numbers came running up. In less than a minute after leaving the battery twelve tremendous reports, following closely one upon another, were heard. The cannon were blown into fragments, killing numbers of the Dahomey men who had just crowded into the battery.

CHAPTER XVI

CAPTIVES IN COOMASSIE

UPON the morning following the successful sortie, not an enemy could be seen from the walls. Swift runners were sent out, and these returned in two hours with news that the enemy were in full retreat towards their capital. The people of Abeokuta were half wild with exultation and joy, and their gratitude to their white allies was unbounded. Mr. Goodenough begged them not to lose an hour in burying their slain enemies, and the entire population were engaged for the two following days upon this necessary but revolting duty. The dead were counted as they were placed in the great pits dug for their reception, and it was found that no fewer than three thousand of the enemy had fallen.

Mr. Goodenough also advised the Abeokutans to erect flanking towers at short intervals round their walls, to dig a moat twenty feet wide and eight deep at a few yards from their foot, and to turn into it the water from the river in order that any future attack might be more easily repelled. The inhabitants were poor, but they would willingly have presented all their treasures to their white allies. Mr. Goodenough, however, would accept nothing save a few specimens of native cloth exquisitely woven from the inner barks of trees, and some other specimens of choice native workmanship. He also begged them to send down to the coast by the first opportunity the cases of specimens which had been collected since the departure of the Fans.

A violent attack of fever, brought on by their exertions in the sun, prostrated both the white travellers a few days after the termination of the siege, and it was some weeks before they were able to renew their journey. Their intention was to ascend the river for some distance, to move westward into upper Ashanti, and then to make their way to Coomassie, whence they would journey down to

Cape Coast and there take ship for England. As soon as they were able to travel, they took leave of their friends at Abeokuta, who furnished them with carriers for their cases and hammock bearers for their journey as far as the Volta. This lasted for a fortnight through an open and fertile country. Then they crossed the river and entered Ashanti, the great rival empire of Dahomey. As Ashanti was at peace with England, they had now no fear of molestation on their journey.

Ashanti consisted of five or six kingdoms, all of which had been conquered, and were tributary to it. The empire of Ashanti was separated by the river Prah from the country of the Fantis, who lived under British protection. The people drew their supplies from various points on the coast, principally, however, through Elmina, a Dutch settlement, five miles to the west of Cape Coast. The Ashantis could not be called peaceable neighbours. They, like the Dahomans, delighted in human sacrifices upon a grand scale, and to carry these out captives must be taken. Consequently every four or five years, on some pretext or other, they crossed the Prah, destroyed the villages, dragged away the people to slavery or death, and carried fire and sword up to the very walls of the English fort at Cape Coast. Sometimes the English confined themselves to remonstrances, sometimes fought, not always successfully, as upon one occasion Sir Charles Macarthy, the governor, with a West Indian regiment was utterly defeated, the governor himself and all his white officers, except three, being killed.

In 1828 we aided the Fantis to defeat the Ashantis in a decisive battle, the consequence of which was the signature of a treaty, by which the King of Ashanti recognized the independence of all the Fanti tribes. In 1844, and again in 1852, a regular protectorate was arranged between the British and the Fantis, the former undertaking to protect them from enemies beyond the borders, and in turn exercising an authority over the Fantis, forbidding them to make war with each other, and imposing a nominal tribute upon them.

In 1853 the Ashantis again crossed the Prah, but, being met with firmness, retired again. After ten years' quiet, in 1863 they again invaded the country, burnt thirty villages, and slaughtered their inhabitants. Governor Price then urged upon the home authorities the necessity for the sending out from England of two thousand troops to aid the native army in striking a heavy blow at the Ashantis, and so putting a stop to this constant aggression. The English government, however, refused to entertain the proposal. In order to encourage the natives some companies of West Indian troops were marched up to the Prah. The wet season set in, and, after suffering terribly from sickness, the survivors returned five months later to Cape Coast.

Up to this period the Dutch trading ports and forts upon the coast were interspersed with ours, and as the tribes in their neighbourhood were under Dutch protection constant troubles were arising between the Dutch tribes and our own, and in 1867 an exchange was effected, the Dutch ceding all their forts and territory east of the Sweet river, a small stream which falls into the sea midway between Cape Coast and Elmina, while we gave up all our forts to the west of this stream. Similarly the protectorate of the tribes inland up to the boundary of the Ashanti kingdom, changed hands. The natives were not consulted as to this treaty, and some of those formerly under British protection, especially the natives of Commendah, refused to accept the transfer, and beat off with loss the Dutch troops who attempted to land. The Dutch men-of-war bombarded and destroyed Commendah.

This step was the commencement of fresh troubles between the Ashantis and the English. The Commendah people were Fantis, and as such the implacable enemies of the Elmina people, who had under Dutch protection been always allies of the Ashantis, and had been mainly instrumental in supplying them with arms and ammunition. The Fantis, regarding the Elmina natives and the Dutch as one power, retaliated for the destruction of Commendah by invading the territory of the Elmina tribe, destroying their villages and blockading the Dutch in their port. Another reason for this attack upon the Elminas was that an Ashanti general, named Atjempon, had marched with several hundred men through the Fanti country, burning, destroying, and slaying as usual, and had taken refuge with his men in Elmina. From this time the desultory war between the Elminas and their Ashanti allies, and the Fantis of the neighbourhood had never ceased. Our influence over our allies was but small, for we in vain endeavoured to persuade them to give up the invasion of Elmina. We even cut off the supplies of powder and arms to the Fantis, whose loyalty to our rule was thereby much shaken.

All these troubles induced the Dutch to come to the decision to withdraw altogether, and they accordingly offered to transfer all their possessions to us. The English government determined not to accept the transfer if it should lead to troubles with the natives, and as a first step required that the Ashanti force should leave Elmina. In 1870 the King of Ashanti wrote to us claiming Elmina as his, and protesting against its being handed over to us.

According to native ideas the King of Ashanti's claim was a just one. The land upon which all the forts, English, Dutch, Danish, and French, were built had been originally acquired from the native chiefs at a fixed annual tribute, or as we regarded it, as rent, or as an annual present in return for friendly relations. By the native customs he who conquers a chief entitled to such a payment becomes the heir of that payment, and one time the King of Ashanti upon the strength of his conquest of the Fantis set up a claim of proprietorship over Cape Coast and the other British forts.

Of a similar nature was the claim of the Ashantis upon Elmina. The Dutch had paid eighty pounds a year, as they asserted, as a present, and they proved conclusively that they had never regarded the King of Ashanti as having sovereignty over their forts, and that he had never advanced such a claim. They now arrested Atjempon, and refused to pay a further sum to the King of Ashanti until he withdrew his claim. In order to settle matters amicably they sent an envoy to Coomassie with presents for the king, and obtained from him a repudiation of his former letter, and a solemn acknowledgment that the money was not paid as a tribute. The king sent down two ambassadors to Elmina, who solemnly ratified this declaration.

The transfer was then effected. We purchased from the Dutch their forts and stores, but the people of Elmina were told that we should not take possession of the place except with their consent; but it was pointed out to them that if they refused to accept our protection they would be exposed as before to the hostility of the Fantis. They agreed to accept our offer, and on the 4th of April, 1872, a grand council was held, the king and chiefs of Elmina announced the agreement of their people to the transfer, and we took possession of Elmina, Atjempon and the Ashantis returning to their own country.

Upon the transfer taking place, Mr. Pope Hennessy, the governor of the colony, sent to the King of Ashanti, saying that the English desired peace and friendship with the natives, and would give an annual present, double that which he had received from the Dutch. At the same time negotiations were going on with the king for the free passage of Ashanti traders to the coast, and for the release of four Germans who had been carried off ten years before by Aboo Boffoo, one of the king's generals, from their mission station on British territory near the Volta. The king wrote saying that Aboo Boffoo would not give them up without a ransom of eighteen hundred ounces of gold, and protracted negotiations went on concerning the payment of these sums.

At the time when Mr. Goodenough and Frank had landed on the Gaboon, early in 1872, nothing was known of any anticipated troubles with the Ashanti. The negotiations between the English and the Dutch were in progress, but they had heard that the English would not take over Elmina without the consent of the inhabitants, and that they would be willing to increase the payment made by the Dutch to the King of Ashanti. It was known too that efforts would be made to settle all points of difference with the king; and as at Abeokuta they received news that the negotiations were going on satisfactorily, and that there was no prospect whatever of trouble, they did not hesitate to carry out the plans they had formed.

Before crossing the Volta, they sent across to inquire of the chief of the town there whether two English travellers would be allowed to pass through Ashanti, and were delayed for a fortnight until a messenger was sent to Coomassie and returned with a letter, saying that the king would be glad to see white men at his capital. With this assurance they crossed the stream. They were received in state by the chief, who at once provided them with the necessary carriers, and with them a guard, which he said would prevent any trouble on their way. On the following day they started, and after arriving, at the end of a day's journey, at a village, prepared to stop as usual for a day or two to add to their collection. The officer of the guard, however, explained to them through Bacon, who spoke the Ashanti language, that his instructions were, that they were to go straight through to Coomassie. In vain Mr. Goodenough protested that this would entirely defeat the object of his journey. The officer was firm. His orders were that they were to travel straight to Coomassie, and if he failed in carrying these out, his head would assuredly be forfeited.

"This is serious, Frank," Mr. Goodenough said. "If this fellow has not blundered about his orders, it is clear that we are prisoners. However, it may be that the king merely gave a direction that we should be escorted to the capital, having no idea that we should want to loiter upon the way."

They now proceeded steadily forward, making long day's marches. The officer in command of the guard was most civil, obtaining for them an abundance of provisions at the villages at which they stopped, and as Frank and his companion were both weakened by fever he enlisted sufficient hammock bearers for them, taking fresh relays from each village. He would not hear of their paying either for provisions or bearers, saying that they were the king's guests, and it would be an insult to him were they to pay for anything.

Ten days after starting from the Volta they entered Coomassie. This town lay on rising ground, surrounded by a deep marsh of from forty to a hundred yards wide. A messenger had been sent on in front to announce their coming, and after crossing the marsh they passed under a great fetish, or spell, consisting of a dead sheep wrapped up in red silk and suspended from two poles.

Mr. Goodenough and Frank took their places at the head of the little procession. On entering the town they were met by a crowd of at least five thousand people, for the most part warriors, who fired their guns, shouted, and yelled. Horns, drums, rattles, and gongs added to the appalling noise. Men with flags performed wild dances, in which the warriors joined. The dress of the captains consisted of war caps with gilded rams' horns projecting in front, and immense plumes of eagles' feathers on each side. Their vest was of red cloth, covered with fetishes and charms in cases of gold, silver, and embroidery. These were interspersed with the horns and tails of animals, small brass bells, and shells. They wore loose cotton trousers, with great boots of dull red leather coming half-way up to the thigh, and fastened by small chains to their waist-belts, also ornamented with bells, horse tails, strings of amulets, and strips of coloured leather. Long leopards' tails hung down their backs.

Through this crowd the party moved forward slowly, the throng thickening at every step. They were escorted to a house which they were told was set aside for their use, and that they would be allowed to see the king on the following day. The houses differed entirely from anything which they had before seen in Africa. They were built of red clay, plastered perfectly smooth. There were no windows or openings on the exterior, but the door led into an open court-yard of some twelve feet in diameter. On each side of this was a sort of alcove, built up of clay, about three feet from the ground. This formed a couch or seat, some eight feet long by three feet high, with a thatched roof projecting so as to prevent the rain beating into the alcove. Beyond were one or more similar courts in proportion to the size of the house. A sheep and a quantity of vegetables and fruits were sent in in the course of the day, but they were told not to show themselves in the streets until they had seen the king.

"We shall be expected to make his majesty a handsome present," Mr. Goodenough said, "and, unfortunately, our stores were not intended for so great a potentate. I will give him my double-barrelled rifle and your Winchester, Frank. I do not suppose he has seen such an arm. We had better get them cleaned up and polished so as to look as handsome as possible."

In the morning one of the captains came and said that the

king was in readiness to receive them, and they made their way through a vast crowd to the market-place, an open area, nearly half a mile in extent. The sun was shining brightly, and the scene was a brilliant one. The king, his Caboceers or great tributaries, his captains, and officers were seated under a vast number of huge umbrellas, some of them fifteen feet across. These were of scarlet, yellow, and other showy colours in silks and cloths, with fantastically scalloped and fringed valences. They were surmounted with crescents, birds, elephants, barrels, and swords of gold, and on some were couched stuffed animals. Innumerable smaller umbrellas of striped stuff were borne by the crowd, and all these were waved up and down, while a vast number of flutes, horns, and other musical instruments sounded in the air. All the principal people wore robes woven of foreign silk, which had been unravelled for working into native patterns. All had golden necklaces and bracelets, in many cases so heavy that the arms of the bearers were supported on boys' heads. The whole crowd, many thousands in number, shone with gold, silver, and bright colours.

The king received them with dignity, and expressed his satisfaction at seeing them, his speech being interpreted by one of his attendants, who spoke English. Mr. Goodenough replied that they had very great pleasure in visiting the court of his majesty, that they had already been travelling for many months in Africa, having started from the Gaboon and travelled through many tribes, but had they had any idea of visiting so great a king they would have provided themselves with presents fit for his acceptance. But they were simple travellers, catching the birds, beasts, and insects of the country, to take home with them to show to the people in England. The only things which they could offer him were a double-barrelled breech-loading rifle of the best English construction, and a little gun, which would fire sixteen times without loading. The king examined the pieces with great attention, and, at his request, Mr. Goodenough fired off the whole contents of the magazine of the repeating rifle, whose action caused the greatest astonishment to the assembled chiefs. The king then intimated his acceptance of the presents, and said that he would speak farther with them on a future occasion. He informed them that they were free to move about in the town where they wished, and that the greatest respect would be shown to them by the people. There was a fresh outburst of wild music, and they were then conducted back to their house.

After the assembly had dispersed the two Englishmen walked about through the town. It was not of great extent, but the streets were broad and well kept. Many of the houses were much larger than that allotted to them, but all were built on the same plan. It was evident that the great mass of the population they saw about must live in villages scattered around, the town being wholly insufficient to contain them. Three days afterwards they were told that the king wished to see them in his palace. This was a large building situated at the extremity of the town. It was constructed of stone, and was evidently built from European designs. It was square, with a flat roof and embattled parapet. They were conducted through the gateway into a large court-yard, and then into a hall where the king sat upon a raised throne. Attendants stood round fanning him.

"Why," he asked abruptly as they took their places before him, "do the English take my town of Elmina?"

Mr. Goodenough explained that he had been nine months absent from the coast, and that having come straight out from England, he was altogether unaware of what had happened at Elmina.

"Elmina is mine," the king said. "The Dutch, who were my tributaries, had no right to hand it over to the English."

"But I understood, your majesty, that the English were ready to pay an annual sum, even larger than that which the Dutch have contributed."

"I do not want money," the king said. "I have gold in plenty. There are places in my dominions where ten men in a day can wash a thousand ounces. I want Elmina; I want to trade with the coast."

"But the English will give your majesty every facility for trade."

"But suppose we quarrel," the king said; "they can stop

powder and guns from coming up. If Elmina were mine I could bring up guns and powder at all times."

"Your majesty would be no better off," Mr. Goodenough said; "for the English in case of war could stop supplies from entering."

"My people will drive them into the sea," the king said. "We have been troubled with them too long. They can make guns, but they cannot fight. My people will eat them up. We fought them before; and see," he said pointing to a great drum, from the edge of which hung a dozen human skulls, "the heads of the white men serve to make a fetish for me." He then waved his hand to signify that the audience was terminated.

"Things look bad, Frank," Mr. Goodenough said, as they walked towards their home. "I fear that the king is determined upon war, and if so, our lives are not worth a month's purchase."

"It can't be helped," Frank said, as cheerfully as he could. "We must make the best of it. Perhaps something may occur to improve our position."

The next day the four German missionaries, who had so long been kept captive, called upon them, and they obtained a full insight into the position. This seemed more hopeful than the king's words had given them to expect. The missionaries said that negotiations were going on for their release, and that they expected very shortly to be sent down to Cape Coast. So far as they knew everything was being done by the English to satisfy the king, and they looked upon the establishment of peace as certain. They described the horrible rites and sacrifices which they had been compelled to witness, and said that at least three thousand persons were slaughtered annually in Coomassie.

"You noticed," one of them said, "the great tree in the market-place under which the king sat. That is the great fetish tree. A great many victims are sacrificed in the palace itself, but the wholesale slaughters take place there. The high brushwood comes up to within twenty yards of it, and if you turn in there you will see thousands of dead bodies or their remains putrefying together."

"I thought I felt a horribly offensive smell as I was talking to the king," Frank said shuddering. "What monsters these people must be! Who would have thought that all that show of gold and silver and silks and bright colours covered such horrible barbarism!"

After chatting for some time longer, and offering to do anything in their power to assist the captives, the Germans took their leave.

CHAPTER XVII

THE INVASION OF FANTI LAND

THE following morning Mr. Goodenough and Frank were called to the door by the noise of a passing crowd, and to their horror saw a man being taken to sacrifice. He was preceded by men beating drums his hands were pinioned behind him. A sharp thin knife was passed through his cheeks, to which his lips were noozed like the figure ∞. One ear was cut off and carried before him, the other hung to his head by a small piece of skin. There were several gashes in his back, and a knife was thrust under each shoulder blade. He was led by a cord passed through a hole bored in his nose. Frank ran horror-stricken back into the house, and sat for a while with his hand over his eyes as if to shut out the ghastly spectacle.

"Mr. Goodenough," he said presently, "if we are to be killed, at least let us die fighting to the last, and blow out our own brains with the last shots we have left. I don't think I'm afraid of being killed, but to be tortured like that would be horrible."

The next day a message was brought them that their retaining private guards was an insult to the king, and that the Houssas must remove to another part of the town. Resistance was evidently useless. Mr. Goodenough called his four men together and told them what had happened. "I am sorry I have brought you into this plight, my poor fellows," he said. "There are now but two things open to you. You can either volunteer to join the king's army and then try to make your escape as an opportunity may offer, or slip away at once. You are accustomed to the woods, and in native costume might pass without notice. You can all swim, and it matters not where you strike the Prah. If you travel at night and lie in the woods by day, you should be able to get through. At anyrate you know that if you try to escape and are caught you will be killed. If you stop here it is possible that no harm may happen to you, but on the other hand, you may at any moment be led out to sacrifice. Do not tell me your decision; I shall be questioned, and would rather be able to say that I was ignorant that you intended to escape. There is one other thing to settle. There is a long arrear of pay due to you for your good and faithful service. It would be useless for me to pay you now, as the money might be found on you and taken away, and if you should be killed it would be lost to your friends. I have written here four orders on my banker in England, which the agents down at Cape Coast will readily cash for you. Each order is for twice the sum due to you. As you have come into such great danger in my service, and have behaved so faithfully, it is right that you should be well rewarded. Give me the names of your wives or relatives whom you would wish to have the money. Should any of you fall and I escape, I will, on my arrival at Cape Coast, send money, double the amount I have written here, to them."

The men expressed themselves warmly grateful for Mr. Goodenough's kindness, gave him the names and addresses of their wives, and then, with tears in their eyes, took their leave.

"Now, Ostik, what do you say?" Mr. Goodenough asked, turning to him.

"I stay here, sar," Ostik said. "Houssas fighting men, creep through wood, crawl on stomach. Dey get through sure enough. Ostik stay with massa. If dey kill massa, dey kill Ostik. Ostik take chance."

"Very well, Ostik, if we get through safe together you shall not have reason to regret your fidelity. Now, Frank, I think it would be a good thing if you were to spend some hours every day in trying to pick up as much of the language here as you can. You are quick at it, and were able to make yourself understood by our bearers far better than I could do. You already know a great many words in four or five of these dialects. They are all related to each other, and with what you know you would in a couple of months be able to get along very well in Ashanti. It will help to pass your time and to occupy your mind. There will be no difficulty in finding men here who have worked down on the coast and know a little English.

If we get away safely you will not regret that your time has been employed. If we have trouble your knowledge of the language may in some way or other be of real use to you. We can go round to the Germans, who will, no doubt, be able to put you in the way of getting a man."

The next day they were again sent for to the king, who was in a high state of anger at having heard that the Houssas had escaped.

"I know nothing about it," Mr. Goodenough said. "They were contented when they were with me, and had no wish to go. Your soldiers took them away yesterday afternoon, and I suppose they were frightened. It was foolish of them. They should have known that a great king does not injure travellers who come peacefully into his country. They should have known better. They were poor, ignorant men, who did not know that the hospitality of a king is sacred, and that when a king invites travellers to enter his country they are his guests, and under his protection."

When the interpreter translated this speech, the king was silent for two or three minutes. Then he said, "My white friend is right. They were foolish men. They could not know these things. If my warriors overtake them no harm shall come to them."

Pleased with the impression that his words had evidently made Mr. Goodenough returned to Frank, who had not been ordered to accompany him to the palace. In the afternoon the king sent a sheep and a present of five ounces of gold, and a message that he did not wish his white friends to remain always in the town, but that they might walk to any of the villages within a circle of three or four miles, and that four of his guards would always accompany them to see that no one interfered with or insulted them. They were much pleased with this permission, as they were now enabled to renew their work of collecting. It took them, too, away from the sight of the horrible human sacrifices which went on daily. Through the German missionaries they obtained a man who had worked for three years down at Cape Coast. He accompanied them on their walks, and in the evening sat and talked with Frank, who, from the knowledge of native words which he had picked up in his nine months' residence in Africa, was able to make rapid progress in Ashanti. He had one or two slight attacks of fever, but the constant use of quinine enabled him to resist their effect, and he was now to some degree acclimatized, and thought no more of the attacks of fever than he would have done at home of a violent bilious attack. This was not the case with Mr. Goodenough. Frank observed with concern that he lost strength rapidly, and was soon unable to accompany him in his walks. One morning he appeared very ill.

"Have you a touch of fever, sir?"

"No, Frank, it is worse than fever, it is dysentery. I had an attack last time I was on the coast, and know what to do with it. Get the medicine chest and bring me the bottle of ipecacuanha. Now, you must give me doses of this just strong enough not to act as an emetic, every three hours."

Frank nursed his friend assiduously, and for the next three days hoped that he was obtaining a mastery over the illness. On the fourth day an attack of fever set in.

"You must stop the ipecacuanha, now," Mr. Goodenough said, "and, Frank, send Ostik round to the Germans, and say I wish them to come here at once."

When these arrived, Mr. Goodenough asked Frank to leave him alone with them. A quarter of an hour later they went out, and Frank, returning, found two sealed envelopes on the table beside him.

"My boy," he said, "I have been making my will. I fear that it is all over with me. Fever and dysentery together are in nine cases out of ten fatal. Don't cry, Frank," he said, as the lad burst into tears. "I would gladly have lived, but if it is God's will that it should be otherwise, so be it. I have no wife or near relatives to regret my loss—none, my poor boy, who will mourn for me as sincerely as I know that you will do. In the year that we have been together I have come to look upon you as my son, and you will find that I have not forgotten you in my will. I have written it in duplicate. If you have an opportunity, send one of these letters down to the coast. Keep the other yourself, and I trust that you will live to carry it to its destination. Should it not be so, should the worst come to the

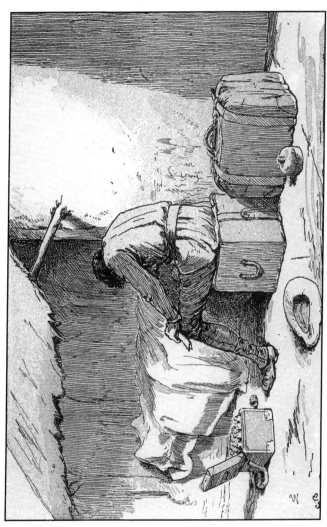

THE DEATH OF MR. GOODENOUGH.

worst, it will be a consolation to you to know that I have not forgotten the little sister of whom you have spoken to me so often, and that in case of your death, she will be provided for."

An hour later Mr. Goodenough was in a state of delirium, in which he remained all night, falling towards morning into a dull coma, gradually breathing his last, without any return of sensibility, at eight in the morning.

Frank was utterly prostrated with grief, from which he roused himself to send to the king to ask permission to bury his friend. The king sent down to say how grieved he was to hear of the white man's death. He had ordered many of his warriors to attend his funeral. Frank had a grave dug on a rising spot of ground beyond the marsh. In the evening a great number of the warriors gathered round the house, and upon the shoulders of four of them Mr. Goodenough was conveyed to his last resting-place, Frank and the German missionaries following with a great crowd of warriors. The missionaries read the service over the grave, and Frank returned heart-broken to his house, with Ostik, who also felt terribly the loss of his master.

Two days later a wooden cross was erected over the grave. Upon this Frank carved the name of his friend. Hearing a week afterwards that the king was sending down a messenger to Cape Coast, Frank asked permission to send Mr. Goodenough's letter by him. The king sent for him.

"I do not wish any more troubles," he said, "or that letters should be sent to the governor. You are my guest. When the troubles are settled, I will send you down to the coast; but we have many things to write about, and I do not want more subjects for talk."

Frank showed the letter and read the address, and told the king that it was only a letter to the man of business of Mr. Goodenough in England, giving directions for the disposal of his property there.

The king then consented that his messenger should take the letter.

At the end of December, when Frank had been nearly three months at Coomassie, one of the Germans said to him:

"The king speaks fairly, and seems intent upon his negotiations; but he is preparing secretly for war. An army is collecting on the Prah. I hear that twelve thousand men are ordered to assemble there."

"I have noticed," Frank said, "that there have been fewer men about than usual during the last few days. What will happen to us, do you think?"

The missionary shook his head.

"No one can say," he said. "It all depends upon the king's humour. I think, however, that he is more likely to keep us as hostages, and to obtain money for us at the end of the war, than to kill us. If all goes well with his army, we are probably safe; but if the news comes of any defeat, he may in his rage order us to be executed."

"What do you think are the chances of defeat?" Frank asked.

"We know not," the missionary said; "but it seems probable that the Ashantis will turn the English out of the coast. The Fantis are of no use. They were a brave people once, and united might have made a successful resistance to the Ashantis; but you English have made women of them. You have forbidden them to fight among themselves, you have discouraged them in any attempts to raise armies, you have reduced the power of the chiefs, you have tried to turn them into a race of cultivators and traders instead of warriors, and you can expect no material aid from them now. They will melt away like snow before the Ashantis. The king's spies tell him that there are only a hundred and fifty black troops at Cape Coast. These are trained and led by Englishmen, but, after all, they are only natives, no braver than the Ashantis. What chance have they of resisting an army nearly a hundred to one stronger than themselves?"

"Is the fort at Cape Coast strong?" Frank asked.

"Yes, against savages without cannon. Besides, the guns of the ships of war would cover it."

"Well," Frank said, "if we can hold that, they will send out troops from England."

"They may do so," the missionary asserted; "but what could

white troops do in the fever-haunted forests, which extend from Coomassie to the coast?"

"They will manage somehow," Frank replied confidently. "Besides, after all, as I hear that the great portion of Ashanti lying beyond this is plain and open country, the Ashantis themselves cannot be all accustomed to bush fighting, and will suffer from fever in the low, swamp land."

Three days later the king sent for Frank.

"The English are not true," he said angrily. "They promised the people of Elmina that they should be allowed to retain all their customs as under the Dutch. They have broken their word. They have forbidden the customs. The people of Elmina have written to me to ask me to deliver them. I am going to do so."

Frank afterwards learned that the king's words were true, Colonel Harley, the military commandant, having, with almost incredible fatuity, and in spite of the agreement which had been made with the Elminas, summoned their king and chiefs to a council, and abruptly told them that they would not be allowed henceforth to celebrate their customs, which consisted of firing of guns, waving of flags, dancing, and other harmless rites. The chiefs, greatly indignant at this breach of the agreement, solemnly entered into with them, at once, on leaving the council, wrote to the King of Ashanti, begging him to cross the Prah and attack the English. Frank could only say that he knew nothing of what was going on at the coast, and could only think that his majesty must have been misinformed, as the English wished to be friendly with the Ashantis.

"They do not wish it," the king said furiously; "they are liars!"

A buzz of approval sounded among the cabooceers and captains standing round. Frank thought that he was about to be ordered to instant execution, and grasped a revolver, which he held in his pocket, resolving to shoot the king first, and then to blow out his own brains, rather than to be put to the horrible tortures which in Ashanti always precede death.

Presently the king said suddenly to him:

"My people tell me that you can talk to them in their own tongue."

"I have learnt a little Ashanti," Frank said in that language. "I cannot talk well, but I can make myself understood."

"Very well," the king said. "Then I shall send you down with my general. You know the ways of English fighting, and will tell him what is best to do against them. When the war is over and I have driven the English away, I will send you away also. You are my guest, and I do not wish to harm you. Tomorrow you will start. Your goods will be of no more use to you. I have ordered my treasurer to count the cloth, and the powder, and the other things which you have, and to pay you for them in gold. You may go."

Frank retired, vowing in his heart that no information as to the best way of attacking the English should be obtained from him. Upon the whole he was much pleased at the order, for he thought that some way of making his escape might present itself. Such was also the opinion of Ostik when Frank told him what had taken place at the palace. An hour later the king's treasurer arrived. The whole of the trade goods were appraised at fair prices, and even the cases were paid for, as the treasurer said that these would be good for keeping the king's state robes. Frank only retained his own portmanteau with his clothes, his bed and rugs, and the journals of the expedition, a supply of ammunition for his revolver, his medicine chest, tent, and a case with chocolate, preserved milk, tea, biscuits, rice, and a couple of bottles of brandy.

In the morning there was a great beating of drums. Four carriers had been told off for Frank's service, and these came in, took up his baggage, and joined the line. Frank waited till the general, Ammon Quatia, whom he had several times met at the place, came along, carried in a hammock, with a paraphernalia of attendants bearing chairs, umbrellas, and flags. Frank fell in behind these accompanied by Ostik. The whole population of Coomassie turned out and shouted their farewells. There was a pause in the marketplace while a hundred victims were sacrificed to the success of the expedition. Frank kept in the thick of the warriors so as to avoid witnessing the horrible spectacle. As they passed the king he said to the general, "Bring me back the head of the governor. I will place it on my drum by the side of that of Macarthy."

Then the army passed the swamp knee-deep in water, and started on their way down to the Prah. Three miles further they crossed the river Dah at Agogo, where the water was up to their necks. The road was little more than a track through the forest, and many small streams had to be crossed.

It was well that Frank had not had an attack of fever for some time, for they marched without a stop to Fomanse, a distance of nearly thirty miles. Fomanse was a large town. Many of the houses were built in the same style as those at Coomassie, and the king's palace was a stone building. That night Frank slept in a native house which the general allotted to him close to the palace. The army slept on the ground. The next morning they crossed a lofty hill, and then descending again kept along through the forest until, late in the afternoon, they arrived on the Prah. This river was about sixty yards wide, and here, in roughly made huts of boughs, were encamped the main army, who had preceded them. Here there was a pause for a week while large numbers of carriers came down with provisions. Then on the 22d of January the army crossed the Prah in great canoes of cotton-wood tree, which the troops who first arrived had prepared.

Had the Ashanti army now pushed forward at full speed, Cape Coast and Elmina must have fallen into their hands, for there were no preparation whatever for their defence. The Assims, whose territory was first invaded, sent down for assistance, but Mr. Hennessey refused to believe that there was any invasion at all, and when the King of Akim, the most powerful of the Fanti potentates, sent down to ask for arms and ammunition, Mr. Hennessey refused so curtly that the King of Akim was grievously offended, and sent at once to the Ashantis to say that he should remain neutral in the war.

About this time Mr. Hennessey, whose repeated blunders had in no slight degree contributed to the invasion, was relieved by Mr. Keate, who at once wholly alienated the Fantis by telling them that they must defend themselves, as the English had nothing more to do with the affair than to defend their forts. Considering that the English had taken the natives under their protection, and that the war was caused entirely by the taking over of Elmina by the English and by their breach of faith to the natives there, this treatment of the Fantis was as unjust as it was impolitic.

Ammon Quatia, however, seemed to be impressed with a spirit of prudence as soon as he crossed the river. Parties were sent out, indeed, who attacked and plundered the Assim villages near the Prah, but the main body moved forward with the greatest caution, sometimes halting for weeks.

The Ashanti general directed Frank always to pitch his tent next to the hut occupied by himself. Four guards were appointed, nominally to do him honour, but really, as Frank saw, to prevent him from making his escape. These men kept guard, two at a time, night and day over the tent, and if he moved out, all followed him. He never attempted to leave the camp. The forest was extremely dense with thick underwood and innumerable creepers, through which it would be almost impossible to make a way. The majority of the trees were of only moderate height, but above them towered the cotton trees and other giants, rising with straight stems to from two hundred and fifty to three hundred feet high. Many of the trees had shed their foliage, and some of these were completely covered with brilliant flowers of different colours. The woods resounded with the cries of various birds, but butterflies, except in the clearings, were scarce. The army depended for food partly upon the cultivated patches around the Assim villages, partly on supplies brought up from the rear. In the forest, too, they found many edible roots and fruits. In spite of the efforts to supply them with food, Frank saw ere many weeks had passed that the Ashantis were suffering much from hunger. They fell away in flesh. Many were shaking with fever, and the enthusiasm, which was manifest at the passage of the Prah, had entirely evaporated.

The first morning after crossing the river, Frank sent Ostik into the hut of the general with a cup of hot chocolate, with which Ammon Quatia expressed himself so much gratified that henceforth Frank sent in a cup every morning, having still a large supply of tins of preserved chocolate and milk, the very best food which a traveller can take with him. In return the Ashanti general showed

Frank many little kindnesses, sending him in birds or animals when any were shot by his men, and keeping him as well provided with food as was possible under the circumstances.

It was not until the 8th of April that any absolute hostilities took place. Then the Fantis, supported by fifty Houssas under Lieutenant Hopkins, barred the road outside the village of Dunquah. The Ashantis attacked, but the Fantis fought bravely, having great confidence in the Houssa contingent. The battle was one of the native fashion, neither side attempting any vigorous action, but contenting themselves with a heavy fire at a distance of a hundred yards. All the combatants took shelter behind trees, and the consequence was that at the end of the day a great quantity of powder and slugs had been fired away, and a very few men hit on either side. At nightfall both parties drew off.

"Is that the way your English soldiers fight?" the general asked Frank that night.

"Yes," Frank said vaguely; "they fire away at each other."

"And then I suppose," the general said, "when one party has exhausted its ammunition, it retires."

"Certainly it would retire," Frank said. "It could not resist without ammunition, you know."

Frank carefully abstained from mentioning that one side or the other would advance even before the ammunition of its opponents was expended, for he did not wish the Ashantis to adopt tactics which, from their greatly superior numbers, must at once give them a victory. The Ashantis were not dissatisfied with the day's work, as they considered that they had proved themselves equal to the English troops.

CHAPTER XVIII

THE ATTACK ON ELMINA

ON the 14th the Fantis took the initiative, and attacked the Ashantis. The fight was a mere repetition of that of a week before, and about mid-day the Fantis, having used up all their ammunition, fell back again to Cape Coast.

"Now," the general said to Frank, "that we have beaten the Fantis we shall march down to Elmina."

Leaving the main road at Dunquah the army moved slowly through the bush towards Elmina, thirty miles distant, halting in the woods some eight miles from the town, and twelve from Cape Coast.

"I am going," the general said, "to look at the English forts. My white friend will go with me."

With fifty of his warriors Ammon Quatia left the camp, and, crossing a stream came down upon the sea-coast, a short distance west of Elmina. With them were several of the Elmina tribe, who had come up to the camp to welcome the Ashantis. They approached to within three or four hundred yards of the fort, which was separated from them by a river.

The forts on the west coast of Africa, not being built to resist artillery, are merely barracks surrounded by high walls sufficiently thick to allow men to walk in single file along the top, to fire over the parapet. The tops of the walls being castellated, the buildings have an appearance of much strength. The fort of Elmina is of considerable size, with a barrack and officers' quarters within it. One side faces the river, and another the sea.

"It is a wonderful fort," the Ashanti general said, much impressed by its appearance.

"Yes," Frank replied. "And there are cannon on the top, those great black things you see sticking out. Those are guns, and each carries balls enough to kill a hundred men with each shot."

The general looked for some time attentively. "But you have castles in the white men's country, how do you take them?"

"We bring a great many cannon throwing balls of iron as big as my head," Frank answered, "and so knock a great hole in the wall and then rush in."

"But if there are no cannon?" the general urged.

"We never attack a castle without cannon," Frank said. "But if we had no cannon we might try to starve the people out; but you cannot do that here, because they would land food from the sea."

The general looked puzzled. "Why do the white men come here? They come to trade," he said presently.

"Yes, they come to trade," Frank replied.

"And they have no other reason?"

"No," Frank said. "They do not want to take land, because the white man cannot work in so hot a climate."

"Then if he could not trade he would go away?" the general asked.

"Yes," Frank agreed, "if he could do no trade it would be no use remaining here."

"We will let him do no trade," the general said, brightening up. "If we cannot take the forts we will surround them closely, and no trade can come in and out. Then the white man will have to go away. As to the Fantis we will destroy them, and the white men will have no one to fight for them."

"But there are white troops," Frank said.

"White soldiers?" the Ashanti asked surprised. "I thought it was only black soldiers that fought for the whites. The whites are few, they are traders."

"The English are many," Frank said earnestly. "For every man that the King of Ashanti could send to fight, England could send ten. There are white soldiers, numbers of them, but they are not sent here. They are kept at home to fight other white nations, the French and the Dutch and the Danes, and many others, just as the

188

kings of Africa fight against each other. They are not sent here because the climate kills the whites, so to guard the white traders here we hire black soldiers; but, when it is known in England that the King of Ashanti is fighting against our forts, they will send white troops."

Ammon Quatia was thoughtful for some time. "If they come," he said at length, "the fevers will kill them. The white man cannot live in the swamps. Your friend, the white guest of the king, died at Coomassie."

"Yes," Frank asserted, "but he had been nearly a year in the country before he died. Three weeks will be enough for an English army to march from Cape Coast to Coomassie. A few might die, but most of them would get there."

"Coomassie!" the general exclaimed in surprise. "The white men would be mad to think of marching against the city of the great king. We should make great fetish, and they would all die when they had crossed the river."

"I don't think, General," Frank said dryly, "that the fetishes of the black man have any effect upon the white men. A fetish has power when it is believed in. A man who knows that his enemy has made a fetish against him is afraid. His blood becomes like water and he dies. But the whites do not believe in fetishes. They laugh at them, and then the fetishes cannot hurt them."

The general said no more, but turned thoughtfully and retired to his camp. It was tantalizing to Frank to see the Union Jack waving within sight, and to know that friends were so near and yet to be unable to stretch out his hand to them. He was now dressed in all respects like a native, the king having, soon after his arrival at Coomassie, sent a present of clothes such as were worn by his nobles, saying that the people would not notice them so much if they were dressed like themselves. Consequently, had the party been seen from the castle walls the appearance of an Englishman among them would have been unobserved. Three days later the general with a similar party crossed the Sweet river at night, and proceeded along the sea-coast to within a few hundred yards of Cape Coast Castle, whose appearance pleased him no more than that of Elmina had done.

The Ashantis were now better supplied with food, as they were able to depend upon the Elmina tribes who cultivated a considerable extent of ground, and to add to the stock, the Ashanti soldiers were set to work to aid in planting a larger extent of ground than usual, a proof in Frank's mind that the general contemplated making a long stay, and blockading Elmina and Cape Coast into surrender if he could not carry them by assault.

The natives of Africa are capable of great exertion for a time, but their habitual attitude is that of extreme laziness. One week's work in the year suffices to plant a sufficient amount of ground to supply the wants of a family. The seed only requires casting into the earth, and soon the ground will be covered with melons and pumpkins. Sweet potatoes and yams demand no greater cultivation, and the bananas and plantains require simply to be cut. For fifty-one weeks in the year the natives simply sits down and watches his crops grow. To people like these time is of absolutely no value. Their wants are few. Their garden furnishes them with tobacco. They make drink from the palm or by fermenting the juice of the cocoanut. The fowls that wander about in the clearings suffice, when carried down occasionally to the port, to pay for the few yards of calico and strings of beads which are all that is necessary for the clothing and decoration of a family. Such people are never in a hurry. To wait means to do nothing. To do nothing is their highest joy. Their tomorrow means a month hence, directly, a week. If, then, the Ashanti army had been detained for one year or five before the English settlements, it would have been a matter of indifference to them, so long as they could obtain food. Their women were with them, for the wife and daughters of each warrior had carried on their head, with the army, his household goods, a tiny stool, a few calabashes for cooking, a mat to sleep on, and baskets piled high with provisions. They were there to collect sticks, to cook food, draw water, bring fire for his pipe, minister to his pleasures. He could have no more if he were at home, and was contented to wait as long as the king ordered, were that time years distant.

Frank was often filled with disgust at seeing these noble warriors lying indolently from morn till night while their wives went miles in the forest searching for pineapples and fruits, bent down and prematurely aged by toil and hardship. Many of the young girls among the natives are pretty, with their soft eyes and skin like velvet, their merry laugh and graceful figures. But in a very few years all this disappears, and by middle age they are bent, and wrinkled, and old. All loads are carried by women, with the exception only of hammocks, which are exclusively carried by men. Thus, then, the Ashantis settled down to what appeared to Frank to be an interminable business, and what rendered it more tantalizing was, that the morning and evening guns at the English forts could be plainly heard.

It was on the 7th of June that Ammon Quatia reconnoitred Elmina, and the news came next day that a hundred and ten white men in red coats had landed from a ship which had arrived that morning off the coast. Frank judged from the description that these must be marines from a ship of war. In this he was correct, as they consisted of marines and marine artillery-men under Lieutenant-colonel Festing, who had just arrived from England. Three days later the Ashanti general, with a portion of his force, moved down close to Elmina; Frank was told to accompany them. Shortly afterwards the news came that the Elminas were all ordered to lay down their arms. They replied by going over in a body to the Ashantis. Ammon Quatia determined at once to attack the town, but as he was advancing, the guns of the ships of war opened fire upon the native town of Elmina, which lay to the west of the European quarter.

The sound of such heavy cannon, differing widely from anything they had ever heard before, caused the Ashantis to pause in astonishment. Then came the howl of the shells, which exploded in rapid succession in the village, from which flames began immediately to rise. After a few minutes' hesitation the Ashantis and Elminas again advanced. The general, who was carried in a chair upon the shoulders of four men, took his post on rising ground near the burning village.

"There," he said, "the English soldiers are coming out of the fort. Now you will see."

The little body of marines and the blue-jackets of the *Barra-conta* deployed in line as they sallied from the fort. The Ashantis opened fire upon them, but they were out of range of the slugs. As soon as the line was formed the English opened fire, and the Ashantis were perfectly astonished at the incessant rattle of musketry from so small a body of men. But it was not all noise, for the Snider bullets swept among the crowded body of blacks, mowing them down in considerable numbers. In two minutes the Ashantis turned and ran. The general's bearers, in spite of his shouts, hurried away with him with the others, and Frank would have taken this opportunity to escape had not two of his guards seized him by the arms and hauled him along, while the other two kept close behind.

As soon as they had passed over the crest of the rise, and the British fire had ceased, Ammon Quatia leaped from his chair and threw himself among his flying troops, striking them right and left with his staff, and hurling imprecations upon them.

"If you do not stop and return against the whites," he said, "I will send every one of you back to Coomassie, and there you will be put to death as cowards."

The threat sufficed. The fugitives rallied, and in a few minutes were ready to march back again. It was the surprise created by the wonderful sustained fire of the breech-loaders, rather than the actual loss they inflicted, which caused the panic. In the meantime, believing that the Ashantis had retired, the naval contingent went back to their boats, when the Dutch vice-consul, having ascended a hill to look round, saw that Ammon Quatia had made a detour with his troops, and was marching against the town from the east, where he would not be exposed to the fire of the fort. He instantly ran back with the news. The marines and the thirty West Indian soldiers in the fort at once marched out, and met the Ashantis just as they were entering the town. The fight was a severe one, and for a time neither side appeared to have the advantage, and Frank, who, under the care of his guards, was a few hundred yards in the rear, was filled with dismay at observing that the Ashantis, in spite of the heavy loss they were suffering, were gaining ground and pressing forward bravely. Suddenly he gave a shout of joy, for on a rise on the flank of the Ashantis appeared the sailors of the *Barraconta*, who had been led round from the boats by Lieutenant Wells, R.N., who was in command. The instant these took up their position they opened a heavy fire upon the flank of the Ashantis, who, dismayed by this attack by fresh foes, lost heart and at once fled hastily. In the two engagements they had lost nearly four hundred men. Frank, of course, retired with the beaten Ashantis, and that evening Ammon Quatia told him that the arms of the white men were too good, and that he should not attack them again in the open.

"Their guns shoot farther, as well as quicker, than ours," he said. "Our slugs are no use against the heavy bullets, at a distance; but in the woods, where you cannot see twenty feet among the trees, it will be different. If I do not attack them, they must attack me, or their trade will be starved out. When they come into the woods you will see that we shall eat them up."

Several weeks now passed quietly. There was news that there was great sickness among the white soldiers, and, indeed, with scarce an exception, the marines first sent out were invalided home; but a hundred and fifty more arrived to take their place. Some detachments of the 2d West Indian regiment came down to join their comrades from Sierra Leone, and the situation remained unchanged.

One night towards the end of August a messenger arrived and there was an immediate stir.

"Now," the general said to Frank, "you are going to see us fight the white men. Some of the big ships have gone to the mouth of the Prah, and we believe that they are going to land in boats. You will see. The Elmina tribes are going to attack, but I shall take some of my men to help."

Taking fifty picked warriors, Ammon Quatia started at once. They marched all night towards the west, and at daybreak joined the Elminas. These took post in the brushwood lining the river. The general, with a dozen men, taking Frank, went down near the mouth of the river to reconnoitre. The ships lay more than a mile off the shore. Presently a half-dozen boats were lowered, filled with men, and taken in tow by a steam launch. It was seen that they were making for the mouth of the river.

"Now let us go back," Ammon Quatia said. "You will see what we shall do."

Frank felt full of excitement. He saw the English running into an ambuscade, and he determined, even if it should cost him his life, to warn them. Presently they heard the sharp puffs of the steam launch. The boats were within three hundred yards.

Frank stepped forward and was about to give a warning shout when Ammon Quatia's eye fell upon him. The expression of his face revealed his intention to the Ashanti, who in an instant sprang upon him and hurled him to the ground. Instantly a dozen hands seized him, and, in obedience to the general's order, fastened a bandage tightly across his mouth, and then bound him, standing against a tree, where he could observe what was going on. The incident had occupied but a minute, and Frank heard the pant of the steam launch coming nearer and nearer. Presently through the bushes he caught a glimpse of it, and then, as it came along, of the boats towing behind. The Elminas and Ashantis were lying upon the ground with their guns in front of them.

The boats were but fifteen yards from the bank. When they were abreast Ammon Quatia shouted the word of command, and a stream of fire shot out from the bushes. In the boats all was confusion. Several were killed and many wounded by the deadly volley, among the latter Commodore Commerell himself, and two or three of his officers. The launch now attempted to turn round, and the marines in the boats opened fire upon their invisible foes, who replied steadily. In five minutes from the first shot being fired all was over, the launch was steaming down with the boats in tow towards the mouth of the river, the exulting shouts of the natives ringing in the ears of those on board.

The position of Frank had not been a pleasant one while the fight had lasted, for the English rifle-bullets sang close to him in quick succession, one striking the tree only a few inches above his head. He was doubtful, too, as to what his fate would be at the termination of the fight.

Fortunately Ammon Quatia was in the highest spirits at his victory. He ordered Frank to be, at once, unbound. "There, you see," he said, "the whites are of no use. They cannot fight. They run with their eyes shut into danger. So it will be if they attack us on the land. You were foolish. Why did you wish to call out? Are you not well treated? Are you not the king's guest? Am I not your friend?"

"I am well treated, and you are my friend," Frank said, "but the English are my countrymen. I am sure that were you in the hands of the English, and you saw a party of your countrymen marching into danger, you would call out and warn them, even if you knew that you would be killed for doing so."

"I do not know," the Ashanti said candidly. "I cannot say what I should do, but you were brave to run the risk, and I'm not angry with you. Only, in future when we go to attack the English, I must gag you to prevent your giving the alarm."

"That is fair enough," Frank said, pleased that the matter had passed off so well, "only another time do not stick me upright against a tree where I may be killed by English bullets. I had a narrow escape of it this time, you see," and he pointed to the hole in the trunk of the tree.

"I am sorry," the Ashanti general said, with an air of real concern. "I did not think of your being in danger; I only wished you to have a good sight of the battle, next time I will put you in a safer place." They then returned to the camp.

The next day a distant cannonade was heard, and, at night-fall the news came that the English fleet had bombarded and burnt several Elmina villages at the mouth of the Prah.

"Ah," the general said, "the English have great ships and great guns. They can fight on the sea-side and round their forts, but they cannot drag their guns through the forests and swamps."

"No," Frank agreed. "It would not be possible to drag heavy artillery."

"No," Ammon Quatia repeated exultingly. "When they are

beyond the shelter of their ships they are no good whatever. We will kill them all."

The wet season had now set in in earnest, and the sufferings of the Ashantis were very great. Accustomed as many of them were to high-lying lands free of trees, the miasma from the swamps was well nigh as fatal to them as it would be to Europeans. Thousands died, and many of the rest were worn by fever to mere shadows.

"Do you think," Ammon Quatia said to Frank one day, "that it is possible to blow up a whole town with powder?"

"It would be possible if there were powder enough," Frank said, wondering what could be the motive of the question.

"They say that the English have put powder in holes all over Cape Coast, and my people are afraid to go. The guns of the fort could not shoot over the whole town, and there are few white soldiers there; but my men fear to be blown up in the air."

"Yes," Frank said gravely. "The danger might be great. It is better that the Ashantis should keep away from the town. But if the fever goes on as at present, the army will melt away."

"Ten thousand more men are coming down when the rains are over. The king says that something must be done. There is talk in the English forts that more white troops are coming out from England. If this is so I shall not attack the towns, but shall wait for them to come into the woods for me. Then you will see."

"Do they say there are many troops?" Frank asked anxiously.

"No; they say only some white officers, but this is foolishness. What could white officers do without soldiers? As for the Fantis, they are cowards, they are only good to carry burdens and to hoe the ground. They are women and not men."

During this time, when the damp rose so thick and steaming that everything was saturated with it, Frank had a very sharp attack of fever, and was for a fortnight, just after the repulse of the attack on Elmina, completely prostrated. Such an attack would at his first landing have carried him off, but he was now getting acclimatized, and his supply of quinine was abundant. With its aid he saved a great many lives among the Ashantis, and many little presents in the way of fruit and birds did he receive from his patients.

"I wish I could let you go," the general said to him one day. "You are a good white man, and my soldiers love you for the pains you take going amongst them when they are sick, and giving them the medicine of the whites. But I dare not do it. As you know when the king is wroth the greatest tremble, and I dare not tell the king that I have let you go. Were it otherwise I would gladly do so. I have written to the king telling him that you have saved the lives of many here. It may be that he will order you to be released."

CHAPTER XIX

THE TIDE TURNED

FROM many of the points in the forest held by the Ashantis the sea could be seen, and on the morning of the 2d of October, a steamer which had not been there on the previous evening was perceived lying off the town. The Ashantis were soon informed by spies in Elmina and Cape Coast that the ship had brought an English general with about thirty officers. The news that thirty men had come out to help to drive back twenty thousand was received with derision by the Ashantis.

"They will do more than you think," Frank said when Ammon Quatia was scoffing over the new arrival. "You will see a change in the tactics of the whites. Hitherto they have done nothing. They have simply waited. Now you will see they will begin to move. The officers will drill the natives, and even a Fanti, drilled and commanded by white officers, will learn how to fight. You acknowledge that the black troops in red coats can fight. What are these? Some of them are Fantis, some of them are black men from the West Indian Islands, where they are even more peaceful than the Fantis, for they have no enemies. Perhaps alone the Fantis would not fight, but they will have the soldiers and sailors from on board ship with them, and you saw at Elmina how they can fight."

The ship was the *Ambriz*, one of the African company's steamers, bringing with it thirty-five officers, of whom ten belonged to the Commissariat and Medical staff. Among the fighting men were Sir Garnet Wolseley, Colonel M'Neill chief of his staff, Major T. D. Baker, 18th Regiment, Captain Huyshe, Rifle Brigade, Captain Buller, 60th Rifles, all of the staff; Captain Brackenbury, military secretary, and Lieutenant Maurice, R.A., private secretary, Major Home, R.E., Lieutenant Saunders, R.A., and Lieutenant Wilmot, R.A., Lieutenant-colonel Evelyn Wood, 90th Regiment, and Major B. C. Russell, 13th Hussars, were each to form and command a native regiment, having the remainder of the officers as their assistants.

The *Ambriz* had left England on the 12th of September, and had touched at Madeira and at the various towns on the coast on her way down, and at the former place had received the news of the disaster to the naval expedition up the Prah.

The English government had been loath to embark upon such an expedition, but a petition which had been sent home by the English and native traders at Sierra Leone and Elmina had shown how great was the peril which threatened the colony, and it had been felt that unless an effort was made the British would be driven altogether from their hold of the coast. When the expedition was at last determined upon, the military authorities were flooded with recommendations and warnings of all kinds from persons who knew the coast. Unfortunately these gentlemen differed so widely from each other, that but little good was gained from their counsels. Some pronounced the climate to be deadly. Others said that it was really not bad. Some warmly advocated a moderate use of spirits. Others declared that stimulants were poison. One advised that all exercise should be taken between five and seven in the morning. Another insisted that on no account should anyone stir out until the sun had been up for an hour, which meant that no one should go out till half-past seven. One said take exercise and excite perspiration. Another urged that any bodily exercise should be avoided. One consistent gentleman, after having written some letters to the papers strongly advocating the use of white troops upon the coast instead of West Indian regiments, when written to by Sir Garnet Wolseley for his advice as to articles of outfit, replied that the only article which he could strongly commend would be that each officer should take out his coffin.

Ten days passed after the landing. It was known in the Ashanti camp that the Fanti kings had been ordered to raise contingents, and that a white officer had been allotted to each to assist him in this work. The Ashantis, however, had no fear whatever on this score. The twenty thousand natives who occupied the country south of the Prah had all been driven from their homes by the invaders, and had scattered among the towns and villages on the sea-coast, where vast numbers had died from the ravages of small-pox. The kings had little or no authority over them, and it was certain that no native force, capable in any way of competing with the army of the assailants, could be raised.

The small number of men of the 2d West Indian regiment at Elmina had been reinforced by a hundred and twenty Houssas brought down the coast. The Ashanti advanced parties remained close up to Elmina.

On the 13th of October, Frank accompanied the Ashanti general to the neighbourhood of this town. The Ashanti force here was not a large one, the main body being nearly twenty miles away in the neighbourhood of Dunquah, which was held by a small body of Houssas and natives under Captain Gordon. At six in the morning a messenger ran in with the news that two of the English war steamers from Cape Coast were lying off Elmina, and that a number of troops had been landed in boats. The Ashanti general was furious, and poured out threats against his spies in Cape Coast for not having warned him of the movement, but in fact these were not to blame. So quietly had the arrangements been made that, until late in the previous afternoon, no one, with the exception of three or four of the principal officers, knew that an expedition was intended. Even then it was given out that the expedition was going down the coast, and it was not until the ships anchored off Elmina at three in the morning that the officers and troops were aware of their destination. All the West Indian troops at Cape Coast had been taken, Captain Peel of the *Simoon* landing fifty sailors to hold the fort in case the Ashantis should attack it in their absence. The expedition consisted of the Houssas, two hundred men of the 2d West India regiment, fifty sailors, and two companies of marines and marine artillery, each fifty strong, and a large number of natives carrying a small Armstrong gun, two rocket tubes, rockets, spare ammunition, and hammocks for wounded.

The few Ashantis in the village next to Elmina retired at once when the column was seen marching from the castle. Ammon

Quatia had taken up his quarters at the village of Essarman, and now advanced with his troops and took post in the bush behind a small village about three miles from the town. The Houssas were skirmishing in front of the column. These entered the village, which had been deserted by the Ashantis, and set it on fire, blowing up several kegs of powder which had been left there in the hurry of the flight. Then as they advanced farther the Ashantis opened fire. To their surprise the British, instead of falling back, opened fire in return, the Houssas, West Indians, and natives discharging their rifles at random in all directions. Captain Freemantle with the sailors, the gun, and rockets made for the upper corner of the wood facing them to their left. Captain Crease with a company of marine artillery took the wood on the right. The Houssas and a company of West Indians moved along the path in the centre. The remainder of the force remained with the baggage in reserve. The Ashantis kept up a tremendous fire, but the marines and sailors pushed their way steadily through the wood on either side. Captain Freemantle at length gained a point where his gun and rockets could play on Essarman, which lay in the heart of the wood, and opened fire, but not until he had been struck by a slug which passed through his arm. Colonel M'Neill who was with the Houssas, also received a severe wound in the arm, and thirty-two marines and Houssas were wounded. The Ashantis were gradually driven out of the village and wood, a great many being killed by the English fire.

Having accomplished this, the British force rested for an hour and then moved on, first setting fire to Essarman, which was a very large village. A great quantity of the Ashanti powder was stored there, and each explosion excited yells of rage among the Ashantis. Their general was especially angry that two large war drums had been lost. So great was the effect produced upon the Ashantis by the tremendous fire which the British had poured into every bush and thicket as they advanced, that their general thought it expedient to draw them off in the direction of his main body instead of further disputing the way.

The English now turned off towards the coast, marching part of the way through open country, part through a bush so dense that it was impossible to make a flank attack upon them here. In such cases as this, when the Ashantis know that an enemy is going to approach through a dense and impassable forest, they cut paths through it parallel to that by which he must advance and at a few yards' distance. Then, lying in ambush there, they suddenly open fire upon him as he comes along. As no idea of the coming of the English had been entertained they passed through the dense thickets in single file unmolested. These native paths are very difficult and unpleasant walking. The natives always walk in single file, and the action of their feet, aided by that of the rain, often wears the paths into a deep V-shaped rut, two feet in depth. Burning two or three villages by the way, the column reached the coast at a spot five miles from Elmina, having marched nine miles.

As the Ashantis were known to be in force at the villages of Akimfoo and Ampene, four miles farther, a party was taken on to this point. Akimfoo was occupied without resistance, but the Ashantis fought hard in Ampene, but were driven out of the town into the bush, from which the British force was too small to drive them, and therefore returned to Elmina, having marched twenty-two miles, a prodigious journey in such a climate for heavily armed Europeans. The effect produced among the Ashantis by the day's fighting was immense. All their theories that the white men could not fight in the bush were roughly upset, and they found that his superiority was as great there as it had been in the open. His heavy bullets, even at the distance of some hundred yards, crashed through the brushwood with deadly effect, while the slugs of the Ashantis would not penetrate at a distance much exceeding fifty yards.

Ammon Quatia was profoundly depressed in spirits that evening. "The white men who come to fight us," he said, "are not like those who come to trade. Who ever heard of their making long marches? Why, if they go the shortest distances, they are carried in hammocks. These men march as well as my warriors. They have guns which shoot ten times as far as ours, and never stop firing. They carry cannon with them, and have things which fly through the air and scream, and set villages on fire and kill men. I have never heard of such things before. What do you call them?"

"They are called rockets," Frank said.

"What are they made of?"

"They are made of coarse powder mixed with other things, and rammed into an iron case."

"Could we not make some, too?" the Ashanti general asked.

"No," Frank replied. "At least, not without a knowledge of the things you should mix with the powder, and of that I am ignorant. Besides, the rockets require great skill in firing, otherwise they will sometimes come back and kill the men who fire them."

"Why did you not tell me that the white men could fight in the bush?"

"I told you that there would be a change when the new general came, and that they would not any longer remain in their forts, but would come out and attack you."

A few days after this fight the Ashantis broke up their camp at Mampon, twelve miles from Elmina, and moved eastward to join the body who were encamped in the forest near Dunquah.

"I am going," Ammon Quatia said to Frank, "to eat up Dunquah and Abra Crampa. We shall do better this time. We know what the English guns can do and shall not be surprised."

With ten thousand men Ammon Quatia halted at the little village of Asianchi, where there was a large clearing, which was speedily covered with the little leafy bowers which the Ashantis run up at each halting-place.

Two days later Sir Garnet Wolseley with a strong force marched out from Cape Coast to Abra Crampa, halting on the way for a night at Assaiboo, ten miles from the town. On the same day the general sent orders to Colonel Festing of the Marine Artillery, who commanded at Dunquah, to make a reconnaisance into the forest from that place. In accordance with this order, Colonel Festing marched out with a gun and rocket apparatus under Captain Rait, the Annamaboe contingent of a hundred and twenty men under their king, directed by Captain Godwin, four hundred other Fantis under Captain Broomhead, and a hundred men of the 2d

West India regiment. After a three-mile march in perfect silence they came upon an Ashanti cutting wood, and compelled him to act as guide. The path divided into three, and the Annamaboes, who led the advance, when within a few yards of the camp, gave a sudden cheer and rushed in.

The Ashantis, panic-stricken at the sudden attack, fled instantly from the camp into the bush. Sudden as was the scare, Frank's guards did not forget their duty, but, seizing him, dragged him off with them in their flight, by the side of Ammon Quatia. The latter ordered the war drums to begin to beat, and Frank was surprised at the quickness with which the Ashantis recovered from their panic. In five minutes a tremendous fire was opened from the whole circle of bush upon the camp. This stood on rising ground, and the British force returned the fire with great rapidity and effect. The Annamaboe men stood their ground gallantly, and the West Indians fought with great coolness, keeping up a constant and heavy fire with their Sniders. The Houssas, who had been trained as artillerymen, worked their gun and rocket tube with great energy, yelling and whooping as each round of grape or canister was fired into the bush, or each rocket whizzed out.

Notwithstanding the heavy loss which they were suffering, the Ashantis stood their ground most bravely. Their wild yells and the beating of their drums never ceased, and only rose the louder as each volley of grape was poured into them. They did not, however, advance beyond the shelter of their bush, and, as the British were not strong enough to attack them there, the duel of artillery and musketry was continued without cessation for an hour and a half, and then Colonel Festing fell back unmolested to Dunquah.

The Ashantis were delighted at the result of the fighting, heavy as their loss had been. They had held their ground, and the British had not ventured to attack them in the bush.

"You see," Ammon Quatia said exultingly to Frank, "what I told you was true. The white men cannot fight us in the bush. At Essarman the wood was thin and gave but a poor cover. Here, you see, they dared not follow us."

On the British side five officers and the King of Annamaboe were wounded, and fifty-two of the men. None were killed, the distance from the bush to the ground held by the English being too far for the Ashanti slugs to inflict mortal wounds.

Ammon Quatia now began to meditate falling back upon the Prah—the sick and wounded were already sent back—but he determined before retiring to attack Abra Crampa, whose king had sided with us, and where an English garrison had been posted.

On the 2d of November, however, Colonel Festing again marched out from Dunquah with a hundred men of the 2d West India regiment, nine hundred native allies, and some Houssas with rockets, under Lieutenant Wilmot, towards the Ashanti camp. This time Ammon Quatia was not taken by surprise. His scouts informed him of the approach of the column, and moving out to meet them, he attacked them in the bush before they reached the camp. Crouching among the trees, the Ashantis opened a tremendous fire. All the native allies, with the exception of a hundred, bolted at once, but the remainder, with the Houssas and West Indians, behaved with great steadiness and gallantry, and for two hours kept up a heavy Snider fire upon their invisible foes.

Early in the fight Lieutenant Wilmot, while directing the rocket tube, received a severe wound in the shoulder. He, however, continued at his work till, just as the fight was ended, he was shot through the heart with a bullet. Four officers were wounded as were thirteen men of the 2d West Indian regiment. One of the natives was killed, fifty severely wounded, and a great many slightly. After two hours fighting, Colonel Festing found the Ashantis were working round to cut off his retreat, and therefore fell back again on Dunquah. The conduct of the native levies here and in two or three smaller reconnaisances was so bad that it was found that no further dependence could be placed upon them, and, with the exception of the two partly disciplined regiments under Colonel Wood and Major Russell, they were in future treated as merely fit to act as carriers for the provisions.

Although the second reconnaisance from Dunquah had, like the first, been unsuccessful, its effect upon the Ashantis was very great. They had themselves suffered great loss, while they could not see that any of their enemies had been killed, for Lieutenant Wilmot's body had been carried off. The rockets especially appalled them, one rocket having killed six, four of whom were chiefs who were talking together. It was true that the English had not succeeded in forcing their way through the bush, but if every time they came out they were to kill large numbers without suffering any loss themselves, they must clearly in the long run be victorious.

What the Ashantis did not see, and what Frank carefully abstained from hinting to Ammon Quatia, was that if, instead of stopping and firing at a distance beyond that at which their slugs were effective, they were to charge down upon the English and fire their pieces when they reached within a few yards of them, they would overpower them at once by their enormous superiority of numbers. At ten paces distant a volley of slugs is as effective as a Snider bullet, and the whole of the native troops would have bolted the instant such a charge was made. In the open such tactics might not be possible, as the Sniders could be discharged twenty times before the English line was reached, but in the woods, where the two lines were not more than forty or fifty yards apart, the Sniders could be fired but once or at the utmost twice, while the assailants rushed across the short intervening space.

Had the Ashantis adopted these tactics they could have crushed with ease the little bands with which the English attacked them. But it is characteristic of all savages that they can never be got to rush down upon a foe who is prepared and well armed. A half dozen white men have been known to keep a whole tribe of Red Indians at a distance on the prairie. This, however, can be accounted for by the fact that the power of the chiefs is limited, and that each Indian values his own life highly and does not care to throw it away on a desperate enterprise. Among the Ashantis, however, where the power of the chiefs is very great and where human life is held of little account, it is singular that such tactics should not have been adopted.

The Ashantis were now becoming thoroughly dispirited. Their sufferings had been immense. Fever and hunger had made great ravages among them, and although now the wet season was over a large quantity of food could be obtained in the forest, the losses which the white men's bullets, rockets, and guns had inflicted upon them had broken their courage. The longing for home became greater than ever, and had it not been that they knew that troops stationed at the Prah would prevent any fugitives from crossing, they would have deserted in large numbers. Already one of the divisions had fallen back.

Ammon Quatia spent hours sitting at the door of his hut smoking and talking to the other chiefs. Frank was often called into council, as Ammon Quatia had conceived a high opinion of his judgment, which had proved invariably correct so far.

"We are going," he said one day, "to take Abra Crampa and to kill its king, and then to fall back across the Prah."

"I think you had better fall back at once," Frank answered. "When you took me with you to the edge of the clearing yesterday I saw that preparations had been made for the defence, and that there were white troops there. You will never carry the village. The English have thrown up breast-works of earth, and they will lie behind these and shoot down your men as they come out of the forest."

"I must have one victory to report to the king if I can," Ammon Quatia said. "Then he can make peace if he chooses. The white men will not wish to go on fighting. The Fantis are eager for peace and to return to their villages. What do you think?"

"If it be true that white troops are coming out from England, as the Fanti prisoners say," Frank answered, "you will see that the English will not make peace till they have crossed the Prah and marched to Coomassie. Your king is always making trouble. You will see that this time the English will not be content with your retiring, but will in turn invade Ashanti."

Ammon Quatia and the chiefs laughed incredulously. "They will not dare to cross the Prah," Ammon Quatia said. "If they enter Ashanti, they will be eaten up."

"They are not so easy to eat up," Frank answered. "You have seen how a hundred or two can fight against your whole army.

207

What will it be when they are in thousands? Your king has not been wise. It would be better for him to send down at once and to make peace at any price."

CHAPTER XX

THE WHITE TROOPS

TWO days later Frank was awoke by a sudden yell. He leaped from his bed of boughs, seized his revolver, and rushing to the door, saw that a party of some twenty men were attacking Ammon Quatia's hut. The two guards stationed there had already been cut down. Frank shouted to his four guards and Ostik to follow him. The guards had been standing irresolute, not knowing what side to take, but the example of the young Englishman decided them. They fired their muskets into the knot of natives, and then charged sword in hand. Ostik drew the sword which he always carried and followed close to his master's heels. Frank did not fire until within two yards of the Ashantis. Then his revolver spoke out and six shots were discharged, each with deadly effect. Then, catching up a musket which had fallen from the hands of one of the men he had shot, he clubbed it and fell upon the surprised and already hesitating conspirators.

These, fortunately for Frank, had not loaded their muskets. They had intended to kill Ammon Quatia and then to disperse instantly before aid could arrive, believing that with his death the order for retreat across the Prah would at once be given. Several of them had been killed by the slugs from the muskets of Frank's guard, and his pistol had completed their confusion. The reports of the guns called up other troops, and these came rushing in on all sides. Scarcely did Frank and his followers fall upon the conspirators than they took to their heels and fled into the wood.

Ammon Quatia himself, sword in hand, had just sprung to the door of the hut prepared to sell his life dearly, when Frank's guard fired. The affair was so momentary that he had hardly time to realize what had happened before his assailants were in full flight.

"You have saved my life," he said to Frank. "Had it not been for you I must have been killed. You shall not find me ungrateful.

When I have taken Abra Crampa I will manage that you shall return to your friends. I dare not let you go openly, for the king would not forgive me, and I shall have enough to do already to pacify him when he hears how great have been our losses. But rest content. I will manage it somehow."

An hour afterwards Ammon Quatia gave orders that the army should move to the attack of Abra Crampa. The place was held by a body of marines and sailors, a hundred West Indians, and the native troops of the king. Major Russell was in command. The village stood on rising ground, and was surrounded for a distance of a hundred and fifty yards by a clearing. Part of this consisted of patches of cultivated ground, the rest had been hastily cleared by the defenders. At the upper end stood a church, and this was converted into a stronghold. The windows were high up in the walls, and a platform had been erected inside for the sailors to fire from the windows, which were partially blocked with sand-bags. The houses on the outside of the village had all been loopholed, and had been connected by breast-works of earth. Other defences had been thrown up further back in case the outworks should be carried. The mission house in the main street and the huts which surrounded it formed, with the church, the last strongholds. For two or three days the bush round the town had swarmed with Ashantis, whose tom-toms could be heard by the garrison night and day.

Frank accompanied Ammon Quatia, and was therefore in the front, and had an opportunity of seeing how the Ashantis commence an attack. The war drums gave the signal, and when they ceased, ten thousand voices raised the war song in measured cadence. The effect was very fine, rising as it did from all parts of the forest. By this time the Ashantis had lined the whole circle of wood round the clearing. Then three regular volleys were fired, making, from the heavy charges used, a tremendous roar.

Scarcely had these ceased when the King of Abra, a splendid looking warrior standing nearly six feet four in height, stepped out from behind the breast-work and shouted a taunting challenge to the Ashantis to come on. They replied with a loud yell, and with the opening of a continuous fire round the edge of the wood. On wall and roof of the village the slugs pattered thickly; but the defenders were all in shelter, and in reply, from breast-work and loophole, from the windows and roof of the church, the answering Snider bullets flew out straight and deadly. Several times Ammon Quatia tried to get his men to make a rush. The war drums beat, the great horns sounded, and the men shouted, but each time the English bullets flew so thick and deadly into the wood wherever the sound rose loudest that the Ashantis' heart failed them, and they could not be got to make the rush across the hundred yards of cleared ground.

At five o'clock the fire slackened, but shortly after dark the attack recommenced. The moon was up and full. Frank feared that the Ashantis would try and crawl a part of the distance across the clearing and then make a sudden rush; but they appeared to have no idea of a silent attack. Several times, indeed, they gathered and rushed forward in large bodies, but each time their shouting and drums gave warning to the besieged, and so tremendous a fire was opened upon them when they emerged from the shadow of the trees into the moonlight, that each time they fell back leaving the ground strewn with dead. Till midnight the attack was continued, then the Ashantis fell back to their camp.

At Accroful, a village on the main road some four miles distant, the attack had been heard, and a messenger sent off to Cape Coast to inform Sir Garnet Wolseley.

In the morning fifty men of the 2d West India regiment marched from Accroful into Abra Crampa without molestation. Later on some Abra scouts approached the Ashanti camp and shouted tauntingly to know when the Ashantis were coming into Abra Crampa.

They shouted in return, "After breakfast," and soon afterwards, a rocket fired from the roof of the church falling into the camp, they again sallied out and attacked. It was a repetition of the fight of the day before. Several times Major Russell withheld his fire altogether, but the Ashantis could not be tempted to show in force beyond the edge of the wood. So inspirited were the defenders that they now made several sorties and penetrated some distance into the wood.

At eight in the morning Sir Garnet Wolseley had marched from Cape Coast with three hundred marines and blue jackets to the relief of the position, but so tremendous was the heat that nearly half the men fell exhausted by the way, and were ordered when they recovered to march back to Cape Coast. The remainder, when they arrived at Assaiboo, five miles from Abra Crampa, were so utterly exhausted that a long halt was necessary, although a faint but continuous fire could be heard from the besieged place.

Chocolate and cold preserved meat were served out to the men, and in the course of another three hours a large number of the stragglers came in. At three o'clock, a hundred of the most exhausted men being left to hold the village, the rest of the force with the fifty West Indians stationed there marched forward to Buteana, where they were joined by fifty more men from Accroful. Just as they started from this place they met the King of Abra, who had come out with a small body of warriors; from him Sir Garnet learned that this road, which wound round and came in at the back of Abra Crampa, was still open.

The Ashantis were too busy with their own operations to watch the path, and the relieving force entered the place without firing a shot. The firing round the town continued, but Ammon Quatia, when he saw the reinforcements enter, at once began to fall back with the main body of his troops, and although the firing was kept up all night, when the besieged in the morning advanced to attack the Ashanti camp they found it altogether deserted.

"It is of no use," the Ashanti general said to Frank. "My men cannot fight in the open against the English guns. Besides, they do not know what they are fighting for here; but if your general should ever cross the Prah you will find it different. There are forests all the way to Coomassie, as you know, and the men will be fighting in defence of their own country, you will see what we shall do then. And now I will keep my promise to you. Tonight your guards will go to sleep. I shall have medicine given them which will make them sleep hard. One of the Fanti prisoners will come to your hut and will guide you through the woods to Assaiboo. Good-bye, my friend. Ammon Quatia has learnt that some of the white men are good and honest, and he will never forget that he owes his life to you. Take this in remembrance of Ammon Quatia." And he presented Frank with a necklace composed of nuggets of gold as big as walnuts and weighing nearly twenty pounds.

Frank in return gave the general the only article of value which he now possessed, his revolver and tin box of cartridges, telling him that he hoped he would never use it against the English, but that it might be of value to him should he ever again have trouble with his own men. Frank made a parcel of the necklace and of the gold he had received from the king for his goods, and warned Ostik to hold himself in readiness for flight. The camp was silent although the roar of musketry a few hundred yards off round Abra Crampa continued unbroken. For some time Frank heard his guards pacing outside, and occasionally speaking to each other. Then these sounds ceased and all was quiet. Presently the front of the tent was opened and a voice said, "Come, all is ready."

Frank came out and looked round. The Ashanti camp was deserted. Ammon Quatia had moved away with the main body of his troops, although the musketry fire round the village was kept up. A Fanti stood at the door of the hut with Ostik. The four guards were sleeping quietly. Noiselessly the little party stole away. A quarter of an hour later they struck the path, and an hour's walking brought them to Assaiboo. Not an Ashanti was met with along the path, but Frank hardly felt that he was safe until he heard the challenge of "Who goes there?" from an English sentry. A few minutes later he was taken before Captain Bradshaw, R.N., who commanded the sailors and marines who had been left there. Very hearty was the greeting which the young Englishman received from the genial sailor, and a bowl of soup and a glass of grog were soon set before him.

His arrival created quite a sensation, and for some hours he sat talking with the officers, while Ostik was an equal subject of curiosity among the sailors. The news that the Ashanti army was in full retreat relieved the garrison of the place from all further fear of attack, and Frank went to sleep before morning, and was only roused at noon when a messenger arrived with the news that the

Ashanti camp had been found deserted, and that the road in its rear was found to be strewn with chairs, clothes, pillows, muskets, and odds and ends of every description. Few Ashanti prisoners had been taken, but a considerable number of Fantis, who had been prisoners among them, had come in, having escaped in the confusion of the retreat. Among these were many women, several of whom had been captured when the Ashantis had first crossed the Prah ten months before.

In the afternoon Sir Garnet Wolseley, with the greater portion of the force from Abra Crampa, marched in, and Frank was introduced by Captain Bradshaw to the general. As the latter was anxious to press on at once to Cape Coast, in order that the sailors and marines might sleep on board ship that night, he asked Frank to accompany him, and on the road heard the story of his adventures. He invited him to sleep for the night at Government House, an invitation which Frank accepted; but he slept worse than he had done for a long time. It was now nearly two years since he had landed in Africa, and during all that time he had slept, covered with a rug, on the canvas of his little camp-bed. The complete change, the stillness and security, and, above all, the novelty of a bed with sheets, completely banished sleep, and it was not until morning was dawning that, wrapping himself in a rug, and lying on the ground, he was able to get a sleep.

In the morning at breakfast Sir Garnet asked him what he intended to do, and said that if he were in no extreme hurry to return to England he could render great services as guide to the expedition, which would start for Coomassie as soon as the white troops arrived. Frank had already thought the matter over. He had had more than enough of Africa, but two or three months longer would make no difference, and he felt that his knowledge of the Ashanti methods of war, of the country to be traversed, the streams to be crossed, and the points at which the Ashantis would probably make a stand, would enable him to render really valuable assistance to the army. He therefore told Sir Garnet Wolseley that he had no particular business which called him urgently back, and that he was willing to guide the army to Coomassie. He at once had

"WHO GOES THERE?"

quarters as an officer assigned to him in the town, with rations for himself and servant.

His first step was to procure English garments, for although he had before starting laid aside his Ashanti costume, and put on that he had before worn, his clothes were now so travel-worn as to be scarce wearable. He had no difficulty in doing this. Many of the officers were already invalided home, and one who was just sailing was glad to dispose of his uniform, which consisted of a light brown Norfolk shooting-jacket, knickerbockers, and helmet, as these would be of no use to him in England.

Frank's next step was to go to the agent of Messrs. Swanzy, the principal African merchants of the coast. This gentleman readily cashed one of the orders on the African bank which Mr. Goodenough had, before his death, handed over to Frank, and the latter proceeded to discharge the long arrears of wages owing to Ostik, adding, besides, a handsome present. He offered to allow his faithful servant to depart to join his family on the Gaboon at once, should he wish to do so, but Ostik declared that he would remain with him as long as he stopped in Africa. On Frank's advice, however, he deposited his money, for safe keeping, with Messrs. Swanzy's agent, with orders to transmit it to his family should anything happen to him during the expedition.

Three days later Frank was attacked by fever, the result of the reaction after so many dangers. He was at once sent on board the *Simoon*, which had been established as a hospital ship; but the attack was a mild one, and in a few days, thanks to the sea air, and the attention and nursing which he received, he was convalescent.

As soon as the fever passed away, and he was able to sit on deck and enjoy the sea-breezes, he had many visits from the officers of the ships of war. Among these was the captain of the *Decoy* gunboat. After chatting with Frank for some time the officer said: "I am going down the coast as far as the mouth of the Volta, where Captain Glover is organizing another expedition. You will not be wanted on shore just at present, and a week's rest will do you good; what do you say to coming down with me—it will give you a little change and variety?"

Frank accepted the invitation with pleasure. An hour later the *Decoy's* boat came alongside, and Frank took his place on board it, Ostik following with his clothes. An hour later the *Decoy* got up her anchor and steamed down the coast. It was delightful to Frank, sitting in a large wicker-work chair in the shade of the awning, watching the distant shore and chatting with the officers. He had much to hear of what had taken place in England since he left, and they on their part were equally eager to learn about the road along which they would have to march—at least those of them who were fortunate enough to be appointed to the naval brigade—and the wonders of the native capital. The *Decoy* was not fast, about six knots being her average pace of steaming; however, no one was in a hurry; there would be nothing to do until the troops arrived from England; and to all, a trip down the coast was a pleasant change after the long monotony of rolling at anchor. For some distance from Cape Coast the shore was flat, but further on the country became hilly. Some of the undulations reached a considerable height, the highest, Mamquady, being over two thousand feet.

"That ought to be a very healthy place," Frank said. "I should think that a sanatorium established there would be an immense boon to the whites all along the coasts."

"One would think so," an officer replied; "but I'm told that those hills are particularly unhealthy. That fellow you see jutting out is said to be extremely rich in gold. Over and over again parties have been formed to dig there, but they have always suffered so terribly from fever that they have had to relinquish the attempt. The natives suffer as well as the whites. I believe that the formation is granite, the surface of which is much decomposed, and it is always found here that the turning up of ground that has not been disturbed for many years is extremely unhealthy, and decomposing granite possesses some element particularly obnoxious to health. The natives, of course, look upon the mountain as a fetish, and believe that an evil spirit guards it. The superstition of the native is wonderful, and at Accra they are, if possible, more superstitious than anywhere else. Every one believes that every malady under the sun is produced by fetish, and that some enemy is casting spells upon them."

"There is more in it than you think," the doctor joined in; "although it is not spells, but poison, which they use against each other. The use of poison is carried to an incredible extent here. I have not been much on shore, but the medical men, both civilian and military, who have been here any time are convinced that a vast number of the deaths that take place are due to poison. The fetish men and women who are the vendors of these drugs keep as a profound secret their origin and nature, but it is certain that many of them are in point of secrecy and celerity equal to those of the middle ages."

"I wonder that the doctors have never discovered what plants they get them from," Frank said.

"Some of them have tried to do so," the doctor replied; "but have invariably died shortly after commencing their experiments; it is believed they have been poisoned by the fetish men in order to prevent their secrets being discovered."

The hours passed pleasurably. The beautiful neatness and order prevailing on board a man-of-war were specially delightful to Frank after the rough life he had so long led, and the silence and discipline of the men presented an equally strong contrast to the incessant chattering and noise kept up by the nnatives.

The next morning the ship was off Accra. Here the scenery had entirely changed. The hills had receded, and a wide and slightly undulating plain extended to their feet some twelve miles back. The captain was going to land, as he had some despatches for the colony, and he invited Frank to accompany him. They did not, as Frank expected, land in a man-of-war's boat, but in a surf-boat, which, upon their hoisting a signal, came out to them. These surf-boats are large and very wide and flat. They are paddled by ten or twelve natives, who sit upon the gunwale. These men work vigourously, and the boats travel at a considerable pace. Each boat has a stroke peculiar to itself. Some paddle hard for six strokes and then easy for an equal number. Some will take two or three hard and then one easy. The steersman stands in the stern and steers with an oar. He or one of the crew keeps up a monotonous song, to which the crew reply in chorus, always in time with their paddling.

The surf is heavy at Accra, and Frank held his breath, as, after waiting for a favourable moment, the steersman gave the sign and the boat darted in at lightning speed on the top of a great wave, and ran up on the beach in the midst of a whirl of white foam.

While the captain went up to Government House, Frank, accompanied by one of the young officers who had also come ashore, took a stroll through the town. The first thing that struck him was the extraordinary number of pigs. These animals pervaded the whole place. They fed in threes and fours in the middle of the streets. They lay everywhere in the road, across the doors, and against the walls. They quarrelled energetically in side lanes and court-yards, and when worsted in their disputes galloped away grunting, careless whom they might upset. The principal street of Accra was an amusing sight. Some effort had been made to keep it free of the filth and rubbish which everywhere else abounded. Both sides were lined by salesmen and women sitting on little mats upon the low wooden stools used as seats in Africa. The goods were contained in wooden trays. Here were dozens of women offering beads for sale of an unlimited variety of form and hue. They varied from the tiny opaque beads of all colours used by English children for their dolls, to great cylindrical beads of variegated hues as long and as thick as the joint of a finger. The love of the Africans for beads is surprising. The women wear them round the wrists, the neck, and the ankles. The occupation of threading the little beads is one of their greatest pleasures. The threads used are narrow fibres of palm leaves, which are very strong. The beads, however, are of unequal sizes, and no African girl who has any respect for her personal appearance will put on a string of beads until she has, with great pains and a good deal of skill, rubbed them with sand and water until all the projecting beads are ground down, and the whole are perfectly smooth and even.

Next in number to the dealers in beads were those who sold calico, or, as it is called in Africa, cloth, and gaudily-coloured kerchiefs for the head. These three articles—beads, cotton cloth, and coloured handkerchiefs—complete the list of articles required for the attire and adornment of males and females in Africa. Besides these goods, tobacco, in dried leaves, short clay pipes, knives, small looking-glasses, and matches were offered for sale. The majority of the saleswomen, however, were dealers in eatables, dried fish, smoked fish, canki—which is a preparation of ground corn wrapped up in palm leaves in the shape of paste—eggs, fowls, kids, cooked meats in various forms, stews, boiled pork, fried knobs of meat, and other native delicacies, besides an abundance of seeds, nuts, and other vegetable productions.

After walking for some time through the streets Frank and his companions returned to the boat, where, half an hour later, the captain joined them, and, putting off to the *Decoy*, they continued the voyage down the coast.

The next morning they weighed anchor off Addah, a village at the mouth of the Volta. They whistled for a surf-boat, but it was some time before one put out. When she was launched it was doubtful whether she would be able to make her way through the breaking water. The surf was much heavier here than it had been at Accra, and each wave threw the boat almost perpendicularly into the air, so that only a few feet of the end of the keel touched the water. Still she struggled on, although so long was she in getting through the surf that those on board the ship thought several times that she must give it up as impracticable. At last, however, she got through; the paddlers waited for a minute to recover from their exertions, and then made out to the *Decoy*. None of the officers had ever landed here, and several of them obtained leave to accompany the captain on shore. Frank was one of the party. After what they had seen of the difficulty which the boat had in getting out, all looked somewhat anxiously at the surf as they approached the line where the great smooth waves rolled over and broke into boiling foam. The steersman stood upon the seat in the stern, in one hand holding his oar, in the other his cap. For some time he stood half turned round, looking attentively seaward, while the boat lay at rest just outside the line of breakers. Suddenly he waved his cap and gave a shout. It was answered by the crew. Every man dashed his paddle into the water. Desperately they rowed, the steersman encouraging them by wild yells. A gigantic wave rolled in behind the boat, and looked for a moment as if she would break into it, but she rose on it just as it turned over, and for an instant was swept along amidst a cataract of white foam, with the speed of an arrow. The next wave was a small one, and ere a third reached it the boat grounded on the sand. A dozen men rushed out into the water. The passengers threw themselves anyhow on to their backs, and in a minute were standing perfectly dry upon the beach.

They learned that Captain Glover's camp was half a mile distant, and at once set out for it. Upon the way up to the camp, they passed hundreds of natives, who had arrived in the last day or two, and had just received their arms. Some were squatted on the ground cooking and resting themselves. Others were examining their new weapons, oiling and removing every spot of rust, and occasionally loading and firing them off. The balls whizzed through the air in all directions. The most stringent orders had been given forbidding this dangerous nuisance; but nothing can repress the love of natives for firing off guns. There were large numbers of women among them; these had acted as carriers on their journey to the camp; for among the coast tribes, as among the Ashantis, it is the proper thing when the warriors go out on the warpath, that the women should not permit them to carry anything except their guns until they approach the neighbourhood of the enemy.

The party soon arrived at the camp, which consisted of some bell tents and the little huts of a few hundred natives. This, indeed, was only the place where the latter were first received and armed, and they were then sent up the river in the steamboat belonging to the expedition, to the great camp some thirty miles higher.

The expedition consisted only of some seven or eight English officers. Captain Glover of the royal navy was in command, with Mr. Goldsworthy and Captain Sartorius as his assistants. There were four other officers, two doctors, and an officer of commissariat. This little body had the whole work of drilling and keeping in order some eight or ten thousand men. They were generals, colonels, sergeants, quartermasters, store-keepers, and diplomatists, all at once, and from daybreak until late at night were incessantly at work. There were at least a dozen petty kings in camp, all of whom had to be kept in a good temper, and this was by no means the smallest of Captain Glover's difficulties, as upon the slightest ground for discontent each of these was ready at once to march away with his followers. The most reliable portion of Captain Glover's force were some 250 Houssas, and as many Yorabas. In addition to all their work with the native allies, the officers of the expedition had succeeded in drilling both these bodies until they had obtained a very fair amount of discipline.

After strolling through the camp the visitors went to look on at the distribution of arms and accoutrements to a hundred freshly arrived natives. They were served out with blue smocks, made of serge, and blue night-caps, which had the result of transforming a fine-looking body of natives, upright in carriage, and graceful in their toga-like attire, into a set of awkward-looking, clumsy warriors. A haversack, water bottle, belts, cap-pouch, and ammunition pouch, were also handed to each to their utter bewilderment, and it was easy to foresee that at the end of the first day's march the whole of these, to them utterly useless articles, would be thrown aside. They brightened up, however, when the guns were delivered to them. The first impulse of each was to examine his piece carefully, to try its balance by taking aim at distant objects, then to carefully rub off any little spot of rust that could be detected, lastly to take out the ramrod and let it fall into the barrel, to judge by the ring whether it was clean inside.

Thence the visitors strolled away to watch a number of Houssas in hot pursuit of some bullocks, which were to be put on board the steamers and taken up the river to the great camp. These had broken loose in the night, and the chase was an exciting one. Although some fifty or sixty men were engaged in the hunt it took no less than four hours to capture the requisite number, and seven Houssas were more or less injured by the charges of the desperate little animals, which possessed wonderful strength and endurance, although no larger than moderate-sized donkeys. They were only captured at last by hoops being thrown over their horns, and even when thrown down required the efforts of five or six men to tie them. They were finally got to the wharf by two men each: one went ahead with the rope attached to the animal's horns, the other kept behind, holding a rope fastened to one of the hind legs. Every bull made the most determined efforts to get at the man in front, who kept on at a run, the animal being checked when it got too close by the man behind pulling at its hind leg. When it turned to attack him the man in front again pulled at his rope. So most of them were brought down to the landing-place, and there with great difficulty, again thrown down, tied, and carried bodily on board. Some of them were so unmanageable that they had to be carried all the way down to the landing-place. If English cattle possessed the strength and obstinate fury of these little animals, Copenhagen Fields would have to be removed farther from London, or the entrance swept by machine guns, for a charge of the cattle would clear the streets of London.

After spending an amusing day on shore, the party returned on board ship. Captain Glover's expedition, although composed of only seven or eight English officers and costing the country comparatively nothing, accomplished great things, but its doings were almost ignored by England. Crossing the river they completely defeated the native tribes there, who were in alliance with the Ashantis, after some hard fighting, and thus prevented an invasion of our territory on that side. In addition to this they pushed forward into the interior and absolutely arrived at Coomassie two days after Sir Garnet Wolseley. It is true that the attention of the Ashantis was so much occupied by the advance of the white force that they paid but little attention to that advancing from the Volta; but none the less is the credit due to the indomitable perseverance and the immensity of the work accomplished by Captain Glover and his officers. Alone and single-handed, they overcame all the enormous difficulties raised by the apathy, indolence, and self-importance of the numerous petty chiefs whose followers constituted the army, infused something of their own spirit among their followers, and persuaded them to march without white allies against the hitherto invincible army of the Ashantis. Not a tithe of the credit due to them has been given to the officers of this little force.

Captain Glover invited his visitors to pass the night on shore offering to place a tent at their disposal; but the mosquitoes are so numerous and troublesome along the swampy shore of the Volta that the invitations were declined, and the whole party returned on board the *Decoy*. Next day the anchor was hove and the ship's head turned to the west; and two days later, after a pleasant and uneventful voyage, she was again off Cape Coast, and Frank, taking leave of his kind entertainers, returned on shore and reported himself as ready to perform any duty that might be assigned to him.

Until the force advanced, he had nothing to do, and spent a good deal of his time watching the carriers starting with provisions for the Prah, and the doings of the nnatives.

The order had now been passed by the chiefs at a meeting called by Sir Garnet, that every able-bodied man should work as a carrier, and while parties of men were sent to the villages round to fetch in people thence, hunts took place in Cape Coast itself. Everybody found in the streets was seized by the police; protestation, indignation, and resistance were equally in vain. An arm or the loin cloth was firmly griped, and the victim was run into the castle yard, amid the laughter of the lookers-on, who consisted, after the first quarter of an hour, of women only. Then the search began in the houses, the chiefs indicating the localities in which men were likely to be found. Some police were set to watch outside while others went in to search. The women would at once deny that anyone was there, but a door was pretty sure to be found locked, and upon this being broken open, the fugitive would be found hiding under a pile of clothes or mats. Sometimes he would leap through the windows, sometimes take to the flat roof, and as the houses joined together in the most confused way the roofs offered immense facilities for escape, and most lively chases took place.

No excuses or pretences availed. A man seen limping painfully along the street would, after a brief examination of his leg to see if there was any external mark which would account for the lameness, be sent at a round trot down the road, amid peals of laughter from the women and girls looking on.

The indignation of some of the men thus seized, loaded, and sent up country under a strong escort was very funny, and their astonishment in some cases altogether unfeigned. Small shopkeepers who had never supposed that they would be called upon to labour for the defence of their freedom and country, found themselves with a barrel of pork upon their heads and a policeman with a loaded musket by their side proceeding up country for an indefinite period. A school teacher was missing, and was found to have gone up with a case of ammunition. Casual visitors from down the coast had their stay prolonged. Lazy Sierra Leone men, discharged by their masters for incurable idleness, and living doing nothing, earning nothing, kept by the kindness of friends and the aid of an occasional petty theft, found themselves, in spite of the European cut of their clothes, groaning under the weight of cases of preserved provisions.

Everywhere the town was busy and animated, but it was in the castle court-yard Frank found most amusement. Here of a morning a thousand natives would be gathered, most of them men sent down from Dunquah, forming part of our native allied army. Their costumes were various but scant, their colours all shades of brown up to the deepest black. Their faces were all in a grin of amusement. The noise of talking and laughing was immense. All were squatted upon the ground, in front of each was a large keg labelled "pork." Among them moved two or three commissariat officers in gray uniforms. At the order, "Now then, off with you," the natives would rise, take off their cloths, wrap them into pads, lift the barrels on to their heads, and go off at a brisk pace; the officer perhaps smartening up the last to leave with a cut with his stick, which would call forth a scream of laughter from all the others.

When all the men had gone, the turn of the women came, and of these two or three hundred, who had been seated chattering and laughing against the walls, would now come forward and stoop to pick up the bags of biscuit laid out for them. Their appearance was most comical when they stooped to their work, their prodigious bustles forming an apex. At least two out of every three had babies seated on these bustles, kept firm against their backs by the cloth tightly wrapped round the mother's body. But from the attitudes of the mothers the position was now reversed, the little black heads hanging downwards upon the dark brown backs of the women.

After the women had been got off, three or four hundred boys and girls, of from eleven to fourteen years old, would start with small kegs of rice or meat weighing from twenty-five to thirty-five pounds. These small kegs had, upon their first arrival, been a cause of great bewilderment and annoyance to the commissariat officers, for no man or woman, unless by profession a juggler, could balance two long narrow barrels on the head. At last the happy idea struck an officer of the department that the children of the place might be utilized for the purpose. No sooner was it known that boys and girls could get half men's wages for carrying up light loads, than there was a perfect rush of the juvenile population. Three hundred applied the first morning, four hundred the next. The glee of the youngsters was quite exuberant. All were accustomed to carry weights, such as great jars of water and baskets of yams, far heavier than those they were now called to take up the country; and the novel pleasure of earning money and of enjoying an expedition up the country delighted them immensely.

Bullocks were now arriving from other parts of the coast, and although these would not live for any time at Cape Coast, it was thought they would do so long enough to afford the expedition a certain quantity of fresh meat; Australian meat, and salt pork, though valuable in their way, being poor food to men whose appetites are enfeebled by heat and exhaustion.

It was not till upwards of six weeks after the fight at Abra Crampa that the last of the Ashanti army crossed the Prah. When arriving within a short distance of that river, they had been met by seven thousand fresh troops, who had been sent by the king with orders that they were not to return until they had driven the English into the sea. Ammon Quatia's army, however, although still, from the many reinforcements it had received, nearly twenty thousand strong, positively refused to do any more fighting until they had been home and rested, and their tales of the prowess of the white troops so checked the enthusiasm of the newcomers, that these decided to return with the rest.

CHAPTER XXI

THE ADVANCE TO THE PRAH

A LARGE body of natives were now kept at work on the road up to the Prah. The swamps were made passable by bundles of brushwood thrown into them, the streams were bridged and huts erected for the reception of the white troops. These huts were constructed of bamboo, the beds being made of lattice-work of the same material, and were light and cool.

On the 9th of December the *Himalaya* and *Tamar* arrived, having on board the 23d Regiment, a battalion of the Rifle Brigade, a battery of artillery, and a company of engineers. On the 18th, the *Sarmatian* arrived with the 42d. All these ships were sent off for a cruise, with orders to return on the 1st of January, when the troops were to be landed. A large number of officers arrived a few days later to assist in the organization of the transport corps. Colonel Wood and Major Russell were by this time on the Prah with their native regiments. These were formed principally of Houssas, Cossoos, and men of other fighting Mahomedan tribes who had been brought down the coast, together with companies from Bonny and some of the best of the Fantis. The rest of the Fanti forces had been disbanded, as being utterly useless for fighting purposes, and had been turned into carriers.

On the 26th of December Frank started with the General's staff for the front. The journey to the Prah was a pleasant one. The stations had been arranged at easy marches from each other. At each of these, six huts for the troops, each capable of holding seventy men, had been built, together with some smaller huts for officers. Great filters formed of iron tanks with sand and charcoal at the bottom, the invention of Captain Crease, R.M.A., stood before the huts, with tubs at which the native bearers could quench their thirst. Along by the side of the road a single telegraph wire was supported on bamboos fifteen feet long.

Passing through Assaiboo, they entered the thick bush. The giant cotton-trees had now shed their light feathery foliage resembling that of an acacia, and the straight, round, even trunks looked like the skeletons of some giant or primeval vegetation rising above the sea of foliage below. White lilies, pink flowers of a bulbous plant, clusters of yellow acacia blossoms, occasionally brightened the roadside, and some of the old village clearings were covered with a low bush bearing a yellow blossom, and convolvuli white, buff, and pink. The second night the party slept at Accroful, and the next day marched through Dunquah. This was a great store station, but the white troops were not to halt there. It had been a large town, but the Ashantis had entirely destroyed it, as well as every other village between the Prah and the coast. Every fruit tree in the clearing had also been destroyed, and at Dunquah they had even cut down a great cotton-tree which was looked upon as a fetish by the Fantis. It had taken them seven days' incessant work to overthrow this giant of the forest.

The next halting-place was Yancoomassie. When approaching Mansue the character of the forest changed. The undergrowth disappeared and the high trees grew thick and close. The plantain, which furnishes an abundant supply of fruit to the natives and had sustained the Ashanti army during its stay south of the Prah, before abundant, extended no further. Mansue stood, like other native villages, on rising ground, but the heavy rains which still fell every day and the deep swamps around rendered it a most unhealthy station.

Beyond Mansue the forest was thick and gloomy. There was little undergrowth, but a perfect wilderness of climbers clustered round the trees, twisting in a thousand fantastic windings, and finally running down to the ground, where they took fresh root and formed props to the dead trees their embrace had killed. Not a flower was to be seen, but ferns grew by the roadside in luxuriance. Butterflies were scarce, but dragon-flies darted along like sparks of fire. The road had the advantage of being shady and cool, but the heavy rain and traffic had made it everywhere slippery, and in many places inches deep in mud, while all the efforts of the engineers and working parties had failed to overcome the swamps.

It was a relief to the party when they emerged from the forests into the little clearings where villages had once stood, for the gloom and quiet of the great forest weighed upon the spirits. The monotonous too-too of the doves—not a slow dreamy cooing like that of the English variety, but a sharp quick note repeated in endless succession—alone broke the hush. The silence, the apparently never-ending forest, the monotony of rank vegetation, the absence of a breath of wind to rustle a leaf, were most oppressive, and the feeling was not lessened by the dampness and heaviness of the air, and the malarious exhalation and smell of decaying vegetation arising from the swamps.

Sootah was the station beyond Mansue, beyond this Assin and Barracoo. Beyond Sootah the odours of the forest became more unpleasant than before, for at Fazoo they passed the scene of a conflict between Colonel Wood's regiment and the retiring Ashantis. In the forest beyond this were the remains of a great camp of the enemy's, which extended for miles, and hence to the Prah large numbers of Ashantis had dropped by the way or had crawled into the forest to die, smitten by disease or rifle-balls.

There was a general feeling of pleasure as the party emerged from the forest into the large open camp at Prasue. This clearing was twenty acres in extent, and occupied an isthmus formed by a loop of the river. The 2d West Indians were encamped here, and huts had been erected under the shade of some lofty trees for the naval brigade. In the centre was a great square. On one side were the range of huts for the general and his staff. Two sides of the square were formed by the huts for the white troops. On the fourth was the hospital, the huts for the brigadier and his staff, and the post-office. Upon the river bank beyond the square were the tents of the engineers and Rait's battery of artillery, and the camps of Wood's and Russell's regiments. The river, some seventy yards wide, ran round three sides of the camp thirty feet below its level.

The work which the engineers had accomplished was little less than marvellous. Eighty miles of road had been cut and cleared, every stream, however insignificant, had been bridged, and attempts made to corduroy every swamp. This would have been no great feat through a soft wood forest with the aid of good workmen. Here, however, the trees were for the most part of extremely hard wood, teak and mahogany forming the majority. The natives had no idea of using an axe. Their only notion of felling a tree was to squat down beside it and give it little hacking chops with a large knife or a sabre.

With such means and such men as these the mere work of cutting and making the roads and bridging the streams was enormous. But not only was this done, but the stations were all stockaded, and huts erected for the reception of four hundred and fifty men and officers, and immense quantities of stores, at each post. Major Home, commanding the engineers, was the life and soul of the work, and to him more than any other man was the expedition indebted for its success. He was nobly seconded by Buckle, Bell, Mann, Cotton, Skinner, Bates, and Jeykyll, officers of his own corps, and by Hearle of the marines, and Hare of the 22d, attached to them. Long before daylight his men were off to their work, long after nightfall they returned utterly exhausted to camp.

Upon the 1st of January, 1874, Sir Garnet Wolseley, with his staff, among whom Frank was now reckoned, reached the Prah. During the eight days which elapsed before the white troops came up Frank found much to amuse him. The engineers were at work, aided by the sailors of the naval brigade, which arrived two days after the general, in erecting a bridge across the Prah. The sailors worked, stripped to the waist, in the muddy water of the river, which was about seven feet deep in the middle. When tired of watching these he would wander into the camp of the native regiments, and chat with the men, whose astonishment at finding a young Englishman able to converse in their language, for the Fanti and Ashanti dialects differ but little, was unbounded. Sometimes he would be sent for to headquarters to translate to Captain Buller, the head of the intelligence department, the statements of prisoners brought in by the scouts, who, under Lord Gifford, had penetrated many miles beyond the Prah.

Everywhere these found dead bodies by the side of the road, showing the state to which the Ashanti army was reduced in its retreat. The prisoners brought in were unanimous in saying that great uneasiness had been produced at Coomassie by the news of the advance of the British to the Prah. The king had written to Ammon Quatia, severely blaming him for his conduct of the campaign, and for the great loss of life among his army.

All sorts of portents were happening at Coomassie, to the great disturbance of the mind of the people. Some of those related singularly resembled those said to have occurred before the capture of Rome by the Goths. An aerolite had fallen in the marketplace of Coomassie, and, still more strange, a child was born which was at once able to converse fluently. This youthful prodigy was placed in a room by itself, with guards around it to prevent anyone having converse with the supernatural visitant. In the morning, however, it was gone, and in its place was found a bundle of dead leaves. The fetish men having been consulted declared that this signified that Coomassie itself would disappear, and would become nothing but a bundle of dead leaves. This had greatly exercised the credulous there.

Two days after his arrival, Frank went down at sunset to bathe in the river. He had just reached the bank when he heard a cry among some white soldiers bathing there, and was just in time to see one of them pulled under water by an alligator, which had seized him by the leg. Frank had so often heard what was the best thing to do that he at once threw off his Norfolk jacket, plunged into the stream, and swam to the spot where the eddy on the surface showed that a struggle was going on beneath. The water was too muddy to see far through it, but Frank speedily came upon the alligator, and finding its eyes, shoved his thumbs into them. In an instant the creature relaxed his hold of his prey and made off, and Frank, seizing the wounded man, swam with him to shore amid the loud cheers of the sailors. The soldier, who proved to be a marine, was insensible, and his leg was nearly severed above the ankle. He soon recovered consciousness, and, being carried to the camp, his leg was amputated below the knee, and he was soon afterwards taken down to the coast.

It had been known that there were alligators in the river, a young one about a yard long having been captured and tied up like a dog in the camp, with a string round its neck. But it was thought that the noise of building the bridge, and the movement on the banks, would have driven them away. After this incident, bathing was for the most part abandoned. The affair made Frank a great favourite in the naval brigade, and of a night he would, after dinner, generally repair there, and sit by the great bonfires, which the tars kept up, and listen to the jovial choruses which they raised around them.

Two days after the arrival of Sir Garnet, an ambassador came down from the king with a letter, inquiring indignantly why the English had attacked the Ashanti troops, and why they had advanced to the Prah. An opportunity was taken to impress him with the nature of the English arms. A Gatling gun was placed on the river bank, and its fire directed upon the surface, and the fountain of water which rose as the steady stream of bullets struck its surface astonished, and evidently filled with awe, the Ashanti ambassador. On the following day this emissary took his departure for Coomassie with a letter to the king.

On the 12th the messengers returned with an unsatisfactory answer to Sir Garnet's letter; they brought with them Mr. Kuhne, one of the German missionaries. He said that it was reported in Coomassie that twenty thousand out of the forty thousand Ashantis who had crossed the Prah had died. It is probable that this was exaggerated, but Mr. Kuhne had counted two hundred and seventy-six men carrying boxes containing the bones of chiefs and leading men. As these would have fared better than the common herd they would have suffered less from famine and dysentery. The army had for the most part broken up into small parties and gone to their villages. The wrath of the king was great, and all the chiefs who accompanied the army had been fined and otherwise punished. Mr. Kuhne said that when Sir Garnet's letter arrived, the question of peace or war had been hotly contested at a council. The chiefs who had been in the late expedition were unanimous in deprecating any further attempt to contend with the white man. Those who had remained at home, and who knew nothing of the white man's arms, or white man's valour, were for war rather than surrender.

Mr. Kuhne was unable to form any opinion what the final determination would be. The German missionary had no doubt been restored as a sort of peace offering. He was in a bad state of health, and as his brother and his brother's wife were among the captives, the Ashanti monarch calculated that anxiety for the fate of his relatives would induce him to argue as strongly as possible in favour of peace.

Frank left the camp on the Prah some days before the arrival of the white troops, having moved forward with the scouts under Lord Gifford, to whom his knowledge of the country and language proved very valuable. The scouts did their work well. The Ashantis were in considerable numbers, but fell back gradually without fighting. Russell's regiment were in support, and they pressed forward until they neared the foot of the Adansee Hills. On the 16th, Rait's artillery and Wood's regiment were to advance with two hundred men of the 2d West Indians. The Naval Brigade, the Rifle Brigade, the 42d, and a hundred men of the 23d would be up on the Prah on the 17th.

News came down that fresh portents had happened at Coomassie. The word signifies the town under the tree, the town being so called because its founder sat under a broad tree, surrounded by his warriors, while he laid out the plan of the future town. The market-place was situated round the tree, which became the great fetish tree of the town, under which human sacrifices were offered. On the 6th, the day upon which Sir Garnet sent his ultimatum to the king, a bird of ill omen was seen to perch upon it, and half an hour afterwards a tornado sprang up and the fetish tree was levelled to the ground. This caused an immense sensation in Coomassie, which was heightened when Sir Garnet's letter arrived, and proved to be dated upon the day upon which the fetish tree had fallen.

The Adansee Hills are very steep and covered with trees, but without undergrowth. It had been supposed that the Ashantis would make their first stand here. Lord Gifford led the way up with the scouts, Russell's regiment following behind. Frank accompanied Major Russell. When Gifford neared the crest a priest came forward with five or six supporters and shouted to him to go back, for that five thousand men were waiting there to destroy them. Gifford paused for a moment to allow Russell with his regiment to come within supporting distance, and then made a rush with his scouts for the crest. It was found deserted, the priest and his followers having fled hastily, when they found that neither curses nor the imaginary force availed to prevent the British from advancing.

The Adansee Hills are about six hundred feet high. Between them and the Prah the country was once thick with towns and villages inhabited by the Assins. These people, however, were so harassed by the Ashantis that they were forced to abandon their country and settle in the British protectorate south of the Prah.

Had the Adansee Hills been held by European troops the position would have been extremely strong. A hill if clear of trees, is of immense advantage to men armed with rifles and supported by artillery, but to men armed only with guns carrying slugs a distance of fifty yards, the advantage is not marked, especially when, as is the case with the Ashantis, they always fire high. The crest of the hill was very narrow, indeed a mere saddle, with some eight or ten yards only of level ground between the steep descents on either side. From this point the scouts perceived the first town in the territory of the King of Adansee, one of the five great kings of Ashanti. The scouts and Russell's regiment halted on the top of the hill, and the next morning the scouts went out skirmishing towards Queesa. The war drum could be heard beating in the town, but no opposition was offered. It was not, however, considered prudent to push beyond the foot of the hill until more troops came up. The scouts therefore contented themselves with keeping guard, while for the next four days Russell's men and the engineers laboured incessantly, as they had done all the way from the Prah, in making the road over the hill practicable.

During this time the scouts often pushed up close to Queesa, and reported that the soldiers and population were fast deserting the town. On the fifth day it was found to be totally deserted, and Major Russell moved the headquarters of his regiment down into it. The white officers were much surprised with the structure of the huts of this place, which was exactly similar to that of those of Coomassie, with their red clay, their alcoved bed places, and their little courts one behind the other. Major Russell established himself in the chief's palace, which was exactly like the other houses except that the alcoves were very lofty, and their roofs supported by pillars. These, with their red paint, their arabesque adornments, and their quaint character, gave the court-yard the precise appearance of an Egyptian temple.

The question whether the Ashantis would or would not fight was still eagerly debated. Upon the one hand it was urged that if the Ashantis had meant to attack us they would have disputed every foot of the passage through the woods after we had once crossed the Prah. Had they done so it may be confidently affirmed that we could never have got to Coomassie. Their policy should have been to avoid any pitched battle, but to throng the woods on either side, continually harassing the troops on their march, preventing the men working on the roads, and rendering it impossible for the carriers to go along unless protected on either side by lines of troops. Even when unopposed, it was difficult enough to keep the carriers, who were constantly deserting, but had they been exposed to continuous attacks there would have been no possibility of keeping them together.

It was then a strong argument in favour of peace that we had been permitted to advance thirty miles into their country without a shot being fired. Upon the other hand no messengers had been sent down to meet us, no ambassadors had brought messages from the king. This silence was ominous; nor were other signs wanting. At one place a fetish, consisting of a wooden gun and several wooden daggers all pointing towards us, was placed in the middle of the road. Several kids had been found buried in calabashes in the path pierced through and through with stakes; while a short distance outside Queesa the dead body of a slave killed and mutilated but a few hours before we entered it was hanging from a tree. Other fetishes of a more common sort were to be met at every step, lines of worsted and cotton stretched across the road, rags hung upon bushes, and other native trumperies of the same kind.

Five days later the Naval Brigade, with Wood's regiment and Rait's battery, marched into Queesa, and the same afternoon the whole marched forward to Fomana, the capital of Adansee, situated half a mile only from Queesa. This was a large town capable of containing some seven or eight thousand inhabitants. The architecture was similar to that of Queesa, but the king's palace was a large structure covering a considerable extent of ground. Here were the apartments of the king himself, of his wives, the fetish room, and the room for execution, still smelling horribly of the blood with which the floor and walls were sprinkled. The first and largest court of the palace had really an imposing effect. It was some thirty feet square with an apartment or alcove on each side. The roofs of these alcoves were supported by columns about twenty-five feet high. As in all the buildings, the lower parts were of red clay, the upper of white, all being covered with deep arabesque patterns.

Fomana was one of the most pleasant stations which the troops had reached since leaving the coast. It lay high above the sea, and the temperature was considerably lower than that of the stations south of the hills. A nice breeze sprang up each day about noon. The nights were comparatively free from fog, and the town itself stood upon rising ground resembling in form an inverted saucer. The streets were very wide, with large trees at intervals every twenty or thirty yards along the middle of the road.

CHAPTER XXII

THE BATTLE OF AMOAFUL

TWO days after the arrival at Fomana the remaining members of the German mission, two males, a female, and two children, were sent in by the king with a letter containing many assurances of his desire for peace, but making no mention of the stipulations which Sir Garnet Wolseley had laid down. The advance was therefore to continue. The rest of the troops came up, and on the 25th, Russell's regiment advanced to Dompiassee, Wood's regiment and Rait's battery joining him the next day. That afternoon the first blood north of the Prah was shed. It being known that a body of the enemy were collecting at a village a little off the road the force moved against them. Lord Gifford led the way, as usual, with his scouts. The enemy opened fire as soon as the scouts appeared; but these, with the Houssa company of Russell's regiment, rushed impetuously into the village, and the Ashantis at once bolted. Two of them were killed and five taken prisoners.

The next halting-places of the advance troops were Kiang Bossu and Ditchiassie. It was known now that Ammon Quatia was lying with the Ashanti army at Amoaful, but five miles away, and ambassadors arrived from the king finally declining to accept the terms of peace. Russell's and Wood's regiments marched forward to Quarman, within half a mile of the enemy's outposts. The white troops came on to Insafoo, three miles behind. Quarman was stockaded to resist an attack. Gordon with the Houssa company lay a quarter of a mile in advance of the village, Gifford with his scouts close to the edge of the wood. Major Home with the engineers cut a wide path for the advance of the troops to within a hundred yards of the village which the enemy held.

Everyone knew that the great battle of the war would be fought next morning. About half-past seven on the morning of the 31st of January, the 42d Regiment entered the village of Quarman, and marched through without a halt. Then came Rait's artillery, followed by the company of the 23d and by the Naval Brigade. The plan of operations was as follows. The 42d Regiment would form the main attacking force. They were to drive the enemy's scouts out of Agamassie, the village in front, and were then to move straight on, extending to the right and left, and, if possible, advance in a skirmishing line through the bush. Rait's two little guns were to be in their centre moving upon the road itself. The right column, consisting of half the Naval Brigade, with Wood's regiment, now reduced, by leaving garrisons at various posts along the road, to three companies, was to cut a path out to the right and then to turn parallel with the main road, so that the head of the column should touch the right of the skirmishing line of the 42d. The left column, consisting of the other half of the Naval Brigade with the four companies of Russell's regiment, was to proceed in similar fashion on the left. These columns would therefore form two sides of a hollow square, protecting the 42d from any of those flanking movements of which the Ashantis are so fond. The company of the 23d was to proceed with the headquarter staff. The Rifle Brigade were held in reserve.

Early in the morning Major Home cut the road to within thirty yards of the village of Agamassie, and ascertained by listening to the voices that there were not more than a score or so of men in the village. Gifford had made a circuit in the woods, and had ascertained that the Ashanti army was encamped on rising ground across a stream behind the village.

Frank had been requested by Sir Garnet Wolseley to accompany the 42d, as his knowledge of Ashanti tactics might be of value, and he might be able by the shouts of the Ashantis, to understand the orders issued to them. The head of the 42d Regiment experienced no opposition whatever until they issued from the bush into the little clearing surrounding the village, which consisted only of four or five houses. The Ashantis discharged their muskets hastily as the first white men showed themselves, but the fire of the leading files of the column quickly cleared them away. The 42d pushed on through the village, and then forming in skirmishing line, advanced. For the first two or three hundred yards they encountered no serious opposition, and they were then received by a tremendous fire from an unseen foe in their front. The left column had not gone a hundred yards before they too came under fire. Captain Buckle of the Engineers, who was with the Engineer labourers occupied in cutting the path ahead of the advancing column, was shot through the heart. A similar opposition was experienced by the right.

The roar of the fire was tremendous, so heavy indeed that all sound of individual reports was lost, and the noise was one hoarse hissing roar. Even the crack of Rait's guns was lost in the general uproar, but the occasional rush of a rocket, of which two troughs with parties of Rait's men accompanied each wing, was distinctly audible.

The 42d could for a time make scarcely any way, and the flanking columns were also brought to a stand. Owing to the extreme thickness of the wood and their ignorance of the nature of the ground these columns were unable to keep in their proper position, and diverged considerably. The Ashantis, however, made no effort to penetrate between them and the 42d. For an hour this state of things continued. The company of the 23d advanced along the main road to help to clear the bush, where the Ashantis still fought stubbornly not two hundred yards from the village, while two companies of the Rifle Brigade were sent up the left-hand road to keep touch with the rear of Russell's regiment.

When the fight commenced in earnest, and the 42d were brought to a stand by the enemy, Frank lay down with the soldiers. Not a foe could be seen, but the fire of the enemy broke out incessantly from the bushes some twenty yards ahead. The air above was literally alive with slugs, and a perfect shower of leaves continued to fall upon the path. So bewilderingly dense was the bush that the men soon lost all idea of the points of the compass, and fired in any direction from which the enemy's shots came. Thus it happened that the sailors sent in complaints to the general that the 23d and 42d were firing at them, while the 42d and 23d made the same complaint against the Naval Brigade. Sir Garnet, who had taken up his headquarters at the village, sent out repeated instructions to the commanding officers to warn their men to avoid this error.

For two hours the fight went on. Then the column to the left found that the Ashantis in front of them had fallen back; they had, however, altogether lost touch of the 42d. They were accordingly ordered to cut a road to the north-east until they came in contact with them. In doing so, they came upon a partial clearing, where a sharp opposition was experienced. The Houssas carried the open ground at a rush, but the enemy, as usual, opened a heavy fire from the edge of the bush. The Houssas were recalled, and fire was opened with the rockets, which soon drove the Ashantis back, and the cutting of the path was proceeded with.

In the meantime the 42d were having a hard time of it. They had fought their way to the edge of the swamp, beyond which lay an immense Ashanti camp, and here the fire was so tremendously heavy that the advance was again completely arrested. Not an enemy was to be seen, but from every bush of the opposite side puffs of smoke came thick and fast, and a perfect rain of slugs swept over the ground on which they were lying. Here Rait's gun, for he was only able from the narrowness of the path to bring one into position, did splendid service. Advancing boldly in front of the line of the 42d, ably assisted by Lieutenant Saunders, he poured round after round of grape into the enemy until their fire slackened a little, and the 42d, leaping to their feet, struggled across the swamp, which was over knee-deep. Step by step they won their way through the camp and up the hill. Everywhere the dead Ashantis lay in heaps, attesting the terrible effect of the Snider fire, and the determination with which they had fought.

Beyond the camp, upon the hill, the bush was thicker than ever, and here, where it was impossible for the white soldiers to skirmish through the bush, the Ashantis made a last desperate stand. The narrow lane up which alone the troops could pass was torn as if by hail with the shower of slugs, while a large tree which stood nearly in the centre of the path and caused it slightly to swerve, afforded some shelter to them from the storm of bullets which the 42d sent back in return. Here Rait brought his gun up again to the front and cleared the lane. The bush was too thick even for the Ashantis. The gun stopped firing and with a rush the regiment went up the narrow path and out into the open clearing beyond. For a short time the Ashantis kept up a fire from the houses, but the 42d soon drove them out, and a single shot from the gun down the wide street which divided the town into two portions, bursting in the midst of a group at the further end, killed eight and drove all further idea of resistance in that direction from their minds.

It was now about twelve o'clock; but although the Ashantis had lost their camp and village, and had suffered terribly, they were not yet finally beaten. They had moved the principal part of the force which had been engaged upon our left round to the right, were pressing hard upon the column there and the 23d, and were cutting in between the latter and the 42d, when a fortunate accident enabled us to meet this attack most effectively. The left column had cut its path rather too much to the east, and came into the road between the 42d and 23d, forming a connecting link between them; while the right column, having at last cut away the whole of the brushwood in which the Ashantis had so long wedged themselves between them and the road, were now in direct communication with the 23d. They had been reinforced by a company of the Rifle Brigade. Our front, therefore, was now entirely changed, and faced east instead of north. The Ashantis in vain tried to break the line, but desisted from their efforts.

The firing died away, and it was thought that the battle was over, when at about a quarter to one a tremendous fire broke out from the rear of the column, showing that the Ashantis were making a last and desperate effort to turn our flank, and to retake the village from which we had driven them at eight in the morning. So near was the rear of the column to the village that the slugs fell fast into the reserve who were stationed there. Three companies of the Rifles were sent up to strengthen the line, and for three-quarters of an hour, the roar of musketry was as heavy and continuous as it had been at any time during the day. Then, as the enemy's fire slackened, Sir Garnet gave the word for the line to advance, sweeping round from the rear so as to drive the enemy northwards before them.

The movement was admirably executed. The Bonny men of Wood's regiment, who had fought silently and steadily all the time that they had been on the defensive, now raised their shrill war-cry, and slinging their rifles and drawing their swords—their favourite weapons—dashed forward like so many panthers let loose. By their side, skirmishing as quietly and steadily as if on parade, the men of the Rifle Brigade searched every bush with their bullets, and in five minutes from the commencement of the advance the Ashantis were in full and final retreat. The battle ended at about half-past one, having lasted five hours and a half.

The Ashantis were supposed to have had from fifteen to twenty thousand men in the field. What their loss was could not accurately be calculated, as they carry off their dead as fast as they fall; but where rushes were made by our troops, as they had not time to do this, they lay everywhere thick on the ground. By the most moderate computation they must have lost over two thousand. Ammon Quatia himself was killed, as well as Aboo, one of the six great tributary kings. The body of the king's chief executioner was also pointed out by some of the prisoners. They fought with extraordinary pluck and resolution, as was shown by the fact that although wretchedly armed, for upwards of five hours they resisted the attack of troops armed with breech-loaders, and supported by guns and rockets. Their position was a good one, and they had, no doubt, calculated upon coming down upon us from the rising ground, either on the flank or rear, with advantage, should we succeed in pushing forward.

Upon our side the loss in killed was very slight, not exceeding eight or ten. The 42d out of a total of four hundred and fifty had a hundred and four wounded, of whom eight were officers. In the right-hand column, Colonel Wood, six naval officers, and twenty men of the Naval Brigade, with many of the native regiment, were wounded. Of the sixty engineer labourers, twenty were wounded; while of their five officers, Captain Buckle was killed, Major Home and Lieutenant Hare wounded, together with several of their white soldiers. Altogether our casualties exceeded two hundred and fifty. Fortunately but a small proportion of the wounds were serious.

While the battle was raging, at one o'clock Quarman was attacked by a strong body of Ashantis coming from the west, probably forming part of Essarman Quatia's force. Captain Burnett, who was in command, having under him Lieutenant Jones of the 2d West Indian regiment, and thirty-five men of that corps and a few natives, conducted the defence, and was well seconded by his men. Although the attacking force was very greatly superior, and took the little garrison by surprise—for they did not expect, while a great battle was raging within a distance of a mile, that the Ashantis would be able to spare a force to attack a detached party—the garrison defended itself with great gallantry and complete success, not only beating off the enemy whenever they attacked, but sallying out and assisting to bring in a convoy of stores which was close at hand when the attack began.

Amoaful was a town capable of containing two or three thousand inhabitants. Great quantities of grain and coarse flour were found here. These were done up in bundles of dried plantain leaves, each bundle weighing from five to fifteen pounds. This capture was of great service to the commissariat, as it afforded an abundant supply of excellent food for the carriers. The troops were in high spirits that night. They had won a battle fought under extreme difficulty, and that with a minimum of loss in killed. There were therefore no sad recollections to damp the pleasure of victory. Frank had been twice struck with slugs, but in neither case had these penetrated deeply, and he was able to sit round the camp fire and to enjoy his glass of rum and water. Two kegs of rum were the only stores which that night came up from the rear, thanks to the consideration of a commissariat officer, to whom the soldiers felt extremely grateful for providing them with an invigorating drink after their long and fatiguing labours of the day.

At about a mile and a quarter from Amoaful lay the town of Bequah, the capital of one of the most powerful of the Ashanti kings. Here a considerable force was known to be collected before the battle, and here many of the fugitives were believed to have rallied. It would have been impossible to advance and leave this hostile camp so close to a station in our rear. Lord Gifford was therefore sent out at daybreak to reconnoitre it. He approached it closely, when twenty men sprang out from the bush and fired at him, fortunately without hitting him. When he returned and made his report, the general determined to attack and burn the place, and orders were issued for a column, consisting of Russell's regiment, Rait's battery, and the Naval Brigade, supported by the 42d and commanded by Colonel M'Leod, to start at one o'clock.

The march was not opposed through the bush, but as the scouts entered the clearing a heavy fire was opened upon them. Lord Gifford and almost the whole of his party were more or less severely wounded when the sailors rushed in to their support. For a short time the enemy kept up a heavy fire from the houses, and then fled leaving about forty of their number dead on the ground. The town, which was about twice the size of Fomana, was burned, and the column returned to the camp.

A great portion of the town was destroyed and the place stockaded, and then all was in readiness for the advance upon Coomassie. Amoaful was to be left in charge of the 2d West Indians, who had now come up. Each man received four days' rations and each regiment was to take charge of its own provision and baggage. The advance started at seven in the morning, Russell's regiment, Rait's battery, and the Rifle Brigade. Then came the headquarter staff followed by the 42d and Naval Brigade. The hammocks and rations went on with the troops. The rest of the baggage remained behind. The road differed in nothing from that which had so long been followed. It bore everywhere marks of the retreating enemy, in provisions and other articles scattered about, in occasional dark stains, and in its plants and grass trampled into the ground, six feet in breadth, showing that the usual native way of walking in single file had been abandoned. The rate of progression was slow, as the country had to be thoroughly searched by the advance. There were, too, many streams to be crossed, each causing a delay.

At one of the villages there was a large camp, where about a thousand men were assembled to make a stand. The defence was, however, feeble in the extreme, and it was evident that they were greatly demoralized by their defeat on the 1st. Russell's regiment carried the place at a rush, the enemy firing wildly altogether beyond the range of their weapons. Several were killed and the rest took precipitately to the bush. A few shots were fired at other places, but no real resistance took place. On reaching the village of Agamemmu, after having taken six hours in getting over as many miles, the column halted, and orders were sent for the baggage to come on from Amoaful. The troops were set to work to cut the bush round the village, which was a very small one, and a breast-work was thrown up round it. The troops were in their little *tentes d'abri* packed as closely together as possible outside the houses, but within the stockade. The carriers slept in the street of the village, where so thickly did they lie that it was impossible for anyone to make his way along without treading upon them.

News came in that night that Captain Butler with the Western Akims had arrived within two days' march of Amoaful, but that without the slightest reason the king and the whole of his army had left Captain Butler and retired suddenly to the Prah. At the same time they heard that the army of the Wassaws under Captain Dalrymple had also broken up without having come in contact with the enemy. From the rear also unpleasant news came up. The attack upon Quarman had been no isolated event. Fomana had also been attacked, but the garrison there had, after some hours' fighting, repulsed the enemy. Several convoys had been assaulted, and the whole road down to the Prah was unsafe. The next morning, after waiting till a large convoy came safely in, the column marched at nine o'clock, Gifford's scouts, Russell's regiment, and Rait's battery being as usual in front. The resistance increased with every step, and the head of the column was constantly engaged. Several villages were taken by Russell's regiment, who, full of confidence in themselves and their officers, carried them with a rush in capital style. It was but six miles to the Dah, but the ground was swampy and the road intersected by many streams. Consequently, it was not until after being eight hours on the road that the head of the column reached the river, three hours later before the whole of the troops and their baggage were encamped there.

CHAPTER XXIII

THE CAPTURE OF COOMASSIE

UPON the afternoon of the arrival of the English column upon the Dah the king made another attempt to arrest their progress, with a view no doubt of bringing up fresh reinforcements. A flag of truce came in with a letter to the effect that our rapid advance had much disconcerted him, which was no doubt true, and that he had not been able to make arrangements for the payments claimed; that he would send in hostages, but that most of those whom the general had asked for were away, and that he could not agree to give the queen-mother or the heir-apparent. These were, of course, the principal hostages, indeed the only ones who would be of any real value. The answer was accordingly sent back, that unless these personages arrived before daybreak the next morning we should force our way into Coomassie.

The Dah is a river about fifteen yards wide and three feet deep at the deepest place. The engineers set to work to bridge it directly they arrived, Russell's regiment at once crossing the river and bivouacking on the opposite bank. It was unfortunate that this, the first night upon which the troops had been unprovided with tents, should have turned out tremendously wet. The thunder roared, the lightning flashed, and the rain came down incessantly. Tired as the troops were there were few who slept, and there was a general feeling of satisfaction when the morning broke and the last day of the march began. The rain held up a little before daybreak, and the sky was clear when, at six o'clock, Wood's Bonny men, who had come up by a forced march the evening before, led the advance. Lieutenant Saunders with one of Rait's guns came next. The Rifles followed in support.

Before the Bonny men had gone half a mile they were hotly engaged, and the combat was for two hours a repetition of that of

Amoaful. Saunders advanced again and again to the front with his gun, and with a few rounds of grape cleared the sides of the path of the enemy. At last, however, the Bonny men would advance no farther, and Lieutenant Eyre, the adjutant of Wood's regiment, was mortally wounded. Lieutenant Saunders sent back to say it was impossible for him to get on farther unless supported by white troops. The Rifles were then sent forward to take the Bonny men's place, and slowly, very slowly, the advance was continued until the clearing round a village could be seen fifty yards away. Then the Rifles gave a cheer and with a sudden rush swept through to the open and carried the village without a check. In the meantime the whole column had been following in the rear as the Rifles advanced, and were hotly engaged in repelling a series of flank attacks on the part of the enemy. These attacks were gallantly persevered in by the Ashantis, who at times approached in such masses that the whole bush swayed and moved as they pushed forward.

Their loss must have been extremely large, for our men lined the road and kept up a tremendous Snider fire upon them at a short distance. Our casualties were slight. The road, like almost all roads in the country, was sunk two feet in the centre below the level of the surrounding ground, consequently the men were lying in shelter as behind a breast-work, while they kept up their tremendous fire upon the foe.

The village once gained, the leading troops were thrown out in a circle round it, and the order was given to pass the baggage from the rear to the village. The operation was carried out in safety, the path being protected by the troops lying in a line along it. The baggage once in, the troops closed up to the village, the disappointed foe continuing a series of desperate attacks upon their rear. These assaults were kept up even after all had reached the cleared space of the village, the enemy's war-horn sounding and the men making the woods re-echo with their wild war-cry. The Naval Brigade at one time inflicted great slaughter upon the enemy by remaining perfectly quiet until the Ashantis, thinking they had retired, advanced full of confidence, cheering, when a tremendous fire almost swept them away.

It was six hours from the time at which the advance began before the rear-guard entered the village, and as but a mile and a half had been traversed and Coomassie was still six miles away, it was evident that if the Ashantis continued to fight with the same desperation, and if the baggage had to be carried on step by step from village to village, the force would not get half-way on to Coomassie by nightfall.

The instant the baggage was all in, preparations were made for a fresh advance. Rait's guns, as usual, opened to clear the way, and the 42d this time led the advance. The enemy's fire was very heavy and the Highlanders at first advanced but slowly, their wounded straggling back in quick succession into the village. After twenty minutes' work, however, they had pushed back the enemy beyond the brow of the hill, and from this point they advanced with great rapidity, dashing forward at times at the double, until the foe, scared by the sudden onslaught, gave way altogether and literally fled at the top of their speed. War-drums and horns, chiefs' stools and umbrellas, littered the next village and told how sudden and complete had been the stampede. As the 42d advanced troops were from time to time sent forward until a despatch came in from Sir A. Alison saying that all the villages save the last were taken, that opposition had ceased, and that the enemy were in complete rout. Up to this time the attack of the enemy upon the rear of the village had continued with unabated vigour, and shot and slug continually fell in the place itself. The news from the front was soon known and was hailed with a cheer which went right round the line of defence, and, whether scared by its note of triumph or because they too had received the news, the efforts of the enemy ceased at once, and scarcely another shot was fired.

At half-past three the baggage was sent forward and the head-quarter staff and Rifle Brigade followed it. There was no further check. The 42d and several companies of the Rifle Brigade entered Coomassie without another shot being fired in its defence. Sir Garnet Wolseley soon after arrived, and taking off his hat called for three cheers for the Queen, which was responded to with a heartiness and vigour which must have astonished the Ashantis. These were still in considerable numbers in the town, having been told by the king that peace was or would be made. They seemed in no way alarmed, but watched, as amused and interested spectators, the proceedings of the white troops.

The first thing to be done was to disarm those who had guns, and this seemed to scare the others, for in a short time the town was almost entirely deserted. It was now fast getting dark, and the troops bivouacked in the market-place, which had so often been the scene of human sacrifices on a large scale. Their day's work had, indeed, been a heavy one. They had been twelve hours on the road without rest or time to cook food. Water was very scarce, no really drinkable water having been met with during the day. In addition to this they had undergone the excitement of a long and obstinate fight with an enemy concealed in the bush, after work of almost equal severity upon the day before, and had passed a sleepless night in a tropical rain-storm, yet with the exception of a few fever-stricken men not a single soldier fell out from his place in the ranks. Nor was the first night in Coomassie destined to be a quiet one. Soon after two o'clock, a fire broke out in one of the largest of the collections of huts, which was soon in a blaze from end to end. The engineers pulled down the huts on either side and with great difficulty prevented the flames from spreading. These fires were the result of carriers and others plundering, and one man, a policeman, caught with loot upon him, was forthwith hung from a tree. Several others were flogged, and after some hours' excitement, the place quieted down. Sir Garnet was greatly vexed at the occurrence, as he had the evening before sent a messenger to the king asking him to come in and make peace, and promising to spare the town if he did so.

Although Coomassie was well known to Frank he was still ignorant of the character of the interior of the chiefs' houses, and the next day he wandered about with almost as much curiosity as the soldiers themselves. The interiors even of the palaces of the chiefs showed that the Ashantis can have no idea of what we call comfort. The houses were filled with dust and litter, and this could not be accounted for solely by the bustle and hurry of picking out the things worth carrying away prior to the hurried evacuation of the place. From the roofs hung masses of spiders' webs, thick with dust, while sweeping a place out before occupying it brought down an accumulation of dust which must have been the result of years of neglect. The principal apartments were lumbered up with drums, great umbrellas, and other paraphernalia of processions, such as horns, state chairs, wooden maces, &c. Before the door of each house stood a tree, at the foot of which were placed little idols, calabashes, bits of china, bones, and an extraordinary jumble of strange odds and ends of every kind, all of which were looked upon as fetish. Over the doors and alcoves were suspended a variety of charms, old stone axes and arrow tips, nuts, gourds, amulets, beads, and other trumpery articles.

The palace was in all respects exactly as the king had left it. The royal bed and couch were in their places, the royal chairs occupied their usual raised position. Only, curiously enough, all had been turned round and over. The store-rooms upstairs were untouched, and here was found an infinite variety of articles, for the most part mere rubbish, but many interesting and valuable: silver plate, gold masks, gold cups, clocks, glass, china, pillows, guns, cloth, caskets, and cabinets, an olla podrida, which resembled the contents of a sale-room.

In many of the native apartments of the palace were signs that human sacrifice had been carried on to the last minute. Several stools were found covered with thick coatings of recently shed blood, and a horrible smell of gore pervaded the whole palace, and, indeed, the whole town. The palace was full of fetish objects just as trumpery and meaningless as those in the humblest cottages. The king's private sitting-room was, like the rest, an open court with a tree growing in it. This tree was covered with fetish objects, and thickly hung with spiders' webs. At each end was a small but deep alcove with a royal chair, so that the monarch could always sit on the shady side.

Along each side of the little court ran a sort of verandah, beneath which was an immense assortment of little idols and fetishes of all kinds. From one of the verandahs a door opened into the king's bed-room, which was about ten feet by eight. It was very dark, being lighted only by a small window about a foot square, opening into the women's apartments. At one end was the royal couch, a raised bedstead with curtains, and upon a ledge by the near side (that is to say the king had to step over the ledge to get into bed) were a number of pistols and other weapons, among them an English general's sword, bearing the inscription, "From Queen Victoria to the King of Ashanti." This sword was presented to the predecessor of King Coffee. Upon the floor at the end opposite the bed was a couch upon which the king could sit and talk with his wives through the little window.

In the women's apartments all sorts of stuffs, some of European, some of native manufacture, were found scattered about in the wildest confusion. The terror and horror of the four or five hundred ladies, when they found that their husband was about to abandon his palace and that they would have no time to remove their treasured finery, can be well imagined.

In almost every apartment and yard of the palace were very slightly raised mounds, some no larger than a plate, others two or even three feet long. These were whitewashed and presented a strong contrast to the general red of the ground and lower walls. These patches marked the places of graves. The whole palace, in fact, appeared to be little better than a cemetery and a slaughter-house in one. A guard was placed over the palace, and here, as elsewhere through the town, looting was strictly forbidden.

All day the general expected the arrival of the king, who had sent a messenger to say he would be in early. At two o'clock a tremendous rain-storm broke over the town, lasting for three hours. In the evening it became evident that he was again deceiving us, and orders were issued that the troops, in the morning, should push on another three miles, to the tombs of the kings, where he was said to be staying. Later on however, the news came that the king had gone right away into the interior, and as another storm was coming up it became evident that the rainy season was setting in in earnest. The determination was, therefore, come to, to burn the town and to start for the coast next morning.

All night Major Home with a party of engineers was at work mining the palace and preparing it for explosion, while a prize committee were engaged in selecting and packing everything which they considered worth taking down to the coast. The news of the change of plan, however, had not got abroad, and the troops paraded next morning under the belief that they were about to march still farther up the country. When it became known that they were bound for the coast there was a general brightening of faces, and a buzz of satisfaction ran down the ranks. It was true that it was believed that a large amount of treasure was collected at the kings' tombs, and the prize-money would not have been unwelcome, still the men felt that their powers were rapidly becoming exhausted. The hope of a fight with the foe and of the capture of Coomassie had kept them up upon the march, but now that this had been done the usual collapse after great exertion followed. Every hour added to the number of fever-stricken men who would have to be carried down to the coast, and each man, as he saw his comrades fall out from the ranks, felt that his own turn might come next.

At six o'clock in the morning the advanced guard of the baggage began to move out of the town. The main body was off by seven. The 42d remained as rear-guard to cover the engineers and burning party. Frank stayed behind to see the destruction of the town. A hundred engineer labourers were supplied with palm-leaf torches, and in spite of the outer coats of thatch being saturated by the tremendous rains, the flames soon spread. Volumes of black smoke poured up, and soon a huge pile of smoke resting over the town told the Ashantis of the destruction of their blood-stained capital. The palace was blown up, and when the engineers and 42d marched out from the town scarce a house remained untouched by the flames.

The troops had proceeded but a short distance before they had reason to congratulate themselves on their retreat before the rains began in earnest, and to rejoice over the fact that the thunderstorms did not set in three days earlier than they did. The marsh round the town had increased a foot in depth, while the next stream, before a rivulet two feet and a half deep, had now swollen its banks for a hundred and fifty yards on either side, with over five feet and a half of water in the old channel. Across this channel the engineers had with much difficulty thrown a tree, over which the white troops passed, while the native carriers had to wade across. It was laughable to see only the eyes of the taller men above the water, while the shorter disappeared altogether, nothing being seen but the boxes they carried. Fortunately the deep part was only three or four yards wide. Thus the carriers by taking a long breath on arriving at the edge of the original channel were able to struggle across.

This caused a terrible delay, and a still greater one occurred at the Dah. Here the water was more than two feet above the bridge which the engineers had made on the passage up. The river was as deep as the previous one had been, and the carriers therefore waded as before; but the deep part was wider, so wide, indeed, that it was impossible for the shorter men to keep under water long enough to carry their burdens across. The tall men therefore crossed and recrossed with the burdens, the short men swimming over.

The passage across the bridge too was slow and tedious in the extreme. Some of the cross planks had been swept away, and each man had to feel every step of his way over. So tedious was the work that at five in the afternoon it became evident that it would be impossible for all the white troops to get across—a process at once slow and dangerous—before nightfall. The river was still rising, and it was a matter of importance that none should be left upon the other side at night, as the Ashantis might, for anything they could tell, be gathering in force in the rear. Consequently Sir Archibald Alison gave the order for the white troops to strip and to wade across taking only their helmets and guns. The clothes were made up in bundles and carried over by natives swimming, while others took their places below in case any of the men should be carried off their feet by the stream. All passed over without any accident.

One result, however, was a laughable incident next morning, an incident which, it may be safely asserted, never before occurred in the British army. It was quite dark before the last party were over, and the natives collecting the clothes did not notice those of one of the men who had undressed at the foot of a tree. Consequently he had to pass the night, a very wet one, in a blanket, and absolutely paraded with his regiment in the morning in nothing but a helmet and rifle. The incident caused immense laughter, and a native swimming across the river found and brought back his clothes.

As the journeys were necessarily slow and tedious, owing to the quantity of baggage and sick being carried down, Frank now determined to push straight down to the coast, and, bidding good-bye to Sir Garnet and the many friends he had made during the expedition, he took his place for the first time in the hammock, which with its bearers had accompanied him from Cape Coast, and started for the sea. There was some risk as far as the Prah, for straggling bodies of the enemy frequently intercepted the convoys. Frank, however, met with no obstacle, and in ten days after leaving the army reached Cape Coast.

Ostik implored his master to take him with him across the sea; but Frank pointed out to him that he would not be happy long in England, where the customs were so different from his own, and where in winter he would feel the cold terribly. Ostik yielded to the arguments, and having earned enough to purchase for years the small comforts and luxuries dear to his heart, he agreed to start for the Gaboon immediately Frank left for England.

On his first arrival at Cape Coast he had to his great satisfaction found that the Houssas who had escaped from Coomassie had succeeded in reaching the coast in safety, and that having obtained their pay from the agent they had sailed for their homes.

Three days after Frank's arrival at Cape Coast the mail steamer came along, and he took passage for England. Very strange indeed did it feel to him when he set foot in Liverpool. Nearly two years and a half had elapsed since he had sailed, and he had gone through adventures sufficient for a lifetime. He was but eighteen years old now, but he had been so long accustomed to do man's work that he felt far older than he was. The next day on arriving in town, he put up at the Charing Cross Hotel and then sallied out to see his friends.

He determined to go first of all to visit the porter who had been the earliest friend he had made in London, and then to drive to Ruthven's, where he was sure of a hearty welcome. He had written several times, since it had been possible for him to send letters, to his various friends, first of all to his sister, and the doctor, to Ruthven, to the porter, and to the old naturalist. He drove to London Bridge Station, and there learned that the porter had been for a week absent from duty, having strained his back in lifting a heavy trunk. He therefore drove to Ratcliff Highway. The shop was closed, but his knock brought the old naturalist to the door.

"What can I do for you, sir?" he asked civilly.

"Well, in the first place, you can shake me by the hand."

The old man started at the voice. "Why, 'tis Frank!" he exclaimed, "grown and sunburnt out of all recollection. My dear boy, I am glad indeed to see you. Come in, come in: John is inside."

Frank received another hearty greeting, and sat for a couple of hours chatting over his adventures. He found that had he arrived a fortnight later he would not have found either of his friends. The porter was in a week about to be married again to a widow who kept a small shop and was in comfortable circumstances. The naturalist had sold the business, and was going down into the country to live with a sister there.

After leaving them, Frank drove to the residence of Sir James Ruthven in Eaton Square. Frank sent in his name and was shown up to the drawing-room. A minute later the door opened with a crash and his old school-fellow rushed in.

"My dear, dear, old boy," he said wringing Frank's hand, "I am glad to see you; but, bless me, how you have changed! How thin you are, and how black! I should have passed you in the street without knowing you; and you look years older than I do. But that is no wonder after all you've gone through. Well, when did you arrive, and where are your things? Why have you not brought them here?"

Frank said that he had left them at the hotel, as he was going down early the next morning to Deal. He stayed, however, and dined with his friend, whose father received him with the greatest cordiality and kindness.

On leaving the hotel next morning he directed his portmanteau to be sent in the course of the day to Sir James Ruthven's. He had bought a few things at Cape Coast, and had obtained a couple of suits of clothes for immediate use at Liverpool.

On arriving at Deal he found his sister much grown and very well and happy. She was almost out of her mind with delight at seeing him. He stayed two or three days with her and then returned to town and took up his abode in Eaton Square.

"Well, my dear boy, what are you thinking of doing?" Sir James Ruthven asked next morning at breakfast. "You have had almost enough of travel, I should think."

"Quite enough, sir," Frank said. "I have made up my mind that I shall be a doctor. The gold necklace which I showed you, which Ammon Quatia gave me, weighs over twenty pounds, and as it is of the purest gold, it is worth about a thousand pounds, a sum amply sufficient to keep me and pay my expenses till I have passed. Besides, Mr. Goodenough has, I believe, left me something in his will. I sent home one copy to his lawyer and have brought the other with me. I must call on the firm this morning. I have also some thirty pounds' weight in gold which was paid me by the king for the goods he took, but this, of course, belongs to Mr. Goodenough's estate."

Upon calling upon the firm of lawyers, and sending in his name, he was at once shown in to the principal.

"I congratulate you on your safe return, sir," the gentleman said. "You have called, of course, in reference to the will of the late Mr. Goodenough."

"Yes," Frank replied. "I sent home one copy from Coomassie and have brought another with me."

"We received the first in due course," the gentleman said, taking the document Frank held out to him. "You are, of course, acquainted with its contents."

"No," Frank answered, "beyond the fact that Mr. Goodenough told me he had left me a legacy."

"Then I have pleasant news to give you," the lawyer said. "Mr. Goodenough died possessed of about sixty thousand pounds. He left fifteen thousand each to his only surviving nephew and niece. Fifteen thousand pounds he has divided among several charitable and scientific institutions. Fifteen thousand pounds he has left to you."

Frank gave a little cry of surprise.

"The will is an eminently just and satisfactory one," the lawyer said, "for Mr. Goodenough has had but little intercourse with his relations, who live in Scotland, and they had no reason to expect to inherit any portion of his property. They are, therefore, delighted with the handsome legacy they have received. I may mention that Mr. Goodenough ordered that, in the event of your not living to return to England, five thousand pounds of the portion which would have come to you was to be paid to trustees for the use of your sister, and the remaining ten thousand to be added to the sum to be divided among the hospitals."

"This is indeed a surprise," Frank said; "and I shall be obliged, sir, if you will at once draw out a paper for me to sign settling the five thousand pounds at once upon my sister. Whatever may happen then she will be provided for."

The accession of this snug and most unexpected fortune in no way altered Frank's views as to his future profession. He worked hard and steadily and passed with high honors. He spent another three years in hospital work, and then purchased a partnership in an excellent west-end practice. He is now considered one of the most rising young physicians of the day. His sister keeps house for him in Harley Street; but it is doubtful whether she will long continue to do so. The last time Dick Ruthven was at home on leave he persuaded her that it was her bounden duty to endeavour to make civilian life bearable to him when he should attain captain's rank, and, in accordance with his father's wish, retire from the army, events which are expected to take place in a few months' time.

Ruthven often laughs and tells Frank that he is a good soldier spoiled, and that it is a pity a man should settle down as a doctor who had made his way in life "by sheer pluck."

THE END

Historiae Dona Repertum

Books by G. A. Henty

For the Temple
The Dragon and the Raven
In Freedom's Cause
By Pike and Dyke
Beric the Briton
St. Bartholomew's Eve
With Lee in Virginia
By Right of Conquest
The Young Carthaginian
Winning His Spurs
Under Drake's Flag
The Cat of Bubastes
Wulf the Saxon
A Knight of the White Cross
St. George for England
With Wolfe in Canada
By England's Aid
The Dash for Khartoum
The Lion of the North
Won by the Sword
Facing Death
The Lion of St. Mark
Bonnie Prince Charlie
In the Reign of Terror
The Tiger of Mysore
A March on London
Under Wellington's Command
At Agincourt
Orange and Green
With Moore at Corunna
To Herat and Cabul

For Name and Fame
With Clive in India
Both Sides the Border
No Surrender
True to the Old Flag
Through Russian Snows
A Jacobite Exile
With the Allies to Peking
The Treasure of the Incas
When London burned
Henty Short Stories Vol. 1
By Sheer Pluck
Out on the Pampas
With Frederick The Great

Study Guides

By Right of Conquest
By Pike and Dyke
With Lee in Virginia
For The Temple

Books by Charlotte M. Yonge

The Little Duke
The Dove in the Eagle's Nest

Other Publications

The Captain (a magazine)
The List, by C. D. Baker
John Smith: Gentleman Adventurer

PrestonSpeed Publications takes great pride in re-printing the complete works of G. A. Henty. New titles are released regularly. Both our hardcover and tradepaper printings include the complete text of the original edition, as well as all maps and illustrations.

For a free catalog contact us at:

PrestonSpeed Publications
51 Ridge Road Mill Hall, PA 17751 USA

or call (570) 726-7844
or visit our web site: www.prestonspeed.com